STUFF THE LADY'S HATBOX

An *I LOVE A MYSTERY* Novel

STUFF THE LADY'S HATBOX

CARLTON E. MORSE

Seven Stones Press

Copyright©1988 by Carlton E. Morse
All rights reserved. No portion of this book may be
reproduced in any form without written permission
from the publisher.
Printed in the United States of America.

ISBN 0-940249-03-0 (Hardcover)
    0-940249-04-9 (Paper)

Cover and book design by David Charlsen

Cover photograph by Sidney Brock

For additional copies of this book check your local bookstore, or
you may write directly to the publisher:

Seven Stones Press
Star Route Box 50
Woodside, CA 94062

Please enclose $16.95 for each hardcover book, or $9.95 for each
paperback, plus $1.50 per book for shipping and handling. California
residents please add appropriate sales tax.

To Jim Harmon
the greatest of
my radio fans

STUFF THE
LADY'S HATBOX

"Whooeee! Turn me over and bake me brown both sides!" Doc laid his poker deck in his lap and wiped his face, neck and hands on a crisp, linen handkerchief large enough to diaper an infant elephant.

"I was sired, whelped and whopped to sinful manhood in the heart of Texas, but I ain't *never* been hot as this! Don't they *ever* need handsome, two-fisted, nature-lovin' private detectives, namely us, to save beautiful babes from fates worse'n death up at the North Pole?"

Jerry Booker's rattley-bang tempo on the typewriter keys didn't miss a beat as she answered over her shoulder, "You wouldn't like it up there, either."

"Says why?" Doc picked up the poker deck from his lap.

"Three reasons; you might have to do a little work."

"Now ain't that a nice way for a full-salaried, self-respectin' female secretary to talk to her boss."

"Straw boss!" Jerry modified. "Two, the penguins are stuffed shirts and would make you feel inferior; three, the native girls are all tubs of blubber, sewed up in their winter underwear."

"I swear to goodness, Jerry honey, how can so much insubordination be crammed in such a neat little powder puff? Which is all beside the point on account I was talkin' about August in Hollywood."

It was 11:17 a.m. and a hundred and three degrees in the second-floor loft office of the Triple A-One Detective Agency; presently at three-fourths of full staff and at the height of the morning's activity.

Jack Packard, who bore the brunt of the organization's brains and all of its leadership without undue strain to his solid, neatly packed five-foot-eleven-and-a-half-inch physique, at the moment sits up to his armpits in a litter of bills, statements, reports on cases pending, and letters of pique or commendation for past services. He never perspired, but his skin seemed to crystallize and glitter as he glowered, muttered and condemned the fateful day he'd let Doc doubletalk him into a formal office routine.

Following Jack, as the tail follows the comet, was the aforementioned Doc Long, the lean, lanky, horsey-faced, redheaded Texan with the washed-out blue eyes, whose nimble fingers played havoc with cards, dice, safes and locks. Mild and easygoing, in trouble and out, it was nonetheless his bone-hard fists, swift as heat lightning and effective as a pair of sledgehammers, that had extricated the Triple A partnership from more than one "techous situation!"

If Doc had any failings, and he did, they were topped by his Casanova instincts, Texas version, which convinced him that every one of God's "female girls" was his dish. He also believed there were two kinds of girls in the world: good and bad, and it was his life work to play Sir Galahad to the former and Sir Studhorse Havoc with the latter.

If Jack cursed the shackles of office routine, Doc, who had conceived and given birth to the idea in the first place

— "so's we'd have a place to hang our hats and give us a respectable address and a reason for havin' a cute little secretary all our own" —was bored to the "raw bone." He despised routine, and held paperwork to be a "sinful waste and an inhuman clutter." He vehemently argued that putting money in a bank was a waste of time and space, "on account you just took it out again" and, finally, "hitchin' three such footloose hombres as me, Jack and Reggie York to an office is like tying millstones around the necks of a pack of whiffet hounds."

So there sat Doc on this broiling August morning, in sportshirt and knife-edged gabardine slacks, lounging deep in a client's chair. His moccasin shoes, with a glassy polish, were cocked up on the corner of Jerry Booker's desk, and his long supple fingers with high-glossed nails riffled a poker deck; the cards dancing in air, only to fall back into a neat, compact pile in the palm of his hand.

"What's Reggie think he's doin' this a.m.?" Doc asked resentfully. "Don't he know all members of the firm s'posed to appear at the office before the noon lunch triangle rings?"

Jerry shrugged. "Reggie reported in to the office at 8:45, got the latest report on the International Air Freight case, and is still out."

"That boy's a gonna die of a sense of misplaced duty afore he's reached his majority."

"Reggie's already twenty-four," Jerry flung over her shoulder.

"In my book, a man's majority is the best part of the years he's a gonna live. Reggie's so hearty he'll prob'ly live to eighty unless he steps in front of some mizzable critter that don't want to die without he takes somebody with him." Doc wiped his hands on his now not so crisp handkerchief, stuck it in his pocket, and continued with certainty. "So that makes Reggie's majority any time after forty—say, forty-two or three."

Jerry shrugged without missing a beat of her typewriter rhythm.

Jerry Booker, last but not least of the agency's quartet despite her pint size, sat facing the office switchboard with her back to Doc, banging the ancient typewriter, relaxed and unperturbed. She was, in Doc's summation, "our very own blonde female shoot of a secretary—that is, a tiny shoot up to her armpits, but from her pulley-bone to her St. Anthony necklace she kinda explodes inside her blouse." Jack maintained that Jerry had an overextended sense of feminine attributes, like a vase of full-blooming American Beauties, but Doc "jus' naturally felt that nature meant her to be somebody's mama, and when Jerry settles down to it, man oh man, what a lucky baby he's a gonna be."

Doc heaved a lugubrious sigh and eyed the straight, efficient back and the short, neatly cropped blonde head of the office's single claim to pulchritude.

"Honest to Christmas in Hades, Jerry honey, how can you look so crisp and cool? This place collects heat like a sponge drinkin' up water. Why we ain't got air conditionin' in this barn, like most civilized places, I don't know."

"Ha!" Jerry commented, not missing a beat on the typewriter.

"Well, I don't." He riffled the cards again, whereupon the ace, king, queen, jack and ten of hearts left the deck in that order and danced up his bare, freckled arm, laying out in perfect rotation.

Jerry's fingers left the keyboard as she turned in her chair, an expression of scathing rebuke in her velvety blue eyes.

Doc meekly recovered the cards and grinned engagingly. "This is what I call my five-finger exercise."

"We don't have air conditioning because the bank balance will just barely cover my Friday paycheck; because you sit around in the office with a deck of cards in your hand instead of turning in your report on the Pedlar-Anchor Insurance case, so I can bill them; because you went down to the Cleary Austin Steel Products Company and got a hundred-dollar advance before I could send them a bill; and," Jerry added, bitingly, "because you are a no-good bum who'd rather play with a handful of pretty pasteboards than play detective."

Doc's eyes opened wide in shocked protest. "Sugar, this ain't *play*, it's *work!* Man never knows when he's a gonna be called on to open a lock or a safe or have to defend hisself in a floating poker game."

Jerry continued unheedingly, "Not to mention your silly airplane that eats up hundred-dollar bills like a billy goat absorbs tin cans. And now you *know* why we haven't air conditioning, nor a janitor, nor draperies on the windows, and live in this warehouse loft instead of a swank new office on the boulevard. Money, money, money!"

"Why shame on you to pieces!" Doc protested. "Don't any of you pretty little whiffs of perfume ever think about anything but money?"

Jerry turned back to her typewriter with a "what's the use" gesture.

Doc's eyes strayed to the far cubicle.

"What's Jack think he's a doin' in yonder?"

Jerry gave the back office a bitter glance. "Shuffling and scattering my files like a cat with a roll of toilet paper. There goes a week's hard filing shot to hell. Talk about a grizzly bear in a trapper's cabin!"

Doc grinned. "Yeah," he agreed, "it sure is a pitiful sight."

Jerry's eyes turned on him sourly. "But at least he's *pretending* to work, which is more than I can say for some people."

"Aw, sugar," Doc drawled placatingly, "you just ain't used to the private detective business. A detective agency ain't supposed to open for business until around noon, workin' the hours we do."

"Uh-huh," said Jerry, her mouth suddenly compressed and a gleam in her eye, "who was that redhead I saw you 'working' last night?"

"You mean that client—" Doc began.

"Client, my foot!"

"Well, potential client. After all, part of my job is scouting for new business."

"You were giving her the business, all right," conceded Jerry, "but I didn't notice anything new about it. Who was she, anyway?"

Doc's eyes lighted. "Jerry, baby, I didn't know you cared."

"I care about you borrowing a hundred dollars of the agency's money and throwing it away on floozies."

"That's just plain jealousy."

"What!"

"Why, sure it is. Admit it, sugar, you're just putty in my hands when Jack ain't here, but with him a castin' his shadow around the office, your soul is torn in two places. And that just don't make sense when there's a redheaded Texas boy available."

"Last night a redhead, tonight a blonde, huh?" Jerry said scornfully.

The switchboard broke into an angry buzz. Jerry flipped a switch. It was Linda Holliday, Hilly Holliday's twin sister and only relative, not counting the bank executors of the Holliday multi-million-dollar estate.

Doc leaned forward, deftly lifting the receiver from a desk phone. "I'll take this one. Plug in the line." Jerry looked doubtfully toward Jack's office, then shrugged and plugged in. She kept the board open, flipping over to a fresh page in her dictation book. It was operational procedure whenever Doc or Jack was on the line with a client.

Doc shook his head violently, but Jerry sat unmoved, staring at him suspiciously.

Doc gave up. "Yeah, hello? The Triple A's number one friend of wealthy young females up to their hairline in another ugly situation; Doc Long speaking, you lucky girl. What's your trouble this time, Miss Holliday, honey?"

A burble of laughter came over the phone. "Good morning, Doc."

"It ain't either, it's hot. 'Course if you're phonin' from a cold shower or the swimming pool, you maybe wouldn't notice. What brand of dragons you got for me to slay this evening, after it cools off, so's I can get my breath?"

Linda Holliday's voice lost its lightness. "It isn't my emergency, Doc. The whole Holliday estate is in trouble."

"Not again!"

"I can't talk on the phone. And it can't wait until this evening. I want a conference with one or two of you boys, preferably all three, at the Stone Canyon Hotel cocktail lounge, right now! How long will it take you to get out to Bel Air?"

"Twenty, thirty minutes, accordin' to traffic. Reggie ain't available, but that bit about the cocktail lounge, all dark and cool with the splashin' fountain, sold me."

Doc hung up muttering, "Wisht I had time to go home and take a shower and change."

"Why?" Jerry said, looking him up and down scornfully, "she doesn't want to smell you, she wants to use you, as always."

Doc grinned. "Now you're soundin' your normal little hunk of self, sugar."

"Well you know it's true! Linda Holliday winds you boys around her trim ankle like pet garter snakes."

"They ain't never been a female client yet that you don't get techous and edgy," Doc said cheerfully, slipping into his coat. "You'd think me and Jack and Reggie lived lives of sin and shame every time we step outside the office, which is a good idea but it just plain ain't practical."

Jerry turned her back and attacked the typewriter viciously. Doc leaned over and kissed the nape of her neck.

"Sugar," he consoled, "they ain't nothin' in this world that keeps us Triple A boys as clean and pure as knowin' we got us a jealous little woman a waitin' back in the office."

He beat a hasty retreat for Jack's office as a *Roget's Thesaurus* breezed by his head. He tiptoed past Jack's desk but to no avail. Jack's nose came up out of a page of figures.

"Who's the girl?"

"What girl?" Doc continued on to the washroom, taking from his pocket a tie on which was painted a bare-back horse straddled by an all-over bare girl.

"That's what I asked you." Jack eyed Doc's excessive care with the four-in-hand knot and carefully slicking-down of his hair, already damp with perspiration.

"Who said anything about a girl?"

"The instant you stepped in here with that glassy shine in your light blue Texas eyes and that smug, virtuous smirk on your long horsey face, the answer was obvious—a girl."

"Oh, playin' detective!" Doc slipped back into his Italian-cut jacket and gave himself a final loving onceover in the mirror.

"And stop being coy! Where do you think you're going?"

The hurt, outraged expression on Doc's visage was as phony as the thousand-dollar bill he carried in his wallet for good luck.

2

"Now looky, Jack, do I always ask you where you're going, the minute you step out of the office? Doggone it, are we partners in a detective office or are you a runnin' a nursery for stray Texas boys?"

"Some dame's yelling for help out in the Stone Canyon cocktail lounge. Doc can hardly wait!" This inelegance from Jerry in the outer office.

"Her and her big mouth," muttered Doc, giving a vicious jerk on his handpainted tie.

"So that's it."

"So what's it?" Doc still wasn't looking at Jack.

"You want to play a knight in shining armor riding to the rescue on a white horse, with plumes."

"No, I don't want to ride no white horse—and what's a plume?"

"Never mind the plume."

"And never mind the white horse—I hate white horses. The only time I ever was throwed was from a white horse; the only time I ever bet on a horse race and got hurt was on a white horse; and just to cinch it, my grandma on my mama's side was a drivin' a span of white horses when she was throwed from a buckboard and broke her neck, and was buried from a hearse drawed by white horses."

"Doc!"

" —and more than that, I once turned down a Texas oil well heiress *flat* on account her papa had a white horse in his corral."

"Doc, will you forget the white horses."

"Well, who brung them up?"

"Never mind—who's the girl?"

"The who?" There's nothing dumber looking than a Texan when he's reluctant.

"The girl in the Stone Canyon cocktail bar."

"Oh her—uh—you wouldn't know her."

"Not until you tell me her name, anyway."

"Linda Holliday!" Jerry was broadcasting from the outer regions again. Doc slammed the office door violently.

"Honest to my grandma, Jack, we ain't got no secretary—we got a built-in receivin' and sendin' set! I always *wondered* what she had in her oversized blouse."

"Is she talking about Hilly Holliday's sister?"

"Okay, okay, so now you know!"

"I think I'd better go along."

"Now looky, Jack, when I need your help, I'll send up smoke signals. In the meantime— "

"In the meantime you'll louse things up by yourself. What kind of trouble's Hilly in this time?" Jack got up and put on his coat, welcoming an excuse to duck the paperwork. He reopened the door, which was making a sweatbox of the office cubicle. Doc watched him with a moody belligerence.

"Looky at all that paperwork a clutterin' up your desk. You aimin' to walk out on a mess like that?"

"Yeah," Jerry's bitter, derisive voice came from down the room. "Slave girl Jerry, the overworked, underpaid office flunky'll clean up the mess, while you two rush out to a nice cool bar and swill liquor and make eyes at a fifty-million-dollar playgirl. Don't think of me."

Jack hastily pushed the door closed again with his foot.

"I asked you a question, Doc. What kind of trouble is Hilly Holliday in now?"

"So far as I know he ain't in any kind of trouble— so far as I know Miss Holliday's just plain lonesome and wants somebody, meaning me, to drink with. In which case three's not only a crowd but a criminal waste of manpower."

Jack reopened the door. "Come on, let's go find out."

"I swear to my grandma on my mama's side, Jack, when I partnered up with you, you'd think I took on a lifetime nursemaid. It's a gettin' so I have to sneak out barefoot with my shoes in my hands to even *look* at a girl anymore."

As they passed by Jerry's desk she glowered at them. Doc, in an equally unwholesome mood, glowered back. Jack nodded cheerfully.

"See you later, Jerry. If we get tied up for the afternoon—"

"And you will, of course."

Doc's face lightened hopefully. "Can you guarantee that?"

The switchboard buzzer interrupted her answer. Jack turned quickly toward the exit gate with Doc hard on his heels.

"Hold it, fellows!" Jerry clamped her hand over the mouthpiece and said with a fatuous smirk. "It's Mr. Alexander F. F. McCracken of the Home and Farm Mutual Insurance Company."

"Tell him we ain't in. Tell him we just flew to the Arctic Circle to take the chill off a hot tip just sent in by penguin post."

Jack crossed around to Jerry's desk. "I'll talk to him."

Jerry took her hand from the mouthpiece. "Yes, Mr. McCracken, both men are here. Jack's coming to the phone." She plugged in a line as Jack picked up the receiver.

"Both men *ain't* here," protested Doc hastily. "Whatcha' want to go say a thing like that, when you know I'm already committed to the Stone Canyon Cocktail Lounge."

Jerry dimpled, "But Doc," she murmured with wide-eyed innocence, "you are here and Mr. McCracken wants both of you."

"You ever hear the motto 'first come, first serve,' which means Linda Holliday got her bid in first and—"

"All right, Jerry," Jack interrupted. "You'll have to call the Stone Canyon Hotel bar and cancel our appointment with Miss Holliday—"

"Why dad-blame you, Jack Packard! You can't *do* that! It ain't ethical. You go ahead and see McCracken and I'll—"

"Come along with me," Jack finished for him. "Go ahead, Jerry, cancel the Holliday appointment."

"It will be a pleasure."

Doc reached for his hat to throw on the floor and then remembered he wasn't wearing one. "Talk about Hitler and the Seven Dwarves," he muttered in sour disgust, "you'd think this place was headquarters for the Gestapo."

3

If it was August-hot in the second-floor home office of the Triple A-One Detective Agency, around the corner from Hollywood Boulevard it was even grimmer. The pavement was a sizzling glare, and a limp circus tent of gray hazy smog hung over the city, holding in the muggy, eye-smarting air.

Doc's copper-red hair glinted, curled and smoldered, his lean muscular shoulders hunched in protest against the heat, and his rangy legs lagged as he followed Packard out to the sidewalk. His pale blue Texas eyes washed out to the color of skim milk as he squinted across the street to the parking lot. "I swear to goodness, Jack," he drawled plaintively, "Los Angeles ain't nothin' more'n a smudge pot with the lid on. You'd think crime'd just wither up and die in such a place."

Jack grinned. "Heat brings out the meanness in some."

The Jaguar in the open-air lot was throwing off heat rays like a logging engine. The seats scorched their pants and saturated their backs with sweat before they'd fishtailed half a dozen blocks down La Brea. All the way out to Wilshire the sun, red-eyed behind the smog, blistered their noses and seared their eyeballs.

Doc slid down in the seat and closed his eyes, prepared to let Jack fight the heat and traffic, but the seat leather burned the back of his neck and he sat up indignantly. "Man can't even scrooch down and suffer decently. What's the Home and Farm Mutual Insurance and Indemnity Company want this time? Blood, sweat and tears?"

"McCracken didn't say."

"We ain't a gonna see him personally." Doc was dismayed. "That coldblooded fish'll have the steam heat turned on in his office. He'll want to give us hot coffee to drink. His mama must of been scairt by a tropic heatwave."

"We're meeting him across the street in the Waverly-Carlton cocktail lounge."

"*He* said that?" Disbelief.

"I said that."

"And he agreed?"

"Reluctantly."

"Then he wants us worse'n he's ever wanted us before. Does he know he's walkin' right smack into air conditionin'? I hope he brings his sweater and overcoat. We don't want no frozen corpses on our hands."

"He's eccentric," Jack agreed. "He's also the smartest insurance investigator in the business."

"You mean like the Home and Farm Mutual refusin' to give me and you any life insurance?"

Jack swung the Jaguar out of the Wilshire traffic and into the Waverly-Carlton parking lot. Inside, the high-

ceilinged foyer was cool and dark. Soft string music floated from far off in a subdued, refreshing cascade. The cocktail lounge was a cool, dark cave just off the lobby. In a
far corner, McCracken sat over a steaming cup of black
coffee, a heavy slip-on sweater under his coat and a woolen scarf about his neck. His face was smooth and pink
for a man in his sixties. There was a pleasant, patient expression about him, until he raised his eyes. There was
nothing eccentric behind the thick lenses—only a mixture
of iron and intelligence frozen into hard agate.

He gave Jack and Doc a bare, grudging nod as they
slipped into the booth, one on each side, and shuddered
over the scotch mist and gin-and-tonic orders.

Doc grinned. "Cold or somethin', Mr. McCracken?"

"Yes." McCracken's words were brittle. "So let me
say what I have to say and get out of here." He paused
to let the waiter put down the drinks and move away, and
then spoke to Jack. "Packard, you've done several jobs ex-
tricating Hilliard Holliday from one sort of insane playboy scrape or another."

"Uh-oh," Doc muttered. McCracken looked at him
sharply. Jack interpreted. "What Doc means to say is, we
just had an emergency call from his sister. We were on
our way out there when you called."

McCracken frowned. "I wondered where she got her
information so fast."

"How about me goin' to find out?" Doc's eager move
to rise was vetoed two to one.

"Sit down, Doc," Jack said.

"Yes, never mind the girl," agreed McCracken.

"You would say that," Doc muttered under his breath.

"Have you ever had any hint of him mixing with the wrong sort of company?" McCracken was looking at Jack.

"Women?" Doc's ears perked up.

"Mobsters, drifters, confidence men—any of the rackets?"

"Why, shuckens, Mr. McCracken," Doc protested, "Hilly ain't nothin' but a poor little rich boy, and his own worst enemy. He's just sufferin' from a rich papa and mama who died too early and left him with too much money and practically no brains."

McCracken still looked at Jack for his answer.

Jack shook his head. "What's happened now?"

"A month ago there was a two-hundred-fifty-thousand-dollar heist on the Chicago Stockyard's First National Bank, in which my company has an insurance stake."

Jack nodded.

McCracken continued. "This morning, Holliday came into the Los Angeles and Truckee Union Bank with a woman's hatbox and withdrew two hundred fifty grand, mostly in thousands or five-hundreds—some hundreds, fifties and twenties—loaded them into the hatbox, walked out and boarded a plane for Las Vegas."

Doc's eyes bugged out. "He took two hundred fifty thousand of foldin' money in a pasteboard hatbox to Las Vegas?"

"If I don't make myself clear," McCracken eyed Doc frostily, "be sure to interrupt."

Doc grinned. "Yeah, I will."

"There's no law against a man carrying his money around in a hatbox, if he's that idiotic," Jack said mildly, "or have they passed a new law since I read the morning paper?"

"Do you suppose it's just accidental that, one, the denominations of the bills were identical with those from the robbery?"

Jack's eyes fastened on McCracken's more intently.

Doc shot his partner a quick glance and then studied his gin and tonic thoughtfully.

"Two, that Holliday, or anyone else for that matter, would know that two hundred fifty thousand dollars in certain denominations would exactly fit into a woman's hatbox? Three, that Lilly Montrose, alias Lois Pallaski, not only boarded the Las Vegas plane with Holliday, but was his seat companion for the trip over?"

"Who the heck's Lilly Montrose, alias Lois somethin' or other?" Doc's interest heightened. "Is she blonde, about five foot two, and kinda explodes in the blouse department?"

McCracken's eyes warmed slightly. "You know her?"

Doc shook his head. "No, but I know a lot of Hilly's women and they all fall into what you might call 'big-busted midgets with towheads.'"

Jack was thumbing through a well-worn little black book. Suddenly he looked up with an anxious frown. "One of Skip Sullivan's girls."

"Heeey!" Doc gulped.

McCracken nodded.

"Skip Sullivan, who has the Las Vegas exlusive on all floating poker games. The boy who cleans out the suckers who are too smart to drop their money in the gambling casinos."

Doc was indignant. "Now why'd Hilly do a thing like that? Even an idiot'd know the tables'll give a man a better run for his money than a floatin' game. Of course," Doc grinned, "present company excluded—meanin' me."

McCracken eyed Doc frostily. "Sometimes I get the idea you really mean that."

Doc looked startled. "Huh?"

"That you're so all-fired good with cards, dice and locks."

Doc's face was bland and innocent of anything save a goodnatured grin, but his light blue eyes grew wary and flinty. "Why, Mr. McCracken," he said in a soft, contented drawl, "I'm surprised at you. Course I believe it—marked or unmarked cards; loaded or unloaded dice; jailhouse locks, safe, strongbox or jus' plain padlocks— " He limbered his long, slim, brown fingers and rubbed the tips together lovingly. "I got brains in the ends of my fingers."

McCracken's eyes wandered about the half-dark cocktail lounge, a look of petulant outrage on his face. He pulled the scarf closer about his neck, but his eyes had taken in and catalogued every face in the place.

"They ever run out of space in the morgue's cold room, they can use this place for an annex." He lifted his steaming coffee cup to his lips, set it down abruptly and looked at Jack.

"You boys have something about five foot two, blonde and—er—curvaceous in your office, if I remember?"

Jack looked amused. "Men usually remember Jerry Booker."

"Heeey, now wait a minute—how'd she get into the conversation?" Doc's protest was lost in McCracken's unbroken attention to Jack.

"She's amenable and trustworthy?"

"Now, looky!" Doc demanded to be heard. "Jerry Booker's a nice, untouchable secretary to the Triple A, no matter how she looks; and whatcha mean 'amenable,' anyhow?"

Jack nodded to McCracken, amused, "She's amenable."

"That's a heck of a way to talk about my girl!" Doc's protest lost some of its vehemence at Jack's quick glance. "Well, *our* girl," he amended, "and if you're a hintin' at what I think you're a hintin' at, Mr. McCracken, she ain't never met Hilly Holliday and she ain't ever gonna' meet him, for my money."

McCracken listened to Doc but kept his eyes on Jack.

"It's the Texas boy version of the Knight in Shining Armor riding a white horse to the defense of maidenly virtue," Jack explained blandly over Doc's head to McCracken.

Doc looked disgusted and swallowed some gin and tonic.

"Women fall into two categories for Doc—good and bad! Those who grow up to be mamas and those who grow up to be red-hot mamas. He's just a little confused about Jerry Booker."

"That just plain ain't funny, Jack."

"Well," said McCracken abruptly, picking up the check, "The three of you can still make the night Vegas plane, and that will leave your Reggie York to hold down the office."

Doc's mouth opened but McCracken was ahead of him.

"Holliday, Lilly Montrose and his hatbox have a four-hour lead on you."

"Which means by the time we get there," Doc predicted sourly, "all that'll be left for us'll be Hilly's corpse under a yucca bush in the sand dunes."

McCracken, about to rise, looked at Jack, who shook his head.

"Not with one of Skip Sullivan's girls in tow. That two hundred fifty grand's already spoken for."

McCracken nodded, satisfied to have his own theory confirmed. "It's my theory there's a second identical two hundred fifty thousand floating around over there someplace—identical, that is, except for the serial numbers on the bills. My company isn't interested in what happens to Holliday or his money; it's the heist money we want, and the boys who have it." He reached inside his coat and slid a brown manila envelope to Jack. "Five hundred on account —five hundred expenses." He got up from the edge of his chair quickly, shuddered as a cool blast of air struck him, muttered profanely and escaped.

4

Jerry Booker angled a seat on the Las Vegas plane next to Jack while Doc was observing a cute stewardess with red hair and a tight skirt which made her hips wiggle like two mischievous, hairless midgets tied in a sack. Jerry understood Doc thoroughly—that's why she liked him—but set her sights on Jack, whom she never hoped to understand. She was a scanty, pint-sized blonde; tiny feet, trim ankles, and nicely proportioned for a bikini or tailored skirt, but from her armpits, she flared alarmingly.

As the three unloaded at the Regal Spa Hotel, the stars in Las Vegas' clean blue night sky were crystal sparks left behind by a fierce but long-gone ball of sun. The dry heat still rose from the desert sands, washed by tentative eddies of mountain air, which before dawn would turn the whole desert into a refreshing oasis.

It was twenty minutes to midnight when Jack and Doc left Jerry in her spacious, glassed third-floor room. This air-conditioned Oriental houri's dream (for such is Las Vegas) overlooked a veritable lake of a swimming pool surrounded by acres of lush lawns, stage-lit by a lighting man sired by Hollywood to resemble a movie version of South Sea island bliss. Beyond the artificial glow, the sandy waste pulsed under the radiant heat and trilled with desert insects; in the distance, shadowy mountains showed vaguely as rising smoke.

W YORK, N.Y.

ST FRANCIS
OF ASSISI

CHURCH OF

While Jerry luxuriated in the shower, preparato
squeezing into something suitable for casino nightli
the strip, Jack and Doc rinsed off in similar plushness
door. While Doc lingered at the washbasin, Jack had
for three phone calls. First he spoke to a Joe Denton,
to police headquarters to clear their private-operative
mits for doing business in Las Vegas; after which he ch
with Lieutenant Tracey Holmes, a long-established
on the bright-lights detail. He asked two questions
Holmes aware that Hilliard Holliday was in town ac
panied by Lilly Montrose, also known as Lois Pallaski
Was Skip Sullivan holding a floating poker session to
and if so where? Jack wrote down three addresses, pa
a question, promised Lieutenant Holmes to keep
informed, and said goodbye in the teeth of more ques

Lord,
make me
an
instrument
of
your
Peace

On their way out, Jack tapped on Jerry's door,
to be informed through the keyhole that the girl ha
rid herself of the day's grime and it would be anothe
minutes before she was properly lotioned, powdered
tinted; moreover, it would be an extra ten minutes b
she'd be out of her skin and into presentable attire

Doc grinned: "We'd better not go in now, Jack.
so teensy we probably couldn't even find her withou
clothes on."

Jack grunted, and called back. "We're going out to case
the town. I'll call or send for you when we're ready."

Going down the elevator Jack speculated that inasmuch as Lieutenant Holmes didn't rise to the bait when
he'd mentioned Hilly Holliday, it was evident the playboy
and the Montrose girl hadn't got off the plane in company,
or Holmes' plainclothes man at the airport was sleeping
on the job. It was also certain that Holliday had only made
his big gesture with the hatbox and two hundred fifty thou-

sand dollars in Los Angeles. Las Vegas generally seemed unaware of the big loot in the pasteboard container.

Doc was thinking about something else. "No casino, no nightclub, and self-service elevators," he grumbled. "Why didn't we stay at the Desert Palace? Over there they got elevator girls in abbreviated bikinis."

Jack, frowning over his own problem, didn't hear. "Which means Skip Sullivan wanted Los Angeles to know Hilly was carrying two hundred fifty thousand dollars under his protection, but not Las Vegas. Why?"

"Why do the girls wear abbreviated bikinis at the Desert Palace?" Doc shrugged, "because they're prettier that way! Because it takes the suckers' minds off their gambling losses—if that ain't a silly question."

Jack's blank look turned to disgust. "You're going to be a great help, I can see that."

Out in the taxi area, the air had cooled another degree. Jack handed the taxi driver a ten-dollar bill. "That's got a brother, if we find what we're looking for in a hurry."

The cabby's grizzled, sun-baked face lit up. A toothless grin didn't add to his beauty. He looked as though he should be driving a pack burro and his voice was a gravel whisper, probably a byproduct of cactus juice and alkali dust. "Beautiful girls?"

Doc's face also brightened, but before he could acquiesce, Jack presented the first of Lieutenant Holmes' three addresses.

The old man's face fell. "What you looking for? Cheap whiskey and bad company?" He ground the taxi into gear.

It, also, was all too familiar with alkali dust and desert sand, but it had speed.

The first address was a weary, seedy hotel in downtown Las Vegas and offered nothing. The second, a wino bar on the fringe of the business area, was equally unfruitful, and the third was a rundown clapboard private house, dark and unresponsive.

"Well, we ain't shook no 'possums out of them trees, so now what?" Doc was as disgusted as the cabby.

"If you're out to see the shabby side of town, you ain't seen anything yet. But it's a hell of a way to spend a night in Las Vegas." He squirted tobacco juice out the window and squinted around at Jack and Doc questioningly.

"I don't suppose you could take us to a nice, quiet floating poker game," Jack said without conviction.

"Well, why didn't you say so half an hour ago?" The taxi shot out like a scared pup. After five reckless minutes the cab cut a fast corner on the outskirts of town and drew up before a dilapidated front with all the earmarks of an abandoned roadhouse. The sandy driveway was heavily shadowed and one bare, sullen light glowed weakly over the entrance. If the place ever had had a name it was sandblasted off the weathered boards now.

Jack stepped out of the cab first. "Doc, you wait here with the driver for now." His shadow momentarily grew long under the garish light and then vanished inside.

"What's the matter?" complained the cabby, "he don't trust me?"

"Jack don't trust nobody," Doc agreed cheerfully, "it's a habit."

After five minutes Jack returned. "The scotch is terrible, but this is the place!" He took a fifty-dollar bill out of his wallet and held it up to the driver. "Go back to the Regal Spa and pick up the blonde in Room 3107 and bring her back with you. This'll be waiting for you if you're back in fifteen minutes."

The grizzled face looked suspicious. "What's her name?"

"You don't have to know a girl's social security number to let her ride in your taxi, do you? Just say her boss and Texas friend sent you."

The old man's eyes alternated between the fifty dollar bill and Jack's face for a moment. Reluctantly he got into the taxi and swung back onto the highway, gathering speed at every turn of the wheels.

The area before the roadhouse was more forbidding without the headlights. Doc stumbled and cussed on the steps. Inside, the lights were dull and gloomy on the heavy oak paneling, dark with smoke and age, to shadow rather than reveal faces at the several tables—all of them mean and all unfriendly.

Doc surveyed the scene distastefully, sitting with reluctance on a bar stool at Jack's elbow. "How come you think this is the place?"

Jack nudged him to silence as the bartender moved in front of them, waiting with sour, grudging inhospitality. "Scotch over rocks out of the bottle this time," Jack said in a friendly tone.

"Why don't you go up on the strip if you want expensive drinking?"

"We're thirsty."

"We only got one kind of scotch."

"Okay, Doc," Jack said agreeably, "then maybe we should have a couple of beers."

Doc opened his mouth to protest, but the bartender had moved away. He complained to Jack in an undertone. "Jack, you know I cain't stomach beer."

"Pour it in your shoe. You wouldn't have any stomach with this other stuff. And keep your voice down." He waited until the reluctant bartender shoved two open bottles and glasses before them, took Jack's money as though it were confederate paper, and thereafter patently ignored them.

"Welcome, strangers," Doc muttered, pouring beer and eyeing it sourly. "The life of a private eye gets lousier and lousier." He sipped from his glass and belched. "Pure bloat! And now could I know how come you think we've found Hilly Holliday?"

"How many people do you know who smoke gold tube Aroma-Romas? Besides," he muttered softly, "I know a lookout man when I see one, and I see two of them at one of the tables. Also, why is the bartender so unfriendly?"

"Maybe his girlfriend ran off with a traveling salesman."

"And if you'll look in the bar mirror, you'll notice a closed door to the right of the Men's room. Too many eyes keep watching that door—even the bartender."

"You figure that's where the poker game is?"

Jack nodded and looked at his wristwatch. "Jerry'll be here any minute. Take this fifty and go out and bring her in."

"Jack, that's something I been a wantin' to talk to you about."

"Later."

"No, dad-blame it, now. In the first place you know that throwin' a little blonde at Hilly Holliday is as wasteful as sacrificin' virgins to hungry dragons. How can you do this to Jerry, the way she feels about you and the way I feel about her?"

Jack grinned.

"Well, how can you?"

"Business before pleasure, Doc."

"She's a nice kid and this is a durned unwholesome place to bring her," Doc insisted doggedly.

"She's also a big girl now. So do you go out and bring her in or do I?"

Doc got up off his stool slowly. "When you're a workin' a case you just plain don't care who gets hurt, so long as you get what you're after."

Outside there was a rush of tires on gravel and the gritty squeak of brakes. Doc accepted Jack's look of urgency and went outside.

Jerry was getting out of the taxi. Doc paused at the top of the steps, scandalized, thinking he'd recognize that pair of legs anywhere, only tonight there seemed to be more of them. Being as she was such a small-sized package, he couldn't help wondering what was left under the dress with so much top and bottom exposed as she slid out of the car.

He had the urge to run down and throw a coat around the Triple A's miniature Lady Godiva, but by the time he was off the porch, she was out and standing up, her whiff of a dress now covering a minimum of essentials, and was adjusting an ounce or so of lacy peekaboo puff around her naked shoulder blades.

He was burned to silence that the desert-rat cabby had enjoyed the unloading of his passenger so obviously, and stuck the fifty dollars in his hands and waved him off. Jerry stood silently watching Doc's disgruntlement until the taxi pulled away. Only then she said, "Hi," and took his arm.

"I swear to my grandma, I don't know what comes over nice girls when the sun goes down."

Jerry looked pleased and flattered, as they went up the steps. "You heard Jack say come loaded for bear."

"Yeah, bear like in big game, not bare like in nude. Besides, no sensible hunter goes around with all his ammunition out to the weather."

Jerry squeezed his arm like a reassuring mother as they stepped inside. She looked around the almost empty bar, surprised. "I thought this was the scene of my downfall—I don't see any action here."

"Jack's yonder at the bar." Doc had one more chance to have his say while they crossed down the bar. "Looky, sugar, they ain't no call for a nice little innocent Hollywood secretary like you a gettin' mixed up in this. If me and Jack can't take care of ourselves without hidin' behind a female petticoat, it's time we got out of the business."

"Female petticoat, my eye! Apparently you weren't looking when I got out of the taxi."

Doc was indignant. "Will you tell me how a man's a gonna winnow the hussies from the future wives and mothers, when a girl talks like that!"

Jerry gave him a fleeting smile, crawled up on the stool next to Jack and wriggled her finger at the bartender for a beer. "How'm I doing, boss?"

"You're going to have to take off those French heels."

"Heeey! Not my shoes! Anything else, okay! Didn't anybody ever tell you it's the heels that gives a girl's ankles that certain look and helps the poise and posture . . . "

"Hilly Holliday likes 'em little, have you forgot?"

Jerry looked around the bar with interest. "Where is he?"

Jack dropped his voice and motioned Doc in closer for the conference. "He's in the back room probably behind a locked door. Doc, you're going to find out if the door is locked and, if so, get it unlocked."

"Why, sure," Doc said, full of sarcasm, "and shall I invite them lookout boys a sittin' around the place to join me or should I knock their heads together first?"

"Stop grousing and listen. How long will it take you to get that door open if it is locked?"

Doc felt in his pocket for a couple of little tools, which he knew beforehand were there. "Thirty seconds, maybe a minute."

"All right, but no longer. Jerry and I can create a diversion, but not for long. See that you get the door unlocked . . . "

"What kind a diversion?"

Jack eyed him coldly. "What's that got to do with you?"

"Because when you're on business you'd sacrifice your mama and papa both if you had any, and for all I know you're just as like as not to strip Jerry down and have her run up and down the bar mother-naked and I wouldn't put it past you."

Jerry looked interested.

"And what's more," Doc went on doggedly, "in her frame of mind she'd do it, too, if you ast her."

Jack gave him a blank stare. "You pay attention to your job and I'll take care of mine. Jerry, slip off one of your shoes and give it to me."

Jerry seemed about to protest, but sighed with resignation and did as she was told.

"See what I mean," Doc muttered, "putty in your hands."

Jerry was looking at Jack. "I want you to know," she warned, "I'm wearing sheer nylons at six dollars a pair and if so much as one thread is damaged they go on my expense account."

"Now get your other foot around here so I can grab it when the time comes." Jack's tone was businesslike. "Doc, ask the bartender the way to the Men's room. It's just beyond the door we're interested in. That'll give you an excuse to get started in that direction without attracting attention. Say it loud so everyone can hear."

"Jack, my mama learned me to go to the bathroom *before* I go out in public—"

"Shut up and listen!" But Doc got a suppressed giggle from Jerry.

"And Jerry, when Doc's almost at the locked door, I'm going to put this one shoe on the bar and grab your foot to try to take off the other. You're going to yell and fight me and naturally your skirt'll fly up a little—"

"Jack, that's just plain disgustin'!"

" —Shut up!"

"Well, it is!" But Doc knew already he'd lost by the excited devilment in Jerry's eyes. "They ain't no excuse—"

"The excuse is that Jerry's my girl, but she's planning to leave with you. I bought those shoes she's wearing and she's not going to walk out of here in my shoes with another man."

"And you're really going to muss me up?" Jerry sounded so pleased Doc muttered, "Honest to my grandma! Women!"

"No, I'm not going to muss you and you see you don't muss yourself. Hilly Holliday's not going to be intrigued by a girl who's already been wrestled to a fall. And don't overdo the exposure! Just enough to keep every man's eyes riveted on us while Doc's at work. All right, get set, Doc!"

Jack turned on his bar stool and called to the bartender at the other end of the bar something to the effect that everything from Texas comes big, including their "output," and where could a Texas boy, indicating Doc, put it. The bartender lost his sour look for a moment and flipped his bar towel toward the washroom, and a glowering Doc was on his way.

"Jack sure knowed his psychology," Doc admitted grudgingly as he received friendly, knowing grins from the few legitimate customers and even the two goons as he crossed the room. The next second every eye was riveted on Jack and Jerry. Doc had time for one quick glance over his shoulder and caught the beginning of their cat and dog fight and a flurry of skirts, legs, and pink skin.

To Doc's practiced fingers the lock was so simple it was pathetic. Hardly more than a flick of the wrist with a little sliver of steel. And then, with the door open so fast, Doc suddenly was inspired. He knew what he should do, even if it wasn't the way Jack had planned it. If he could slip through and case the poker game and maybe break it up and save Hilly's hatbox without using Jerry for bait, why not?

As he slipped inside he heard Jerry "a cussin' and a caterwaulin' like a mama bobcat cornered by a papa bobcat," and heard Jack say in a mean voice, "I paid for those shoes and you're not going to walk out in them with that redheaded Texan!"

Doc saw Jack watching out of the corner of his eye, so he gave a quick wave and shut the door, but not before he'd seen more lady-doodads, black garters, and girl than a doublespread in a color art magazine, and Jerry a lovin' every second of it. Shame on her for over-actin'! This hardened Doc's resolve to play it his way.

He left the door unlocked in case Jack could follow. Besides, he just might need a quick exit. He found himself in a dimly lit back hall with a turn in it, and from around the corner he could hear the clink of poker chips and low voices. Doc grinned. "Now ain't that a nice warm homey feelin' a drawin' me like a candle in a purty female's window."

He checked his wallet, which had an interesting bulge from half of the Home and Farm Insurance allowance money, slipped his phony thousand-dollar goodluck bill on top, and was set to tiptoe for the happy hunting ground. Abruptly a door marked Ladies opened almost at his elbow, and out stepped little Miss Las Vegas herself— "blonde, right out of an expensive bottle, and a whole dress full of invitin' goodies sheathed in a slinky black evening contraption."

But her eyes weren't inviting—not after the first startled look. Doc took her in and decided she had to be Lilly Montrose or Lois Pallaski, or whatever her name; Skip Sullivan's blonde.

Her voice was flat and husky. "What do you want?"

"Why," Doc said with open friendliness, "there's only three things a Texas boy ever wants in Las Vegas—the Men's room . . . ''

The girl relaxed at that, all except her eyes and voice. "And?"

He reached in his hip pocket and pulled out his wallet. "And a pretty, blonde female ladyfriend, and one of them famous floatin' poker games we're always hearin' about down Texas way."

Her eyes got hot and interested at the sight of the bulge in Doc's pocketbook, especially when the thousand-dollar bill poked into sight.

It's kinda frightenin', Doc thought soberly, the way a thousand-dollar lettuce leaf'll relax a female.

"Well, well," she murmured to herself, "this must be my night." She slipped her hand under Doc's arm and effectively melted on his coat sleeve, and he could tell by instinct she wasn't leading him to any Men's room.

Around the corner the voices and clink of chips was clearer, and, as Doc had anticipated, there was a lookout lounging outside the door. The gorilla stiffened and Doc saw his right hand "all of a sudden got terrible nervous," until Lilly gave him the wink and said, "A Texas customer to see the boss, Mike."

Mike still looked doubtful, saying something about the boss being busy right now.

Lilly smirked right back at him, "Well, he's going to be busier."

To make it an easier decision for Mike, Doc pulled out his wallet and watched the greedy little eyes fasten on the tip of the big bill and the fat bulge. It was the magic gesture all right, and when Doc said, "Howdy, Mike, I'm Doc Long from Big Water, Texas, with my bushy tail over my shoulder and one night in Las Vegas to howl. Let's not stand in the way of progress, son."

Mike gave a toothy grin and opened the door.

Only one man looked up from the green baize, accepting Lilly with a blank indifference. When he saw Doc not a line changed in his gray, still, poker face, but a hard glint froze his eyes. "Like I'd seen," Doc thought, "when a player with what looked like a cinch hand suddenly was bumped to the limit on the last card." He'd found Skip Sullivan for sure.

When Sullivan laid his hand face down on the table, Doc admired the slow and easy catlike way he got to his feet. The other four ringers looked up and a tense, suspended animation froze the table. Doc could see why Hilly wasn't interested, even with his back to him. The bottle on the table was more than half-empty and so was the hatbox on the floor beside his chair.

Sullivan came over to where Doc and his escort were standing as though he had all the time in the world, gave Lilly and Mike a flinty look and asked Doc in a soft, indifferent tone, "Well, friend, what's *your* problem?"

Doc showed him his pocketbook. "It's too heavy. You got anyplace a Texas man could sit down for a while and rest hisself?"

5

Doc Long's own flamboyant version of his invasion of the unlicensed Las Vegas floating poker game in the shabby roadhouse out among the cactus, sagebrush, yucca and sandy waste on the far edge of town will bear repeating in his own words:

"I seen right at once Skip Sullivan's mind wasn't as enticed by the bulge in my pocket, like it was with Lilly Montrose and the lookout, Mike. Naturally my little contribution to the game was chicken pickin's to what Hilly Holliday had brung from L.A. in his silly hatbox. So naturally I was a gonna have to use my winnin' Texas personality to wring a invitation out of Skip's reluctant heart.

"I had a kinda idea I might bust two birds with the same board, if I played it right and, more important, if Hilly'd hold still for it. He looked bruised enough from the beatin' he'd already taken from the sharpies to maybe follow my lead and keep his yap shut. Only thing, I knowed Hilly from the past and he knowed me, and he was mainly noted for two things—doin' the wrong thing at the wrong time, and losin' his head over baby blondes.

"Anyway, I had to risk it, so I waltzes over to the table next to Hilly, keepin' my fingers crossed. Crossin' over from the door was like walkin' through a nest of rattlesnakes all up on their fat tails and pulled back for the strike, but I played it like I was a rich uncle at a family barbecue.

"I poured out a little of Hilly's whiskey in his empty glass and tipped it to Skip. 'Here's to an oasis in a dusty desert,' I said and took a gulp, and then spit it out in disgust before it touched my tonsils.

" 'You call that drinkin' liquor? Honest to Christmas, if the boys that stomped out that corn didn't forget to take off their socks, I'll put in with you.'

"A couple of Skip's boys kinda grinned and relaxed, which showed I was on the right track. Only Hilly looked up for the first time and I could see for a minute the whole show was a hangin' by a thread. I still don't know whether it was me comin' down hard with my heel on his foot or his own plain gumption that made his eyes glaze and his open mouth snap shut."

Doc put down the glass, picked up the poker deck in front of Hilly, shuffled it a couple of times before anyone could interfere, and slapped the stack down in front of Lilly. At the same instant he flicked out the phony thousand-dollar bill, on the theory that a little deft brashness and a series of unexpected moves would stimulate the gamblers' curiosity to see more.

"This was my big double bid, and I was a bankin' heavy on Skip holdin' still for it out of curiosity, knowin' he could have me throwed out the minute he got fed up with my antics. My first play was to keep him and the boys from gettin' bored and, second, to get enough foldin' money on the table to buck the game without havin' to let Skip in on the horrible truth, which was that the bulge in my wallet was only two hundred and fifty in ones and fives.

"All the time I was a manipulatin' the cards and the phony bill I kept up a runnin' lingo:

" 'Us Texas boys is just plain credulous on a couple of gospel truths about gamblin' that's as sacred as a widow-woman's second chance. One is that it's lucky to have the human scent of a beautiful female woman on the cards, so, sugar, if you'll cut the deck, we'll proceed with the business in hand.' I didn't give Lilly a chance to hesitate or look at Skip for instructions, but took her hand and put it on the deck. I could tell by the way her fingers trembled and the cold feel in them she knowed she was bein' suckered into something, but it was done and over before she could think twice.

" 'And the second gospel us Texas boys live by is, you never plunge in until you get your feet wet. So if Mr. What's-his-name here'll cut for high card, we'll see whether my lonesome thousand strays into his corral or whether I get me a stablemate for my money.' "

Doc shoved the deck in front of Hilly, banking on Skip's gambling instinct to wait for the payoff. He knew if Hilly hesitated even a second, the play was over, "but bless his buttons," he shoved out a couple of five-hundreds and reached for the deck. He cut the queen of spades.

"Why, son," Doc said, full of Texas persiflage and friendliness, "You don't *never* want to ask a female to do a man's work," and cut the king of hearts, pulling the two five-hundreds and the phony thousand in front of him, but leaving them exposed invitingly as he looked about him, happily confident and sociable.

"Can you do that again?" Which was exactly what he'd hoped to hear Skip say, even though his voice grated ominously.

"I dunno, but here's two thousand ready and willin' to find out. If Miss Beautiful here'll do the honors again." Doc picked up the deck, but Skip took them out of his hands and tossed them across the table to the pasty, long-nosed, longfingered, young-in-the-face, old-in-the-eyes sharpy with a white streak in his patentlike hair.

"Max, you shuffle 'em."

Max with the sharp nose and the skunk streak grinned, and with a slow, lazy grace whiffled through the cards a couple of times and laid two stacks of hundreds clipped together.

Doc pushed in his phony thousand and Hilly's two five-hundreds.

Max fluffed the cards once more, making them dance in his hands like a trained chorus, and laid the pack down for the cut.

Doc picked up the whole deck but one card and showed the ace of spades—which settled that. A soft sigh went around the table and Doc kept his ear cocked for any sudden movement behind him, but all Skip did was pat his shoulder and say with amused friendliness, "Well, Mr. Long from Texas, are your feet wet enough for the plunge?"

Doc knew how he was figuring. First, there was four thousand dollars Skip didn't intend to let walk out of the room in someone else's pocket. Second, no matter how good Doc was at one-card draws, in a seven-man game with five sharpers rigging the cards, Doc was still meat for the table.

"Why, thank you, friend," Doc agreed, making it just a shade too eager. "Now you mention it, us Texas boys do hate to wear out shoe leather when the seats of our pants is double-reinforced."

All the while that Doc had been maneuvering and even while a chair was being shoved up for him, Hilly Holliday hadn't looked up from fingering the stack of bills and chips in front of him, as though regretting how big they had once been and how they had dwindled.

As Doc sat down, Hilly poured another drink, but in Doc's opinion "he had a lot of regrets to cauterize before the stuff could begin to bring him any comfort and there just plain wasn't enough liquor left in the bottle." Doc had had a look in the hatbox while he was standing beside Hilly, and while there were still a lot of bills left, they were mostly tens, twenties and fifties. The boys had skimmed off most of the cream.

Doc found himself settled in between Skip on his right and Max's "ciffy cat streak" on his left. He'd made the grade so far, but it was plain there was still considerable treacherous climbing ahead. He grinned happily to himself, wondering if Jack and Jerry were a havin' theirselves as much fun out yonder.

6

Jack Packard, on his stool at the bar, with Jerry's neat, outrageously exposed leg in his hand, cursed himself. To let Doc within a mile of a floating poker game was pure irresistible temptation. He'd known it the minute the Texan had unlocked the door across the room, while he and Jerry were tied down at the bar with their combination wrestling match and leg show for the edification of the few customers, the two lookouts, the bartender, and a mug now identified as the bouncer.

Jack had been right in his theory that he and Jerry could hold the undivided attention of the barroom, but he'd reckoned without Jerry. She was enjoying her playacting with more gusto than the occasion demanded. He was beginning to feel like the man who'd caught himself a wildcat and now couldn't let go.

Jerry's highly colored recollection confirmed Jack in every detail:

"So when Doc ambled across the dark, old barroom in his long-legged, redheaded shamble, and Jack swung me around on the bar stool and grabbed my leg and yelled, 'I paid for those shoes and you're not going to walk out of here in them with another man,' and tried to yank one of them off, I put on such an exhibition of outraged virtue and maidenly doodads, for a while I wasn't sure whether I was wearing a cocktail dress or a parachute. But naturally all good things have to come to an end, which happened just after he yanked off my second shoe.

"That was when the bruised-faced bouncer eased up behind Jack and tapped him on the shoulder, which I think he hated to do, as I was just warming up to my act, what with all the attention I was getting. I was just getting the idea that maybe striptease was my life's work and I'd been hiding my lights under too many clothes as the humdrum secretary in the Triple A-One Detective agency."

As the bouncer tapped Jack's shoulder, he reluctantly released Jerry's leg, or rather Jerry reluctantly took it back.

"Trouble, friend?" The bouncer sounded more friendly than he appeared. He was waiting for the bartender to move in on the scene.

"Not at all." Jack waved Jerry's size-one French heels under his nose and shoved them in his coat pockets. "These are mine, and if you want to see the bill of sale—"

"You'd let the little lady walk out of here barefoot?" The bartender, a bottle of cheap whiskey held by the neck, had moved around the bar to close in behind Jerry.

"She can walk out of here on her hands and knees." Jack shifted on the stool. He was anxious to go find Doc before he loused up things in the back room. He still sat, but now his feet were on the floor.

Jerry was watching for a cue and Jack gave her a quick wink. Either she was a mind reader or the mood for exhibition still was on her.

"I'm neither drunk nor in a frenzy. I've got what I want," Jack patted the shoes in his coat pockets. "But I would like the use of your Men's room before I go."

Neither of the hostile pair budged an eyelash, until Jerry shrugged and again lifted an attractive silken leg a little too high and began tugging at the top of her stocking. Interest in Jack diminished considerably. Even more when she added, "Let the lug go. Barefoot girls can be interesting, too."

Jack eased his way gently out of the situation, content to let Jerry take it from there. He worried a moment when the two lookouts for the floating game joined Jerry's admirers at the bar, and the other eyes in the room fastened hopefully on her new antics. However, he reminded himself they'd been hired to run down a slight matter of two hundred fifty thousand dollars, not campaign against masculine weakness nor rescue dubious virtue.

As Jack slipped through the now unlocked door to the corridor beyond, one over-the-shoulder glance reassured him that no curious eyes were on him. The reason was all too obvious. Jerry was fishing up under her dress, apparently in search of a misplaced garter, and was including everyone in her smile and friendly, bedroom eyes. Jack noted mentally, "That girl definitely has talents the Triple A has been neglecting."

The muffled click of poker chips and subdued voices came from around the corner of the dimly lit corridor. A third lookout for the floating game lounged large and lonesome against a door jamb some fifteen feet down the hall. He looked big and ominous, but Jack suspected some of his size was shadow. He was dividing his boredom between flipping and catching a man-sized switchblade and picking his teeth with the knife.

Jack watched thoughtfully. How had Doc got by him, or hadn't he? Beyond the lookout was the end of the hall and an outside door, probably to a backyard. It was possible Doc was out there, a basket case for the morgue, although Jack hardly troubled himself with that thought, for whatever else were Doc's failings, he fought hard and he fought loud, and wouldn't have gone down without giving an account of himself that would have been heard out front. Besides, the lookout would have sustained a few bruises and the poker game wouldn't be still in session with a corpse or even a severe casualty out back.

Jack's problem was to get by the lookout without disturbing the game. He tiptoed back from the corner to think about it, and noticed for the first time the door marked Ladies. There wouldn't be two such comfort stations in this layout, so obviously if Jerry felt a call to powder her nose, this was where she'd have to come. The problem was threefold: Could he signal Jerry what he wanted of her? Would the lookouts in front refuse her the common courtesy of temporary retirement? And finally, would his passkeys relock the passage door which Doc had unlocked? An unlocked door at this stage would not go unnoticed.

It was a simple old-fashioned inside lock and Jack's passkey did the rest. Satisfied, he unlocked the door again and opened it the barest crack. Jerry still was holding her audience. In fact, Jack's first impression was, she'd begun a striptease in dead earnest. She was now sitting on the bar, one leg dangling tantalizingly bare while she demurely stripped its mate. One of the lookouts was holding the first stocking, a silly smirk on his ugly mug, and the rest of the group was in the throes of a typical Minsky audience reaction. Jerry, aglow with all the enthusiasm of a happy artist at a private showing, was relieving herself not only of hose but of some rather pointed opinions about "the bums who'd brung her."

" —and, furthermore, these stockings are six dollars a pair and if I'm going to walk home barefooted, it'll be on the skin, and not the first time."

But she was casting anxious glances across the room, and the minute she saw Jack she yanked off the second stocking and tossed it in the air. The eager scramble for even this small favor gave her a moment to concentrate on her boss's obvious if crude signal of instruction. She looked startled for an instant and then grinned and pulled the bouncer over to whisper in his ear.

Quickly Jack closed the door and relocked it. Outside, raucous amusement indicated Jerry's immediate needs had been communicated to the group at large. Jack retreated down the hall, entered the Ladies room, and waited. If there was a second such room or the lookouts refused admittance—and then another worry started nagging the back of Jack's mind. As long as Jerry had been out there keeping them occupied, no one was thinking about Doc's overlong retirement to the Men's room. But with her gone, would someone investigate; and if so, what then?

Then came the sound of a key in the lock, the door opening, and Jerry's voice thanking someone, followed by the heavy steps of the third lookout and a flurry of sharp queries and replies. In the midst of male protests and expostulations came Jerry's pathetic appeal, "Jeepers, have a heart," after which there was laughter, a few conciliatory exchanges, and the door was again locked.

Jerry's voice came nearer as she explained her predicament. "You're a lamb, Mike, and when I come out you can send me back to the bar, though will you tell me why they keep a twenty-four-hour watch on the Women's restroom?"

Mike guffawed. "That's almost as mysterious as why a little dame like you is parading around Las Vegas in her bare tootsies."

"A no-good bum bought me a pair of shoes this afternoon and then yanked 'em off when I made eyes at a good-looking jerk, who likewise walked out on me. Excuse me a minute."

Jerry came in so precipitously Jack had to flatten himself against the wall to keep out of Mike's line of vision. Apparently Jerry hadn't expected him in this holy of holies. Her eyes bugged out and her mouth dropped open, but she remembered just in time that Mike was just outside. "You and your funny games," she gave Jack out of the side of her mouth as she crossed to a dressing table at the far end of the lounge and sat down. Without missing a beat she took out her compact and lipstick and began a fresh make-up at the mirror, in plain view if the door should be opened.

Jack followed and sat on the floor behind a davenport out of the line of sight from the door, but still where he could see her face in the mirror. They weren't more than three feet apart. "Keep your voice down," Jack warned her.

"Brother, what's happened to me tonight shouldn't happen to Little Orphan Annie!"

Jack grinned. He'd often speculated about what went on in a ladies' lounge, and now he was getting a partial treatment. But it didn't keep Jerry from talking. "First you steal my shoes and I have to go barefooted to save my stockings and this tile floor is damned cold. Then for fifteen minutes I have to put on Exhibits A, B and C, and if Sally Rand and Lili St. Cyr can face the cold, bare spotlight that long and still tantalize the public . . . "

"And you still have your clothes on."

"Do I? I feel like a cross between a Christian slave on the auction block and a side of beef in a butcher's window."

"Okay, simmer down. We've got business."

"You've been giving me the business all evening. I've had it. If this is how you Triple A detective boys handle your affairs— "

"I'll get you a return trip back to Hollywood the first thing in the morning."

Jerry completed a neat provocative curve with her lipstick and grinned at Jack maliciously. "Since when did the general send the G.I. home for blowing off a little steam? Where's Doc?"

Jack had been reasonably sure that was how Jerry felt, but he'd wanted her to say it. "That's what I want to find out. I think he's made the poker game down around the corner, but before I can find out I've got to get rid of Mike."

"Oh no! You lured me in here to wrestle that ape? I thought you big fearless boys— "

"Any sort of a melee would interrupt the poker game. When you're ready, step out into the hall and stay near the door; but angle Mike with his back to me."

"I get it," she said with heavy sarcasm, "you want to kick him in the pants."

Jack told her what he wanted while she finished her face, which was looking fresher and more dewy by the second.

Running through Jerry's mind as Jack talked was something far away from Las Vegas: "If dear benign, stooped, white-haired, antiquated Father McFarland had seen this far into the future that day my wisp of a mother held me in her arms at the baptismal font with my shock-haired father, red in the face from too tight a collar and Irish whiskey, exuding alcohol fumes with every proud breath and garage mechanic's oil, grease and gasoline fumes from every pore, I don't doubt the scandalized old priest would have disallowed the prefix 'Mary' from the 'Mary Geraldine' so lovingly bestowed upon me, and might then and there have disposed of me in the bowl of holy water.

"In fact if my mother and father had been endowed with foresight, they might have aided and abetted him. Perhaps it's just as well for Father McFarland's peace of mind that he went to his just reward while I was still a scrawny pigtailed squab, and just as well for *their* peace of mind that Ma and Pa brought me to Los Angeles and died of California sunshine, lonesomeness and making a wrong and disastrous turn into heavy traffic, while I was still only sixteen and still untainted by the Triple A-One Detective Agency and three masterminds—ha—detectives, namely, Jack Packard, Doc Long and Reggie York."

Jerry knew these reflections had no place at the moment, but she thought of them just the same as she sat at the mirror in the godforsaken women's lounge freshening her face, her bare feet cold from the tile floor, and missing nothing of Jack's instructions for the next round.

She made Operation Facelift last as long as possible; first, because she was still out of breath and not a little shaken by her leg show at the bar. She hoped Father McFarland wasn't peering down over the wall of heaven at the time. But mainly she had a cringing sensation at the thought of having to walk out into the hall where the big gorilla, Mike, was waiting and maneuver him into position for Jack.

If Doc had been present, at least he'd have put his arm around her and given her a big Texas buss on the cheek and encouraged her with the fiction that she was a big brave girl and important, and anyway it was a simple matter and not the least bit dangerous. And Jerry admitted she'd have swallowed it hook, line and sinker, and gone out full of self-approval and confidence, mightily encouraged, hiding from herself the truth; which was, there wasn't a word of truth in any of it.

Thinking of Doc alone in the room down the hall, almost certainly in more trouble than he knew what to do with, kept Jerry from further stalling.

When she stood up, all she got from Jack was: "Get Mike swung around with his back to the door. I'll take care of the rest."

"Oh, brother!"

Jack tiptoed to the door with her and backed up against the wall as she pulled it open, and of course Mike was right there, "the ape to end all apes," with a grin of welcome on his blemished face and "a gleam of you know what," in his little pig eyes.

Jerry admitted afterwards, "If you don't think it took intestinal fortitude to keep walking and let that door swing shut behind me, try it sometime. And on top of that, try meeting grin for grin and gleam for gleam with an ape."

Mike's lustful grab wasn't exactly a half-nelson or a bodylock, but it was substantial and twice as rough, and Jerry would never have maneuvered Mike anywhere because her feet weren't even touching the floor, but out of "sheer, sweet ecstasy" Mike pivoted of his own accord.

What happened after that Jerry was never quite sure. She knew Jack stepped out, Mike whirled still holding her and there was a loud, snappy smack in the vicinity of Mike's chin just over her head, and suddenly she was a free woman again. As Mike staggered and began to sag, Jack hooked him under the arms and dragged him back into the lounge.

Jerry thought he looked quite peaceful laid out on the tile floor. She followed them in and leaned against the wall until the room got steady again.

Jack was all business. "Give me something to gag and tie him," he said, looking up from feeling Mike's pulse and pulling back the lid of his left eye.

"I don't wear any ribbons with this hair-do and my handkerchief is three inches square; *you* have my shoes, so you know there are no laces, and I threw my six-dollar stockings to the wolves in the bar; everything else is essential to decency and morality."

Jerry was trying to sound flip as a prop to her courage and show Jack she really was a big, brave girl, but he just looked at her the way he sometimes looked at Doc, when he horsed around and wasn't paying attention to essentials.

"Get me five or six towels from the rack at the washstand."

They were nice strong towels, but Jack ripped them into strips and tied them into a rope, and the quick, efficient way he gagged and tied Mike was good for Jerry's morale. For the first time in her two years with the Triple A Agency she had an inkling why Jack and Doc never lacked for clients, and she suddenly was sure somehow, some way, this whole crazy mess was going to come out all right.

Jerry never knew whether it was his professionalism, his instinct as a detective, or just pride in what a whale of a sock he'd landed that made Jack feel Mike's pulse and look into his eye again before they left—anyway, he did, and gave a grunt of satisfaction. Then he went through Mike's pockets, took his switchblade, a gun from a shoulder holster and two loose keys. When he got up, he grinned at Jerry. She suddenly felt shy and complimented, sure a word of approval was coming; but all she got was: "Gird your loins, honey, the next ordeal won't be so easy." What a way to send a girl to her destruction. Well, at least she had got a "honey" out of it, which was some comfort.

"I don't know what Doc's got himself into, so we're going to have to play this by ear—listen to what Doc says, if he can talk—and to what I say, and follow the lead. Keep out of it, if you can." He put the switchblade in his pocket and looked at the gun dubiously, as though undecided; finally he shrugged and slipped it in the back of his waist-band.

In the dim hallway Jack hesitated a moment outside the gambling room. The ruffle of cards and the clink of poker chips and growl of voices floated out through an open transom. All at once there was a sharp exclamation of anger and then Doc's cheerful, happy voice: "Well, will you looky at me! Come to papa!" Following this came the flurry of crisp paper and the clink of cartwheels as someone, quite evidently Doc, pulled in the pot.

Jack grinned, relieved, and motioned Jerry to stay where she was while he tiptoed on down the hallway to the back door. She could see it was locked and Jack was trying Mike's keys. Presently he came back with a quick nod and only one key, which he inserted into the gambling room door so quietly even Jerry, standing at his elbow, heard nothing. The lock slid back soundlessly and the door gave under Jack's cautious pressure. He gave Jerry a warning glance and bending to her ear barely breathed, "Remember you're here and barefooted to fascinate Hilly. But watch it, that may not be the right play, now that we're in it." With that he swung the door open, pushed Jerry ahead of him, and they were in.

Inside was surprise, a stillness and a tension that sent the cold shivers up Jerry's back. Everything seemed to be in slow motion for her and she saw more clearly than she'd ever seen before in her whole life. Doc was sitting between a frightening man wearing a neat pinstriped suit and a chiseled, hard, cruel death's head for a face, and a little nervous man with a long nose and a fascinating streak of yellow-white, almost peroxide blonde, in his sleek, black hair. In front of Doc was a mountain of chips and big bills; behind him a green-eyed, babyfaced blonde in a slinky black dress with, to Jerry's eyes, "a disgusting bibful of chest."

Hilly Holliday was on the death's head's right, his startled face staring at Jack and Jerry over his shoulder, like a forlorn, sick-to-his-stomach animal in a steel trap. Jerry knew it was Hilly because of his playboy antics and his too-often picture in the news.

The other three goons at the table were exactly that—goons! There were five men at the table besides Doc and Hilly, and Jerry had a horrible sensation she could feel five guns on her and Jack as certainly as though they were in view. Jerry didn't know about the doll in the slinky black, but the way she gripped her handbag, she had her suspicions.

Jerry admitted later the suspended animation probably lasted no more than two seconds, but it seemed a week before Doc let out a yowl.

"Heeey, Jack, you can't come in here! I found this gold mine and I've staked my claim. How about that, fellers?"

"You know these people?" the death's head said out of the corner of his mouth, without taking his eyes from Jack.

"Course, I know him! He's my sidekick, Jack Packard! We heared about your floatin' game the minute we hit Las Vegas, but could I get Jack to come out and find you? No, not Jack! He had to go out and find hisself a female woman." Doc grinned at Jerry. "Where'd you win barefoot Josie with her cheeks of drugstore blushes?"

Jerry was outraged. So she was being cast as something Jack'd picked up off the streets. She knew exactly what Doc had in mind; he was cutting her out of the pack and making her just a bystander in case he and Jack came out second best in what was to follow. The only comfort for her in the whole situation was the way Hilly Holliday's dull eyes had started to glow. Jack had wanted her to make a conquest and she had made it. The boy's eyes hadn't left her for a moment and she could see he was getting acquainted with her slowly from "my evershowing pink toenails right up the whole alignment," and was mentally casting up leg, thigh, hip and chest measurements with expert x-ray eyes and growing enthusiasm. "That boy was avid!"

Doc reached down beside his chair and lifted up Hilly's hatbox which was heaped again with greenbacks, and that wasn't counting the heavy stacks in front of him on the table. If Doc suspected he was seated at a table with five mean, angry gunmen, no one would ever have guessed it, except Jack. His enthusiasm was boyishly naive and typically Doc. "Mr. Holliday over yonder didn't need the hatbox no more after he'd scraped the bottom, so he sold it to me for a hundred simoleons, and it's a good thing, on account who's got a takehome bag for totin' this kinda swag?"

The death's head said in a purring voice: "You heard Doc. We don't want you in the game." A menace crept into his voice. "However, I think you'd better stay with us until I find out what's happened to my two lookouts in the front of the house and why Mike isn't outside the door where he belongs."

"Yeah, fella, stick around," Doc encouraged as though it were Jack's choice. "About the only thing I ain't won yet is Lilly here, who's a keepin' me company and smells so good. After I've won her, I'll cut you cold for your barefoot girlfriend, only what I'll do with two blondes, I swear to grandma, I can't think."

The slinky peroxide blonde really looked at Jerry then, as though it had just occurred to her she was female and possible competition.

"You'd have thought I smelled bad, the way her predatory nose wrinkled and her too-thin mouth curled," Jerry recounted later. "I will say this for her, she did have nice teeth—if they were hers—nice sharp teeth that went with her long clawlike fingernails. She definitely belonged to the cat family."

Lilly's greenish eyes got a little malicious when she saw Hilly's attention fixed on Jerry, and she said: "You'll have to make that a three-way cut, Doc—looks like Mr. Holliday's got a stake in the slave girl."

Doc grinned at Hilly, who was paying no attention. "Why sure, Mr. Holliday, you're in, only before we get to the chattels, we still have a little more business with Uncle Sam's best grade of paper."

Nobody else was paying any attention to Doc's byplay. Jerry saw that death's head seemed to be waiting for Jack to make his move and the four henchmen were waiting for their boss. Jack was just waiting. Finally he reached for his coat pockets and, quicker than light, five hands went for shoulder holsters.

"I thought maybe you were wondering what made my coat pockets sag," he said in an accommodating voice, pulling out one of Jerry's evening slippers from each pocket. "I've found the best way to hold a girl, once you get her, is to keep her barefooted."

The goons stared in disbelief and then laughed.

Doc laughed loudest in admiration. "Honest to Christmas, Jack, you kill me. A good-looking hombre like you don't need to make women prisoners. Their precious little heart'll do that, if you'd only break down and show 'em a little Christian charity. How many times I gotta tell you that?" He looked at Jerry. "Honey, what's your name?"

"Jerry Booker."

"Jerry, huh? Well, looky, Jerry honey, is your love for Jack a growin' any with him keepin' you barefoot?"

"Ha!"

"You see it's like I always told you, Jack, you gotta make a girl comfortable if you want her mind to concentrate on the better things of life. Cold feet, cold heart!"

The men around the table were enjoying Doc's lecture and there was a general relaxation, which obviously was his aim. Only old death's head was still stony-faced. Doc noticed, too. He whipped up the deck of cards and whiffed through them. "Come on, whose deal? The march of progress is bein' impeded and me and the boys here is gettin' impatient."

"Just a minute, Doc." The chill in their leader's voice wiped the grins off the men's faces. "I still want to know what's happened to Ferris and Benny on lookout in the bar."

Jack shrugged. "They're still out there—or they were when they let Jerry and me in."

"And Mike?" He wasn't accepting it.

"Well, I must admit, we didn't take Mike into our confidence." Jack grinned. "We waited until he went into the women's lounge."

"What's he doing in there?"

Jack's grin broadened.

Doc laughed. "Now ain't *that* a silly question. Because they ain't no men's lounge in the corridor out yonder."

Three of the goons grinned, but the number-one man wasn't being conned and neither was the sharp-nosed man with the streak in his hair, on the other side of Doc.

Death's head talked across Doc to him. "Logan, go out and check on those two stupid characters in the bar and then find Mike and bring him back here."

The yellow-white streak nodded and got up, shrugged his shoulder harness into position and casually patted the faint bulge on his left chest.

Casually, as an afterthought, the other added: "Take Doc's friend with you."

Jerry couldn't see Jack's face because she was right beside him, but she saw Doc's quick glance and some instant intelligence pass between them and a happy grin light Doc's face. "And while Corporal Logan's out a checkin' the Indian scouts, Mister, let's me and you keep the action rollin' by cuttin' for Lilly."

Death's head looked almost human and just barely amused. Lilly laughed and slid up on the arm of Doc's chair.

"Mmm-mmm," Doc rubbed his nose in her arm and inhaled, "I don't know when I smelled anything so good since the mornin' glories come a bloom down in Big Water, Texas. They growed all over my gran'ma-on-my-mama's-side's hog pen." Jack and Yellowstreak were just going out the door when Doc called out, "Hurry back, Jack, to get in on the cut for little goodie no-shoes. Oh, yeah, and don't go off with her shoes! Female shoes is expensive and they go with the girl."

Jack grinned over his shoulder and dropped Jerry's shoes on the floor as he went out the door ahead of Logan. The door had an ominous click as it was pulled shut—to Jerry, anyway—because she knew as well as Jack and Doc must have known that this maneuver was to separate the boys.

7

Given full rein, Doc Long would happily turn this entire "wamper-jawed Las Vegas scramble for the two-hundred-fifty-thousand-dollar bank loot," into a first-person-singular account. Triple A-One company policy against a one-man point of view and instinct for a fair division of final credit still found his colorful and unexpurgated Texas verbiage dominating some phases of the affair—especially in the area of the backroom floating poker game here on the outskirts of Nevada's city of liquor, women, and gambling. How could anyone but Doc have presented the following:

"Well, looky where we're at, now! All my whoopin'-it-up horseplay to convince Skip Sullivan and his gun slingin' and lightfingered card sharps that me and Jack was just a couple of countrified soozys out for a big time just plain wasn't bein' swallowed.

"There was Jack somewheres out in the back hall with Logan on his back, him with the streak of ciffy-cat yellow-white in his hair and somethin' more potent than a bad smell in his stinger; and there was me and Jerry left inside the gamin' room with four 'techous' hombres that could of shivered us with hot lead anytime they'd a mind to—not to mention the hot little drugstore blonde in the black satin sack, Lilly Montrose, already pegged as Skip Sullivan's everlovin' and well-stacked mama.

"And after all the trouble I'd gone to tryin' to make out like our girl Jerry was just a accidental bystander; what does she do but drape herself on the arm of Hilly Holliday's chair at the poker table like a squirmy young flirt— and Hilly a lovin' every minute of it, as though losin' a whole hatbox of important money was a mere side issue.

"Course I knowed she done it on account of this here Lilly Montrose movin' in on me, when I suggested me and Skip cut the cards for the little lady's affections; but blame it all, Jerry, bein' the Triple A's favorite secretary, should have knowed it was just my way to keep Skip's mind off the main problem until I could see how Jack and Logan made out on their preliminary bout out in the hall.

"Anyway, there was Lilly at my elbow and Jerry across the table a warmin' up to Hilly, with me a shufflin' the poker deck and plunkin' it down in front of Skip.

" 'Course,' I kinda hinted to Skip, 'I don't blame you if you don't throw Lilly up for stakes, on account I won more female women and lettuce in one-card draws than the law of averages allows. It's just that I'm lucky that way, and they ain't nobody a gonna say you're chicken if you don't jeopardize a girlfriend on a sure thing.'

"A kinda intent, malicious grin come on the faces of Skip's three henchmen, still at the table, and a sort of glaze frosted the big boy's eyes. I could hear a soft little chortle of anticipation deep in Lilly's throat. Jerry leaned down and says somethin' snide in Hilly's ear and he looked where I was a sittin' and grinned.

"Kinda slow and easy Skip cut the deck and shoved it at me for the first draw. I cut my card and laid it face down in front of me. Skip give me a quick glance as though he'd expected me to face it up.

" 'We'll turn 'em over at one and the same time; what could be fairer'n that?' "

The flintfaced man shrugged, making it a matter of pure indifference, and his hand hovered like an anxious guardian angel for a second, finally resting on the deck lovingly; then with a twist of the wrist he flipped over the top card. It was the ace of clubs. Doc had to have the ace of diamonds, hearts or spades.

"Which naturally of course I had."

He told Lilly to reach out and turn his card. It was the ace of hearts.

The girl's breath sucked in and she gave her boss a scared, desperate look. Something passed between her and the stony face, and to quote Doc, "All a sudden Lilly was as happy as a young heifer in high grass. She slipped off the arm of the chair into my lap and 'give me the business.' The way her arms entwined my neck and her mouth smothered me I could've thought I was on the hangin' tree and my number up, only my horoscope says my end is fire and water, not a rope. So I knowed it must've been true love.

"The only good part about it was, I got a peek at Jerry in the midst of all this ecstasy, and her eyes was so green and mixed with disgustedness, I knowed for sure she felt Lilly was a trespassin' on her private property."

Doc was just beginning to wonder what next he could do to keep the interest of the poker session, when the door opened and Jack was back. Logan wasn't with him and Jack was looking more than a little worried. But only one part as worried as the boys in the back room. It didn't show on the leader's crusty face but there was a flick of surprise and disillusion in his eyes.

Doc admired the soft, sure way Jack "come across to the table and said, kinda as though he was in charge of the whole shebang: 'Logan's having trouble with your two lookouts in the front bar. He thinks you'd better come out there yourself.' "

Only Sullivan's lips moved: "Why?"

"There's a Lieutenant Tracey Holmes with several men from the racket squad, asking questions and—"

"Well, whooeeee!" recalled Doc, "You never seen such a busy scramble of men and equipment as Skip's three gun boys in Operation Scat. The way them poker chips and cards vamoosed was pure magic, and durin' the pawin' and rakin' in, I naturally concentrated on the long green that was in my vicinity on the table. I had my hatbox so stuffed in no time, I hardly could get the lid on.

"All the while Skip just set there, not movin' a muscle and not missin' a beat. Even when the poker table was lifted practically off his lap, folded up and rolled out, he still just set there. In a couple of minutes at most, the room was empty as my grave, and the three goons was out the door and down the hall to the back entrance. I noticed Jack took occasion to make sure they went out the back way.

"You gotta hand it to Jack. The name of Lieutenant Holmes was first class magic in the Las Vegas bright lights, and he sprung it at the right minute. But that's my boy Jack for you—psychological!

"And all the time Skip just set there and Lilly stuck to me like flypaper, Lieutenant Holmes or *no* Lieutenant Holmes. She sure was a lovin' little filly, only it kinda troubled me that I kept feelin' it was the hatbox full of greetings from the United States mint that really filled her yearnin' heart."

Sullivan slowly got to his feet with as near a grim flick of amusement as he was capable of. "Lieutenant Holmes's an old acquaintance. Shall we go welcome him?"

During the clean-up, Jerry and Holliday appeared to have retreated into their own world, which according to Doc, "from the looks on their faces was a bower of pure apple blossoms in spring, rampant with young love—and not too young at that. You'd of thought me and Jack wasn't even there. There I was a tryin' to herd 'em to the door after Jack and Skip Sullivan, a shooin' 'em with my hatbox of loot in one hand and a armload of Lilly on the other, when Jerry pipes up with: " 'How about Hilly and me slipping to the back way, and meeting you boys at the Regal Spa? Hilly's got his car outside.'

"Skip stopped in the doorway and turned like he was a gonna veto the suggestion, but he never got it out, on account of Jack's fist come up against his chin with such a pop I swear to goodness I could hear splinters of jawbone flyin' like shrapnel. That made me kinda mad, Jack a showin' off like that, when he knowed that was my department. Anyway, Skip kinda sighed in a dissatisfied manner and slumped down like a sack of overripe last-year's tomatos.

" 'We'll all go out the back way,' Jack told Jerry, a rubbin' his fist. I could see he'd skinned a knuckle and that disgusted him, on account they ain't nothin' that puts him out like disfigurin' his hands, which Jerry once said belonged to the artist type, or maybe a surgeon, like Jack set out to be and then didn't.

"While Jack was a bendin' over Skip, playin' doctor like he does when somebody's hurt, even the enemy, I felt Lilly's fingernails a diggin' into my coat sleeve and looked around. By the dark color of her eyes and the sick-cat white under her make-up I could see she'd been jolted almost as bad as Skip. Hilly was kinda gulpin' for air, and Jerry, even though she still was a hangin' onto his arm, was ado-rin' Jack with wide dewy eyes, like a languishin' calf. That made me feel better. Maybe Jerry wasn't as het up over Hilly as she was a actin'. Anyway, Jack nodded over Skip, satis-fied, and got up off his knees and motioned for us to come out into the corridor.

"And then's when I balked! 'Now looky, Jack, we still got Lilly, here!' I could see Lilly tensin' up and lookin' scared, but dad-rat it, she was Skip Sullivan's female, not mine, and I said so."

"But she is yours, Doc," Jerry insisted, dripping with sweetness and malice. "You won her fair and square."

Hilly nodded and Jack grinned.

"And see how scared and helpless she is," Jerry twisted the knife a little, "and look how lovingly she clings to you. I thought all Texas boys had protecting hearts for the frail and innocent."

"She's not *my* frail and she ain't innocent and more'n that she's a stickin' to this hatbox of you-know-what!"

During the interchange Lilly was standing closer to Doc, big-eyed and uncertain, looking from one to the other, but mostly appealing to Jack who she instinctively knew was going to have final say.

"You won her, Doc; she's yours. This is no place to decide what to do with her. So come on."

"What about this Lieutenant Holmes out front?" Hilly wanted to know. Even Jerry looked at him pityingly.

Jack just said: "I'll call him when we get to the Regal Spa. He'll be surprised to learn he was raiding a second-rate roadhouse tonight."

8

The night was freshening under a velvety blue-black canopy thick with star clusters. The backyard was full of deep shadows and rocky sand. That's when Jerry remembered she was barefooted and her shoes still on the floor in the back room. Jerry complained bitterly and soiled her pretty lips with short scandalous words of execration when Doc proposed she ride him piggyback.

Doc was encumbered with his hatbox of money and Lilly, but Jack moved ahead watchfully in anticipation of an ambush. There was no movement or sound save the incessant whir, tinkle and chirp of desert insects. Hilly Holliday's rental car was where he'd said it was parked.

The one pale bare globe still lighted the front door, but otherwise the debilitated old roadhouse showed no sign of life, crouching low and mean in its own humble shadow.

Doc's version of the ride back to the Regal Spa on the strip had its own special significance: "Jack sat between Jerry and Lilly and was welcome, on account the more them two members of the weaker sex (ha!) associated, the more they just plain loathed each other. I was a sittin' in the front alongside Hilly, a daddlin' my hatbox of cabbage on my lap like a everlovin' mama on the way home from the maternity ward with her first ketch. I caught sight of a store clock as we come through the business section and it said 3:15 in the mornin'.

"I looked back at Jerry, and except for a kinda pout-in', and payin' no attention to Lilly like she was a playin' 'see no evil, hear no evil,' she was as fresh and spunky and honey-colored as when she'd swished into the Triple A-One office yesterday a.m., which goes to prove that female women got more'n their share of adrenalin glands, and thrive on big trouble, given a chance. Me, I'd had it and was glad we was a headin' for home.

"I could feel Lilly's fingers on the back of my seat a touchin' my shoulderblades as though she wanted to feel I was still there, and her fingers was a movin' like they was itchin' to go-for-grabs in my hatbox. I never *did* see such a one-tracked female; I sure was glad she didn't feel attached to me, a man'd *never* get shet of that kind of attachment! 'Course I knowed her kind of girl couldn't never love any-thing like she loved the root of all evil. Here she was prac-tically in the hands of the enemy (same bein' us), and not knowin' whether we was a gonna turn her over to Jack's friend Lieutenant Holmes, or toss her in the nearest sand dune, and yet settin' there a yearnin' her heart out for what I was a holdin' in my lap.

"Hilly was a payin' no more attention to the hatbox since I won it, than if I was carryin' home a Easter bon-net. It was like as if he'd had the pretty money and lost it, and now all he was interested in was a swivelin' around so's he could enjoy the next pretty bauble, namely Jerry. The dress Jerry was a wearin' wasn't no high-neck affair in the beginnin', but the way she was sittin' didn't help con-cealment much, so Hilly had plenty of bauble to enjoy.

"Jack was just a sittin' there nursin' the knuckle of his skinned fist, until Jerry took notice. 'Your hand hurting?' she asked kinda anxious and motherly.

"He opened and closed it careful-like, askin' for pity and admiration, which he wasn't a gettin' from me. If he wanted to play the heroic hatchet man, which I'm better at, why, let him take the consequences.

" 'Why didn't you hit him on the Adam's apple instead of going for bone, like I told you a dozen times? It's just as effective and ten times as sure.'

" 'Why thank you, Doc, for your sincere commiseration,' he come back with a kinda amused glint, 'but as I've told you, medically speaking a knockout jolt on the epiglottis can be extremely dangerous to the recipient.'

" 'And I suppose you busted your fist on recipient Mike, the lookout, and recipient Logan, the guy with the ciffy cat streak, likewise.'

" 'That's right,' Jerry remembered. 'What happened to Logan when you went out into the corridor together and you came back alone?'

"Jack smiled kinda dreamy. 'The last I saw of him, he was happily sleeping, stretched out in the women's lounge beside Mike.' He looked at me kinda sour. 'You're always talking about hitting people on the Adam's apple, but I notice every time there's hitting to be done either you've got your hands full of poker chips or pretty women.'

"And that's how we pulled up in the driveway in front of the Regal Spa at 3:30 a.m. and assembled on the sidewalk one lovesick playboy, Hilly Holliday; two explosive blondes; a sizable slice of Fort Knox; and me and Jack. In a way it was unfortunate and pretty durned unprofessional that neither me nor Jack thought to look back at the big black shiny sedan until it pulled up behind us. I say, in a way, on account it might have prevented the shambles that busted out on the Regal Spa's front steps. But shucks, think of the fun we'd of missed.

"Me and Jack both seen what was a comin' as five plug-uglies scrambled out of the black car. Only Jack had the sense to grab the hatbox out of my hands and give it to Jerry and shove her towards the hotel entrance; and she had the sense to skitter into the lobby. The last I seen, her skirt tail was a snappin' and a crackin' for cover, with Lilly a breathin' fire and brimstone down her neck, tooth and nail unsheathed."

9

The unexpected descent of the goon squad, plus Jack's quick hatbox shift from Long to Booker, and his violent shove that sent Jerry lunging into the lobby doorway, had the Triple A-One's blonde, barefoot, junior-size amanuensis' adrenalin glands pumping like a five-alarm fire, with sirens piercing her ears and her perception momentarily looking out through a blood-red haze.

Her final glimpse of Jack and Doc was all she needed to recognize the emergency—the settled, grim, fortresslike aspect of Jack and the pure malicious, pale light in Doc's faded blue eyes and the happy-go-lucky smirk on his horsey face, along with the tightening pantherlike grace of his lean, lanky frame, told her everything she didn't want to know about sudden death and destruction.

The first Jerry realized, to quote, "sister Lilly was my everloving shadow" was three steps inside the lobby, when she felt the other's claws in her bare shoulder and a vicious yank on the low neckline of her dress that "damn near unhorsed me."

There was a rending tear from neck to hem and a gusty breeze that told Jerry an awful truth; she now had a southern exposure more interesting than lawful.

Well, that was too much. Now she was fighting for more than Hilly Holliday's hatbox. That was a two-hundred-and-twenty-five-dollar cocktail dress Lilly ruined. Two could play at that game!

Jerry Booker, secretary, now a small blonde tiger, dropped the two-hundred-fifty-thousand-dollar pasteboard container in a lobby chair and turned on her natural foe just as the latter's fingers reached out for her hair. Jerry ducked, grabbed the hem of Lilly's skirt, butted her in the stomach and came up fast, whipping the circular skirt up over Lilly's head, popping buttons from the bodice and splitting the waistband of her slip. For one precious moment Jerry had the girl's head and arms in a sort of sack. From the armpits down there was nothing but pure girl, draped in a lacy, fig-leaf-size, black bikini.

Busy as Jerry was, she got one glimpse of the grandfather of all night clerks behind the reception desk, his ancient eyes popping and his grizzled mustache alert and quivering over an open mouth! The callow bellhop looked as though he'd suddenly been transported into the delights of a Turkish harem.

But Lilly wasn't holding still for this cat-in-a-sack gambit, and before Jerry could get her breath, Miss Las Vegas had yanked herself free of her shreds and tatters and came at her, intent on the kill. Before Jerry could recover, Lilly came down on her bare foot with a sharp French heel. Pain exploded in Jerry's foot, shot up her leg, and burst out her eyes in hot sparks and tears. Even in blind excruciating pain she felt Lilly's fiery fingernails run down her neck and chest and fasten in the front of her blouse. A second more and Jerry was as unencumbered with the refinements of civilization as Lilly herself.

"Two things I remembered thinking," Jerry recalls, "in the midst of the tempest and lightning: One, I had on prettier, more expensive underwear than Lilly; two, thank the powers that be, Jack and Doc had given me plenty of time for a good hot bath and I'd taken the trouble to lay on a nice, heavy, evenly applied coat of dusting powder. Even under the exertion I still looked smooth and satiny and Lilly was shiny and streaked with perspiration."

Jerry couldn't remember who hit the floor first, "but I know we had stopped reaching for clothes and had closed in on the essential girl, and went down in a tangle of arms and legs. I was on top, sitting on Lilly's heaving stomach when Jack, Doc and Hilly came into the lobby with two of Las Vegas's finest. I wouldn't have known it then, except Lilly stopped clawing at me and looked up over my shoulders, scared. That's when I came to and realized we were surrounded by a covey of grinning male faces."

Doc started to lift Jerry to her feet saying, "Atta old fight, sugar; so this is what you been a hidin' from us all this time down at the Triple A-One office"—only Hilly stepped in ahead of him and gathered up the girl. One of the policemen slipped what looked like an Indian horse blanket around her nakedness.

Lilly got up by herself and the other officer draped her in a second blanket. Jerry couldn't help but feel a moment of pity for Lilly's wilted dejection now the war was over. Forlorn, bedraggled and disheartened, she was contemplating her immediate future in smoldering anger and despair. Jerry even had a grudging affection for Doc when he crossed to Lilly and comforted her with, "It was a good try, honey, and it's just a darned shame everybody couldn't of won."

Lilly's hand shot out and slapped him with all the hateful anger still pent up in her. She wasn't having any sympathy and Jerry suddenly felt better. The policemen laughed and after a dazed moment Doc said, polite and meek, "Well, 'scuse me," and turned away.

That was the first time Jerry noticed the big black and blue mouse under Doc's left eye and the ugly gash on his chin. She looked quickly at Jack and saw his right arm in a makeshift sling, his tender, swollen nose, and his cut lip. Both men's suits showed the ravages of their sidewalk battle, and it was then Jerry remembered Lilly's and her bout in the lobby hadn't been the main event. As she recalled the reason for it all, she looked toward the chair where she'd dropped the hatbox. It wasn't there!

"The hatbox— " but that's all she got out because Jack gave her such a thundercloud of a warning glance, the rest choked up in her throat. She was relieved to hear the unspeakable, moaning siren as the paddy wagon whipped into the driveway to distract the questioning eyes on her. Another policeman came to the lobby door and signaled inside, and one of the cops picked up the rags and tatters and asked Lilly which were hers. She snatched her slinky black remnants out of his hand, gave Jerry a dirty look and walked out to the sidewalk. The other officer shook hands with Jack and Doc, nodded at Hilly and smirked at Jerry, "Sorry, lady, duty calls, so could I have my blanket back?"

According to Jerry's version, "Everyone stopped whatever he was doing or thinking and concentrated on me expectantly. I gave a quick estimate of the draperies still intact underneath the blanket and knew doggone well he could be arrested for aiding and abetting indecent exposure if he insisted on his blanket. It was one thing to be ripped and stripped in the heat of action, something else to stand forth in the flesh, a child of nature in the lobby of even a Las Vegas hotel. Besides, I didn't like the avid look on the old goat of a night clerk, who'd never moved from behind the reception desk during the whole fracas; nor the grinning leer of the bellhop leaning in the doorway of the nearest elevator; nor Hilly Holliday's amused, hopeful expectancy; and most of all, Jack's mildly withdrawn attitude, as though something more important were on his mind. His own secretary facing a choice between Godiva without a horse and a trip down to the police station; because I knew doggone well the cop was going to take

the blanket, either with or without me. And my boss was
thinking about something else!

"Well, Doc wasn't thinking of something else, bless
his Sir Lancelot (Texas version) heart, always at the service
of a maiden in distress.

" 'Come on, sugar, get in the phone booth. That'll hide
your sin and shame whilst I rustle you up somethin' else.'
He held a quick exchange of words and money with the
bellhop, and they went across to the checkroom. A minute
later Doc shoved a man-sized raincoat into the phone booth
and I gave him the horse blanket.

"Even when I'd turned up the sleeves and buttoned
the collar, you could have your choice of whether I was
a barefoot South Sea native in a missionary's mother hub-
bard, or a large turtle poking its silly head out of an over-
size shell! Brother, being secretary to a couple of private
detective characters was rough on blondes."

10

By the time Doc had Jerry out of fig leaves and under temporary cover, the police wagon was loaded. Two of the thugs were still completely tranquilized, another was spitting out a loose tooth, and the fourth and fifth were nursing meaty noses, split ears and dizzy spells in the head. Jack had returned outside and was nosing around, haveing a final "say so" with a police sergeant.

When Doc joined them everything was friendly and he got a grin from the wagon crew and had to shake hands with the sergeant. "I could see right off Jack had been a spreadin' on the malarkey, the way the sergeant pumped my hand," Doc afterwards reported modestly.

"I've heard about you Texas boys," the sergeant approved, "and now I've seen the results with my own eyes. I'm only sorry I wasn't around to see how it was done."

"All me and Jack done was stand back to back and kinda persuade the boys they was makin' a mistake."

The officer grinned and climbed up into the front of the wagon beside the driver and waved: "We'll see you down at the station at three this afternoon," he called and nodded to the driver.

Doc got a glimpse into the back as the wagon swung around out onto the highway, and the last thing he saw was Lilly huddled in her blanket. She looked up and her eyes spit fire as she said something Doc was just as glad, for his morale, he couldn't hear, but the policeman sitting beside her looked back and laughed.

"Well, that ties a knot in the tail of *that* possum," Doc said contentedly, "and I'm plumb glad. It's been a long day and a little pillow time's a gonna feel just dandy."

"You think so?" Jack turned back into the lobby.

"Huh?"

"Where's the hatbox?"

"Ain't Jerry got it?"

"Did you see it in the lobby?"

"No."

"No, because it wasn't there."

"But maybe she knows where it is?"

"You weren't listening. She doesn't know. Lilly didn't have enough on to conceal a ring box until the policeman put the blanket around her, so she's clean. It was gone when we came into the lobby, so one of the policemen couldn't have taken it, and anyway I had my eyes on them every minute. Besides, I made sure it wasn't anywhere in the wagon while they were loading the goons."

"Well, that just plain don't make sense," Doc protested. "Jerry's bound to know *somethin'*."

Inside, Jerry was sitting in the corner of a davenport in her tent of a raincoat with her feet tucked up under her. It was plain to Doc that "Hilly didn't care much about me and Jack horning in just then. Jerry's eyes was big, moony and bedroomy, but the rest of her looked kinda beat and I had a hunch she was plenty relieved to see us. She still was a playin' Hilly like Jack had told her, and for why I couldn't see, on account I'd won all Hilly's money, and anyway the loot had vamoosed."

Doc wondered at the empty lobby, which was surprising for a Las Vegas hotel even at four in the morning. He took in the night clerk, still behind his desk, and the bell-hop who'd joined him and noticed "they was kinda keepin' an eye on us, as if waitin' for the next explosion and passin' eager comments out of the corners of their mouths, like they was a tellin' each other their versions of what they'd seen up to now."

Hilly swung his legs around reluctantly when Jack sat down next to him, and Doc dropped on the arm of the davenport next to Jerry.

She looked at Jack anxiously and he shook his head. "Just what happened when you ran in here with the hat-box?" he asked.

"Everything," Jerry said wearily. "Lilly was right on my tail. She grabbed my dress and ripped me down the back. You can see the nail marks on my shoulders. Jack, I *had* to drop the hatbox to defend myself."

"Where'd you drop it?"

She pointed to the armchair not too far away.

Jack went over, looked at the chair for a couple of seconds, tipped it up, looked under it and then came back. "And that's the last you saw of it?"

Jerry nodded her head meekly.

"You and Lilly were fighting quite a way from the chair when we came in."

"We were all over the lobby. And if you think I had any time for hatboxes with that she-cat climbing my frame—" She signed dejectedly. "I'm sorry, boss. I guess I should have hung onto the box, no matter what!"

Jack didn't say anything, as though he hadn't heard her humble confession.

Doc heard and came to Jerry's defense. "Honest to Christmas, Jack, when you get on a problem you ain't got no more milk of human kindness than a fish!" He looked down from his height on the arm of the davenport to Jerry. "Honey, you done good! When I seen the muscles you got under that baby flesh and the way you was a layin' into that Las Vegas tart—"

Hilly leaned forward with a new glimmer of interest and a sudden smirk of amusement.

"Am I to understand from all this that my former two hundred and fifty thousand dollars, now the property of Doc, has vanished right under his nose?"

Jack looked at him sourly. "What's so hilarious? The money still belonged to you."

Hilly looked like he'd been kicked in the stomach.

Doc did too. He admitted it. "And why not? On account of, this was all news to me. I worked my finger-bones to the knuckles a winnin' that money—"

Jack went right on talking, but looking at Doc as though reading his mind. "Doc and I hired out to come over here and round up a certain two hundred fifty thousand dollars and get it safely back to a bank. Doc's winning at the poker table was part of the job."

"Well, how do you like that sack of turnips! If that ain't somethin' to throw to the hawgs!" Jack opened his mouth but Doc stopped him. "Not that I'm a gonna cross you, son! You said it, and me and you are partners and you've been top man too long for me to start a argument this late." However, Doc appealed to Jerry but she didn't blink an eye, which left him feeling she accepted Jack's verdict all the way, "which the same as settled the matter."

Hilly just stared. Finally he got out a weak, silly grin and held out his hand to Doc across Jerry.

Doc took it grudgingly. "For what?" he asked. "It ain't *my* money that's missin' —it's yours." Doc could feel some of the enthusiasm oozing out of the handshake, but Hilly was game.

"Thanks for the good try," he said.

Jack got up. "You folks wait here a minute," he said, and started across the lobby, "to where," Doc saw, "the night clerk and bellboy was still a leerin' and poppin' their eyes at us. The oh so casual way Jack ambled over, I knowed just as well as right's right and wrong's wrong, he had somethin' definite in mind, and it was probably trouble, so there was nothin' for me to do but trail along, him with his arm in a sling from too much piston action already, and maybe more called for."

11

To reach the Regal Spa's reception desk from their davenport rendezvous, Jack and Doc had to wade through a half-acre of thick, sand-colored pile in the vast, dimly lit four-in-the-morning desert of a lobby.

They left Hilly Holliday, an intently thoughtful and sobered playboy, chewing on the fact that he'd had in his hands, and lost, two hundred fifty thousand dollars; which was impressive, even in Las Vegas. For the moment it took his mind off the pint-sized Triple A-One Detective agency's secretary, Jerry Booker, whom he'd chosen by divine right as a decidedly acceptable consolation prize.

At the other end of the davenport sat Jerry, a brooding female Buddha, wrapped in moody contemplation of the excesses required of a private detective's girl friday, and little else. She was barefooted and so close to mother-naked under the borrowed oversized man's raincoat, it was neither decent nor funny.

As he and Jack approached, the ancient on the night desk at one and the same time riled Doc and tickled his funnybone. "This throwaway, withered old apple core, in his standup collar and goat's eyes, behind old-fashioned pinch-nose glasses on a black cord, kinda reared up as he seen us a comin'. His Adam's apple in his skinny neck began to pump up and down, like a auxiliary heartbeat, and his skimpy mouth come open in a kinda snarlin' grin, showin' a full set of store teeth. His puny arms come up in a sorta sissy show of self-defense, only his heart wasn't in it. He'd of been happier if we'd just went away.

"I had to admire the bellboy. He was a tough, wiry kid and he'd just seen the slaughter me and Jack was capable of, but he stood there polite and interested, with a kinda impudent smirk on his face. You could see the rough-and-tumble, knockabout life he'd had in this Nevada gamblin' and floozy town. He didn't expect nothin' but trouble and he knew how to stand, wait for it, and grin. I liked him just as much as I didn't like grandpa, but it was seepin' through my thick skull what was in Jack's mind, and if what he was a thinkin' was the answer, then sonny boy was our man.

"As we come up to the desk, the kid's grin widened. 'Mr. Kinder here, and I, was tossing up which fight we liked the best, Mr. Packard. The one you and Mr. Long put on out in front or the one Miss Booker and the other dame settled here in the lobby.'

"Jack kinda leaned on the counter lookin' at the night clerk, as if he hadn't heard the kid. 'Keys to 3107 and 3109, please, and if you've got a room for our friend, Mr. Holliday, for one night, I'll sign for it.'

"The relief on Mr. Kinder's face and the eager fumblin' for keys and the sign-in card was real comical. When Jack had put the keys in his pocket and signed up for Hilly, he turned to the kid, who'd quit grinnin' at being ignored.

" 'You saw both fights?'

"The young feller's eyes lighted up again and he give Jack another nice, white, even-toothed grin.

" 'It was like a three-ring circus,' he confided. 'It kept us looking in two directions, but we didn't miss much.'

" 'Didn't, huh?'

" 'Well, there was a few minutes when Miss Booker and the other dame was doing their striptease act and Mr. Kinder's attention got pretty locked in—' (A mean, sickly smile and a high pink on Mr. Kinder's bony face didn't add nothin' to his beauty.) '—but to me, dames is dames with or without, and I've never seen the way you and Mr. Long backed up to each other and used your fists. That was something to look at.'

" 'Without a doubt your sidewalk act was the bloodiest, but the lobby performance was the fleshiest.' Mr. Kinder gave a dry cackle that cut off with a gulp when we all looked at him, and a blank sick-chicken film come over his eyes, shuttin' out the not very nice gleam that was behind. Especially when I said, 'Why, shame on you, grandpa—a old man like you!'

"Jack butted in, lookin' at him more friendly. 'I'm glad you didn't miss anything in the lobby, Mr. Kinder. That's important, I have it on good authority that you didn't move from behind your desk here.'

"Mr. Kinder nodded kinda uneasy and suddenly looked wary.

"Jack shifted his eyes to the kid. 'Then you must have seen our young friend here pick up Miss Booker's hatbox.'

"I moved in closer to the kid, but all he done was look surprised.

" 'Heeey, what is this?' he asked, 'I put it in the checkroom, Mr. Long knows that.'

"I guess it was my turn for my mouth to flop open. Both Mr. Kinder and the bellboy was a lookin' at me, brimmin' over with suspicion.

"Jack looked at me kinda disgusted, the way he has. 'Now wait a minute, Jack, I'm a two-tailed hipponauserous if I know what he's a talkin' about, and I bet he don't neither.'

" 'Now look, Mister,' the kid stuck out his bony chin at me, 'that kind of talk could lose both Mr. Kinder and me our jobs. When you came over to get that raincoat for Miss Booker, I not only found you the coat, but I gave you a check for the hatbox.'

"Well, I swear to my grandma, that's the first time I'd even thought about it. I fished down in my pocket for the stub. 'You mean this is for Jerry's hatbox?'

" 'What else?' he asked real sarcastic. 'When the two dames were romping over each other they didn't have any time to think about new hats. For all I knew they could have sat on it. Besides, they were so busy, anybody could have come in and walked off with it, which isn't so unusual in this town. That's the first rule of the house; anything left unattended in the lobby has to be put in the checkroom, pronto.'

" 'Well, strike me pink and call me blue boy!' I just stood there and let Jack take the stub out of my hand.

"Jack took out his wallet and put a twenty on the desk. 'Thank you, Mr. Kinder, for keeping an eye on the lobby,' he said all friendly. He peeled off another twenty and give it to the bellboy. 'That's not only for being on the job, but to help you forget how stupid a Texas boy can be. Let's go redeem the hatbox.'

"That made me plumb mad. Why'd he have to say that? I stood there a glarin' at grandpa, just hopin' he'd give me one of his store-tooth grins or smirks or somethin', but he tucked the twenty away and just waited nice and polite, blank as cardboard.

" 'Something else, Mr. Long?'

" 'Yeah, go have your dirty mind wrenched out by one of them brainwashers!' I turned on my heel just in time to hear the bellboy, on his way across the lobby.

" 'Of course, as soon as I picked up the hatbox I knew it wasn't a hat inside, by the heft of it. Out-of-town visitors carry the craziest things in the craziest packages.'

" 'Real crazy,' Jack agreed. 'Imagine our Miss Booker lugging a hatbox of sexy paperback romances around Las Vegas. But that just shows how starved some girls are for love.'

"Jerry heard that and so did Hilly. He grinned as Jerry lurched up off the davenport, forgettin' all about the long raincoat, and stepping on the hem she fell kerflop in Hilly's lap. He just folded her to him and still was a kissin' her when she busted out of his arms like a catamount on a catapult and stalked off to the elevator in a barefoot stomp.

" 'We're all coming, Jerry,' Jack called from the checkstand, taking the hatbox from the bellboy. 'Don't be in such a snit. Besides, I've got your door key.'

"Jerry just set down on the bench inside and sulked. In a minute the rest of us crowded in. Jack pressed the third-floor button. And there we was, Jerry sulkin'; Hilly tryin' to decide which he was most interested in, Jerry or the hatbox Jack was a carryin'; and me, still insulted. So nobody said anything, and we all got out on the third floor feeling frazzled and techous."

When they came to Jerry's door, she yanked the key out of Jack's hand, opened it herself and then slammed it shut, locking it from the inside. The expectant look faded out of Hilly's eyes, but then they lit on the hatbox and got hopeful again. They were still looking hopeful when they came to Jack and Doc's suite. "Get some sleep, Hilly; you want to be fresh and clearheaded this afternoon for our date with Lieutenant Holmes."

"The police want to see me?" Hilly was taken aback.

"Or maybe you'd like to tell us first why you brought two hundred fifty thousand dollars to Las Vegas in a hatbox," Jack paused a moment and then added, "making sure everyone in Los Angeles knew about it."

"And maybe it's none of your business." Hilly's brusqueness sounded more defensive than mean.

"You don't even want to tell us why you chose to bring exactly two hundred and fifty thousand or why you selected the denominations you did?"

"No!" But Hilly looked uneasy.

"Nor why you had Lilly Montrose for a traveling companion on the flight over?"

"I just happened to meet her on the plane. She sat beside me."

"By prearrangement?"

"What?"

"I suggest it was arranged for Lilly to meet you in Los Angeles and escort you to the floating poker game here in Las Vegas." Hilly's eyes went blank, but he was listening to Jack. "Also, you were told the amount of money to draw out of the bank and the exact denomination of bills to bring; also it was part of the plot to use a woman's hatbox."

Hilly flared. "I still don't know how it concerns you, much less the police."

"Then you're not aware the amount and the denominations you withdrew in Los Angeles coincide with the bills in a recent Chicago bank robbery?"

The green tinge of Hilly's complexion wasn't acting; he was hit squarely between the eyes. "I don't know anything about a bank robbery."

Jack nodded as though he believed him. "Oh, it was a frame, all right—but don't you think it's about time you gave out with a little information?"

Hilly cased the corridor both ways with nervous eyes, "Let's go inside."

Jack nodded and unlocked the suite. Hilly ducked inside, with Jack and Doc on his heels. One of the sliding glass panel doors onto a balcony was open, letting in a mixture of desert night sounds and alternating currents of desert heat and cooler mountain air.

Hilly crossed the room quickly, looked out anxiously, then slid the panel shut. "What about the men out at the roadhouse?" he worried.

"It's took you a long time to start worryin' about them." Doc looked amused, and Jack added, "The police have been sweeping up after us."

Doc looked surprised. "Huh, when'd you have time to report in?"

Jack grinned. "You don't have to report in to Lieutenant Holmes. Why do you think I tipped him off before we started out?"

"And he cleaned out the roadhouse after we got out?"

"The paddy wagon sergeant said they had quite a collection under lock and key down at the station."

"On what charge?"

"Disturbing the peace; operating an unlicensed floating poker game, which is a serious offense in a town that makes its profits out of gambling. Oh yes, there's also something about them being 'held without bail, pending further information.' "

Hilly's eyes grew suspicious. "What information?"

"Why, your information," Jack said innocently.

Hilly shrugged. "Sorry, I can't help."

"Try."

"All I know is a friend of mine in Hollywood called me on the phone and said he could put me onto something hot if I wanted a little fast action in Las Vegas and was willing to do a favor for a 'power behind the scenes.' "

"You want to name any names?"

"Names?" You'd have thought Jack was talking a foreign language.

"This friend in Hollywood?"

Hilly hesitated and then confessed. At least it sounded like a confession. "He's not actually a friend—I've met him at parties; he's about my age and build; good dresser; the women are crazy about him."

Doc's Texas grin widened.

Jack's face grew more sardonic as Hilly babbled on. "He's got a name?"

"Uh—Charlie."

"Charlie what?"

Hilly shrugged helplessly.

"Well, we know two things for certain, Jack," Doc's voice sounded tolerantly amused. "It ain't Charlie Chan, on account he's in Honolulu; and it ain't Charlie Chaplin, on account he's in Switzerland."

"What about the name of this Las Vegas 'power behind the scenes?' "

Hilly's lips tightened.

"Another blank?"

"He was to contact me here after I'd completed my favor for him."

"And the favor?"

"Just bring the two hundred fifty thousand in certain required denominations in a woman's hatbox which was delivered to my Beverly Hills apartment yesterday morning."

Jack's eyes grew more intent. "It had to be a certain hatbox?"

"I don't know. I just thought they brought me a hatbox for convenience."

"Was there a name on it—describe it?"

Hilly shrugged; "No name—just a plain black and white box—white box with a black top—you're holding it right there in your lap."

"And that's all?"

Hilly nodded gloomily. "Except Lilly would meet me in the terminal and I was to follow her lead after we got to Las Vegas."

"You didn't get off the plane together?"

"No, Lilly said she was known here; always too many eyes around the airport, checking on the new arrivals—suckers. She got off alone, and took a taxi. I got a rental car and picked her up at a gas station on the outskirts of town."

"And?"

"That's all, except on our way out to the roadhouse, she had to stop at a shop downtown to pick up a hat."

Doc's ears pricked up but Jack pretended he wasn't interested.

"She got it?" Doc wanted to know.

Hilly nodded vaguely.

"How'd she look in it?" Doc had straightened as though he'd suddenly sniffed Indians.

Hilly looked puzzled. "In what?"

"In the new bonnet?"

"She wasn't wearing it. She had it in a hatbox."

Doc looked at Jack, who shook his head slightly. He said, as though it were a matter of indifference, "I don't suppose you noticed what kind?" Hilly looked blank. Jack elucidated, "What kind of a hatbox?"

Hilly threw himself in a chair, at the end of his patience. "How do I know what kind? Just a hatbox! I was driving, I wasn't paying any attention. She just came out, heaved it in the back seat with my luggage, and we drove on out to the roadhouse. We had a lousy dinner, and then Skip Sullivan and his poker game showed up."

"And what became of Lilly's hatbox?"

"She took it with her, what else?"

Jack studied Hilly's sulky face and waited. Nothing came.

"Any other comment?"

"Yes," Hilly said angrily, "I'm damn sick of all this. I'm fed up to here with you two. That poker game had been set up to pay me off for the favor I was doing this Mr. Big. So what happens? Doc, here, comes barging in and wins everything—loused up the whole deal."

Doc's mouth dropped open; his eyes bugged. "Why, son," he said in a hurt voice, "I saved you from a fate worse than death. When I come into the game they already had all the important money skimmed off your hatbox—and little Jerry a sacrificin' herself for you right down to her bare hide, and Jack with his hand in a sling! Now ain't that gratitude for you!"

Jack wasn't listening. He was unfastening the buckle of the leather strap across the top of the hatbox. He'd just lifted the lid on the heap of bills—so much paper didn't look real; it was like stage money, too much stage money provided by an overenthusiastic prop man—when there was a knock at the door. An imperious, demanding knock! He put the lid carefully back on the box and nodded to Doc.

12

The sudden light of interest in Doc's eyes, the springy eagerness of his step across the room, belied his previous protestations of weariness. "More trouble," he surmised to Hilly as he brushed by him.

"Then don't open the door." Hilly sounded as though he meant it. If ever a man looked as though he'd had his belly full of Las Vegas, he was the man.

Doc's enthusiasm was in his voice. "Why, son, they ain't *nothin'* me and Jack like more'n trouble, except vittles and women—and naturally I'm a speakin' for myself on that last item."

He opened the door and exclaimed, "Whoooeee, will you looky what we got!"

Jerry Booker stalked in, a tiny bauble of shimmering light in a wisp of a negligee that didn't pretend to cover a pair of outrageous see-through pajamas. Holliday stared with appreciation, Jack with disapproval, as the girl descended on him, thrusting out a sheet of paper.

"What's this?" Jack took the sheet of hotel letterhead dubiously.

"I've been lying across the hall getting madder and madder," Jerry fumed. "I can't sleep until I get tonight's expense account settled."

Jack looked at the list in his hand and grinned.

"And just in case you can't read my handwriting, it says," Jerry's manicured finger pointed at the sheet, item by item, "one pair of evening shoes, $25; one cocktail dress, $225; lingerie, frayed and soiled, $35; medical expenses for Lilly's claw marks and a bruised instep from her French heel, $125; $500 for the humiliation of being publicly torn to shreds and denuded in public; and," her eyes grew bright with malicious venom, "$500 for the crude, uncalled-for remark to the effect of my 'being starved for love.' "

"Yeah, Jack, you shouldn't ought to of said that!" Doc had been listening with appreciation. "That last item sure is justified."

"Total," Jerry read, unheeding, "fourteen hundred ten dollars. Do I get it?"

"You sure do, sugar," Doc agreed, "every penny! If more secretaries was to approach us bosses in such a beguilin' spirit of give and take, this world would be a happier place."

Jerry was listening but her eyes were on Jack.

"You ask me," Doc persisted, "you're makin' a mistake in not askin' for a raise from the Triple A, while you got everybody in the mood."

"You're too generous with the agency's money," Jerry told Doc severely. "My salary as secretary is perfectly satisfactory. Besides, the agency can't afford it!" She turned back to Jack, "These items are another matter. They can be charged to the client as out-of-pocket expenses."

Jack folded the paper and put it in his coat pocket. "This'll be taken under advisement at the proper time and place." Jerry's ruffled-kitten outrage was stifled as Jack continued in a matter-of-fact tone. "However, I'm glad you're here," he said, handing Jerry a slip of paper from his billfold. "I want you to check the serial numbers on the thousand-dollar bills in this hatbox against this list, while I call Lieutenant Holmes."

Curiosity burned some of the resentment out of the girl's eyes, and the instincts of a trained secretary did the rest. Jack lifted the lid from the box and put it in his chair. Jerry curled up on the floor with the list and Doc squatted on his heels beside her. Hilly, suspicious, was torn three ways between the girl, the money, and Jack's conversation on the phone.

It was brief and consisted chiefly of five questions: Was Skip Sullivan in condition to talk? Would Lieutenant Holmes bring Sullivan and Lilly Montrose to the Regal Spa, Suite 3107, for questioning? Had the lieutenant by any chance picked up a hatbox in the raid on the roadhouse? Jack gave a grunt of disappointment. Could he find out whether Skip Sullivan had had a falling-out with a Mr. Big here in Las Vegas? Apparently Lieutenant Holmes would have to look for an answer to that. Jack frowned. And finally, did the lieutenant know, and if not, could he check on, a social lion in the Hollywood film colony named "Charlie"? Jack listened a moment, nodded and said, "Yes, I'm beginning to get a picture," and hung up.

"Any luck?"

Jerry held up her list—twenty-five of the thousand-dollar bills were checked off, and now she was beginning on the second bundle in its neat elastic straps.

Holliday yawned, stretched prodigiously and got slowly to his feet. "I'm just not up to any more of this tonight. When you got me a room here, I thought it was for sleep. I'm checked in down the strip at the Mocomber."

Jack didn't even look up from the list. "Don't do anything silly, Holliday," he advised.

Hilly hesitated in surprise, and then said sulkily, "I've seen all I want to see of Skip Sullivan and that Montrose dame. And I don't want to get mixed up with the police."

"Shouldn't you oughta of thought of that before you launched out on this quarter-million-dollar wing ding?" Doc asked sympathetically. "And anyway, what's one more front page splash to a playboy of your standin'?"

Holliday looked at Doc, and then with a bored shrug, sat down in his chair again.

Doc looked disgusted, but he remained in the vicinity of the door.

13

When Lieutenant Holmes and party arrived, dawn was pink and hot in the east; the night breezes had retreated to the mountains, and the early blue light was pulsing with heat.

Two plainclothes men accompanied the lieutenant with the girl and Sullivan, whose sullen, granite face looked gray and grotesquely meaty and lopsided in the left area of his chin. For some reason Lilly's eyes were dark with fright and darted about the bedroom "a lookin'," Doc thought, "like scairt beetles, hopin' for some cranny to crawl in." Someone had replaced the horse blanket in which she'd left the Regal Spa earlier with slacks and a blouse, obviously from her own wardrobe, but her hours in jail hadn't done much for her hair and make-up.

One of the accompanying policemen took up a post on the balcony outside the sliding glass panels. Jack pulled the curtain. The second man stayed in the hall, closing the door behind him.

Holliday watched the new arrivals with distaste, ignoring Skip Sullivan and Lilly completely, and barely acknowledging an introduction to Lieutenant Holmes.

Immediately on entering, Lilly had sidled over close to Doc, which was just about as far as she could get from Sullivan.

96

Jerry, from her place on the floor beside the hatbox, frowned at her through narrow eyes. "You're Skip Sullivan's girl, remember?" she said vindictively. "Go sit beside him."

Lilly took Doc's arm. He could feel her hand tremble, but she made her voice sound bold and cocky. "Doc won me in the poker game. I'm his."

Doc glanced at Sullivan, but his eyes were brooding and far away.

"Sure, he hooked you, but he threw you back."

Lilly's only response was to raise pleading eyes, appealing to Doc. He patted her hand and grinned at Lieutenant Holmes, who'd been watching with considerable interest.

"How about callin' the meetin' to order, Lieutenant?"

Holmes' eyes went to Jack questioningly.

"Well, to begin with," Jack said, "Skip Sullivan recently had been making himself rather unpopular with some pretty important people here in Las Vegas." Sullivan's bleak eyes searched Jack's face for an instant and then returned to his far-off gaze. "The probabilities are, Sullivan didn't realize he was biting off more than he could chew. Most warped mentalities don't." The gambler's eyes turned back to Jack with a flick of surprise and stayed there.

"Item two," Jack went on, nodding at the hatbox on the chair, "here we have two hundred fifty thousand dollars taken in a recent Chicago bank holdup." Sullivan's eyes widened, and Doc could feel Lilly's hand tighten on his arm. Lieutenant Holmes rose and crossed over to the box of money. Jack handed him the check list. "McCracken of the Home and Farm Mutual Insurance Company gave me these serial numbers before we left Los Angeles." Holmes returned thoughtfully to his chair beside Sullivan.

"Naturally," Jack went on, "this being hot money, it wasn't smart to put it into circulation. How or when it arrived in Las Vegas is a matter for Lieutenant Holmes and the FBI. Doc and I simply were hired to get the money back to the insurance company and that's where it's going."

There was a yelp of protest from Hilly Holliday. "But you said— " He choked off the rest, but he wasn't happy.

Jack nodded, "I thought it was your money at the time I said it. However, that was before you helped me put the puzzle together."

Lieutenant Holmes suddenly reached out and yanked Skip Sullivan back into his chair. The man didn't even seem to notice. His eyes were on Lilly, hard and cruel. The girl's eyes were wide and blank with fright and she trembled so as Doc had to hold her. He eased her down into the chair and sat on the arm, still holding her hand.

"I see you're beginning to get the drift, Sullivan," Jack said dryly. "You're right. Lilly's the key to the whole setup. You thought you were the one who sent Lilly to Los Angeles to contact Hilly Holliday and entice him to bring a quarter-million sucker money for your poker game, but it was a double-cross set up by this Mr. Big you've been feuding with. He got to Lilly, and made the setup. You swallowed it!"

Lieutenant Holmes was fascinated. "Some place along the line Lilly switched hatboxes?"

Jack nodded. "After Lilly and Holliday got off the plane, she had Hilly stop his rental car at a shop downtown, where she picked up an identical hatbox, with this bank holdup loot. She dumped it in the back of the car with Holliday's luggage, and when they got out at the roadhouse, Lilly switched boxes. Holliday thought nothing about it because he supposed there was a hat in Lilly's box and his box was heavy with money."

"I still don't see the point," Hilly protested. Everyone looked disgusted except Sullivan, who still sat boring Lilly with a hateful glare, and Lilly, who shivered in her chair.

"Honest to goodness, Hilly, even you can't be that dumb," Doc told him. "Right now, if me and Jack hadn't butted in, Mr. Big would have had your two hundred fifty thousand of good money and Skip Sullivan here'd be holdin' the bag for the two hundred fifty grand of bank loot, a plucked pigeon all set up for the FBI." Doc's eyes flicked to the gambler. "Actually, Skip, you owe us a debt of gratitude for savin' you from thirty, forty years in some lonely Federal pokey." Any gratitude Sullivan felt wasn't in evidence.

Hilly Holliday still wasn't satisfied. "But somebody's got my money."

Lieutenant Holmes waved him off. "You'll be lucky if you're not charged with conspiracy and handling stolen money along with some other people in this town I could mention." He looked sideways at Sullivan and turned back to Jack. "I'm checking this 'Charlie' playboy in Los Angeles. What's he got to do with the setup?"

Jack shrugged, "Probably unimportant, except he might turn out to be an interesting witness, if he'll sing. He was Mr. Big's contact with Holliday; sold Hilly on bringing his clean money to Las Vegas, arranged the whole hat-box deal."

The Lieutenant frowned and nodded. "I left word at the station to call here if they get a line on him." He stood up. "Well, if that cleans things up— "

Jack looked surprised. "Well, there are a couple of more items." He seemed to hesitate and his eyes, which for a puzzled second had fastened on Lieutenant Holmes, slid away to Holliday. "For one, I still can't figure why Mr. Big here in Las Vegas wanted Hilly to make that display of a hatbox full of money in Los Angeles. That doesn't make sense. In fact, if he'd withdrawn the money quietly and put it in the hatbox after he'd left the bank, Doc and I'd never have been sent out on this job."

"That's exactly what he was supposed to do." Lilly's voice pierced the room on a high note of hysteria. "But, no, he had to make a grandstand play! Hilly Holliday makes another big gesture! And louses up the whole deal!" Every eye fixed on the unnerved girl. "Lieutenant Holmes," she shrilled, "you didn't tell me—"

Her words were drowned in a gun blast and a gasping exhaling moan. She would have pitched forward to the floor, had Doc not caught her.

At the same instant there was a cursing shout from Lieutenant Holmes and he had Skip Sullivan on the floor, the two men wrestling desperately for the lieutenant's gun. It was all over in an instant; the second explosion, the ugly hole in Sullivan's head, and a panting, shaken officer rising unsteadily to return the revolver to his holster.

The guard on the balcony came into the room, gun in hand, and the second guard in the corridor beat frantically at the door.

"It's all right, Simms, everything's under control," the lieutenant reassured his aide. "Sullivan grabbed my gun and shot the girl and I had to kill him to get it back." The pounding on the door infuriated him. "Go out there and tell that fool to stop pounding, and call the morgue."

The plainclothes man hesitated a moment and then went into the hall, pushing his frantic partner back and pulling the door closed. Jerry hadn't moved from her place on the floor, her eyes round with horror; nor Holliday from his chair, a waxwork figure of a gaping, terrified idiot.

Doc was holding Lilly in his arms. Now he picked her up carefully and laid her on the bed. "She's still a breathin'. "

Jack came across to the opposite side of the bed, and Lieutenant Holmes leaned over the girl beside Doc. "Can't really tell much until we get her clothes off and—"

Jack didn't wait to unbutton the blouse. He ripped it down the front in one quick motion, and bent over the wound under her left breast.

With sudden, apparently unreasoning rage, Doc raised up swiftly, plunged his fist into Lieutenant Holmes's stomach, bending him over in agony, and whipped a left and right to the unguarded chin, knocking the man sprawling to his back.

"What'd you do that for, you crazy idiot?" Jack was using a sheet to staunch the wound. "Jerry, get on the phone and call for a house doctor up here, fast."

Jerry, stunned and wide-eyed, responded to the boss's voice, stepping over the lieutenant's body and around Doc, who was busy twisting the officer's arms behind his back and fastening them there with his own handcuffs.

Jack glanced up. "Have you gone out of your mind?"

"Sullivan never shot Lilly," said Doc as he got up. "This two-tailed ciffy cat done it hisself, and then turned the gun on Sullivan. Skip wasn't fightin' to hang onto the gun. He was tryin' to fight Holmes off."

Jack nodded, still working over the girl. "You saw it?"

"Yeah, out of the corner of my eye. I just plain couldn't believe it. Murder, right before our eyes. I still don't get it!"

Jerry hung up the phone. "A doctor's on his way up."

"Reach in my hip pocket and take out my wallet. There's a number in the first compartment. Call it. Ask to speak to Joe Denton." Jack was holding a bloody bandage against the wound with one hand and feeling the girl's wrist for a pulse with the other. He still had time for Doc. "You don't understand what?"

"Why a lieutenant of the police would go berserk and do what he done."

"Would it make sense if Lieutenant Holmes turned out to be Hilly's 'power behind the scenes'?"

"Mr. Big? *Him?*" Doc's eyes lighted up. "You know that for a fact?"

Jerry reached for the phone, as it rang sharply. Her eyes asked Jack for instructions; he nodded and she lifted the receiver. She listened a moment, said "Just a minute," and then put her hand over the mouthpiece. "Somebody wants Lieutenant Holmes."

"Put the receiver to my ear." Jerry did. "Sorry, Lieutenant Holmes is on another line. He asked me to take the message." Jack listened, grunted a couple of times, and said, "Thanks, I'll tell him," and nodded for Jerry to hang up. Jerry did so, waited a moment for the switchboard operator to clear the lines, and then put in her own call.

"What was that all about, Jack?" Doc wanted to know.

"Report on Hilly's friend 'Charlie' in Hollywood."

"Yeah?"

"Charlie conveniently fell out of a twelve-story hotel window in Beverly Hills about an hour ago."

Jerry gasped, but went on with her call. Doc chewed on it for a moment. "Then Lieutenant Holmes's phone call to Los Angeles wasn't to check on Charlie. It was to check him out."

"What do you think?"

There was a rap at the door.

"There's the doctor." Then Doc remembered something. "Hey, what about them two guards outside the door? They hoods or real policemen?"

"Let me take it." Jack rose from the bed, wiping his hands on a pillow case. He opened the door a crack. "Oh, come in, Doctor." He opened the door just enough to pull in the plump, reluctant, fussy little man and then closed it to a crack again. "Lieutenant Holmes is on the phone. He wants you two men to stay on guard out here until the homicide boys get here." He closed the door quickly in the two protesting faces.

Doc had led the medic to the bed.

"Gunshot wound," the doctor raised suspicious disapproving eyes to Doc and transferred them to Jack, as he joined them. Then for the first time he took in the whole room—the unconscious, manacled police officer, the body of Skip Sullivan, the idiotic horror of the frozen Holliday, the hatbox that seemed to be filled with thousand-dollar bills, and finally, Jerry Booker on the phone, carefully keeping her back to the corpse. Each item seemed to put a heavier strain on his credulity, but the little blonde in the provocative transparent pajamas and negligee hit him the hardest.

Jerry smiled wistfully into his bulging eyes and nodded to Jack, holding out the phone. Jack came over and took it out of her hands, turned his back and spoke in a low tone.

Doc jabbed the little doctor gently in the ribs. "Only one who needs your attention just now, fella," he reminded, "is Lilly here. How bad is she?"

The medic pulled his scattered thoughts back into focus with effort. "A charnel house," he muttered.

"Ain't it the truth," Doc agreed amiably, "but what about Lilly?"

"Close one," he said, "bullet was deflected by a rib; shock and superficial wound." Then his troubled mind veered again. "What is this?" he said in a troubled voice, "a slaughterhouse? A gangster's hangout? Or a love nest?"

Jerry lifted her small chin haughtily. Doc grinned. "Yeah," he agreed, "it has the elements of all of 'em, don't it." He sobered. "I'm sure glad to hear Lilly's a gonna survive. They ain't nothin that makes me feel so bad as to lose one single pretty girl out of this old world. We need 'em all."

Jack turned from the phone.

"Good news, Jack," Doc said. "Doctor here says Lilly's gonna stay with us." Jack nodded. Doc looked inquiringly, "Reinforcements on the way?"

"Ten minutes. The FBI's moving in—they're bringing the police chief with them."

"You mean *he's* in on this, too?"

"No. Lieutenant Holmes is one of his men. More diplomatic to let him make the arrest. The Feds like to have the local police clean out their own nests. Helps to counteract the bad smell of a crooked officer; keeps the public confidence in local law enforcement." Jack took the little doctor by the arm. "Have a look at Holliday over here. He's been sitting like that since the shooting started."

The pompous little man pulled his arm from Jack's grasp fussily and crossed to Hilly, felt his pulse, looked into his glazed eyes and shrugged. "Shock, hypertension," he muttered, taking a hypodermic needle and a small vial from his bag. "Take off his coat and roll up his sleeve." Doc helped Jack. It was like undressing a store window dummy. The medic swabbed Hilly's arm and made the injection. The fixed expression on Hilly relaxed and the rigidity oozed from his limbs.

"Just lay him out on the floor," the doctor ordered, "he'll feel better when he wakes up."

Jack lost interest in Holliday. He walked over and looked down at the unconscious lieutenant, studying him thoughtfully. He got down on his knees and began to search his pockets. He piled the contents in a neat little heap on the floor, discarding article after article, until he came to a key ring in a leather container, which he examined closely. Satisfied, he pocketed the keys and went to the door.

"You a walkin' out now?" Doc sounded incredulous.

Jack paused with his hand on the doorknob. "I'll be back in five minutes. Keep everything just as it is." He opened the door and backed out, saying, "All right, Lieutenant Holmes, I'll take care of it right away." He closed the door quickly, but not before those inside had caught the surprised expression on the two plainclothes men outside the door.

Mr. Kinder, still behind the reception desk, and the young bellhop eyed Jack suspiciously as he crossed the lobby and continued out into the parking lot. The suspicion was intensified by disbelief, when he came back a few minutes later with a second identical white hatbox with a black lid. Placing the hatbox on the counter, Jack said "Now look, boys, I've been thinking this over and I don't see why either one of you should get involved in this mess. I'm sure you don't want to get caught with hot money from a bank heist in your possession; especially with the FBI hot on the trail."

The ancient Kinder paled as his false teeth chattered. The skin on the bellhop's thin cheeks tightened and a sigh escaped. Otherwise he looked at Jack without expression.

Jack shrugged. "It's up to you, of course, but if you want to return the money—there's considerable missing from the box—I'll just put it back and we'll forget all about it."

Mr. Kinder's hand fumbled eagerly in his inside coat pocket and came out with a heavily loaded envelope, which he pushed across the counter with shaking fingers. Jack nodded and looked at the bellhop. The boy shot the old man a bitter, scornful glance, hesitated, and then reluctantly drew a second envelope from inside his uniform.

Jack unsealed the two flaps, looked inside, nodded and put them in his pockets. "Thanks, we'll all sleep better now," he said, and walked to the elevator.

On the third floor the two plainclothes men stared with interest at the hatbox, but otherwise ignored Jack. As he let himself back into the room Jerry's eyes widened and Doc's mouth dropped open, but not as far as the fussy little doctor's when Jack took the lid off the second hatbox and displayed the second heap of money.

"Imagine a mere police lieutenant carrying two hundred fifty thousand dollars in the luggage compartment of his car," he said complacently.

Doc got his breath. "Well, whoooeee, if this other box is the bank loot, then that's got to be Hilly's money. But how'd you know where to look for it?"

Jack shrugged. "Didn't Hilly tell us Lilly had taken her hatbox into the roadhouse? It was obvious that when Lieutenant Holmes's men were making their raid on the place after we left, he picked up the hatbox she'd stashed away for him. He might have hidden it away someplace, but he's been a pretty busy man tonight and anyway, who's going to pry open a police officer's car?"

"Well, ain't Hilly a gonna be a happy boy when he wakes up and hears what we done for him tonight. Now we got *all* the money."

Jack shrugged. He removed the two envelopes from his pocket and dumped the contents in the box of stolen money. "Now we have!"

"Huh, where'd that come from?" Doc demanded.

"Contributions from a couple of sticky-fingered friends."

Doc caught on. "Grandpa and the bellhop?"

Jack nodded. "But they're clear now."

"I thought grandpa was awful jittery about somethin'." Doc was always first-rate on hindsight; "but when the kid was so honest about checkin' the hatbox and givin' it back—what give you the idea, Jack?"

"You don't imagine a bellhop, expecting to pick up a hatbox with only a hat in it, and coming up with anything as heavy as a quarter-million in long green, isn't going to be curious. And once he'd investigated," Jack shrugged, "well, he'd figure one of two ways. Either two or three thousand wouldn't be missed out of that pile, or the owners would be so glad to get the bulk of it back, they wouldn't bother to investigate."

14

It had been a long night. As full morning flooded the suite, Jack, Doc and Jerry Booker were still waiting for the chief of police, an ambulance, the morgue wagon and the federal agent, Joe Denton. Jerry was moody, Doc sleepy and Jack was prowling while keeping an eye on the two hatboxes stuffed with half a million, which was what Chief Jordan and agent Joe Denton wanted. The dead wagon was for Skip Sullivan, the ambulance for Hilly Holliday and Lilly, and the police wagon for Lieutenant Holmes and his two uniformed hoods in the hallway.

"Well, that mighty near winds up the clock," yawned Doc, stretching his six-foot-two lanky frame, which gave the impression of something like ten feet with his arms over his head. "Soon's the company gets here." He relaxed and leered at Jerry. "Ain't you had enough exposure for one evenin', sugar, or you want to go out and do the town in that gauze-nettin' nighty?"

"Gauze netting, my eye," snapped Jerry. "This is sheer silkworm silk. I knew the silkworms personally."

"Sheer ain't the word for it," agreed Doc with enthusiasm. "We been too busy to notice details 'til just now."

"Well, get a good gander, brother, for it's the one and only time you're likely to see me in them."

"Oh, I know, savin' 'em for Jack."

Jerry's face flushed and her eyes rested for a moment on Jack, across the room on his knees beside Hilly Holliday.

"The hell with you," Jerry turned resentful eyes on Doc.

"Aw, I'm sorry." Doc's voice was sincerely apologetic, not for himself, but for Jack. "You could walk up and down in front of that cold fish mother-naked and all he'd see was the thread of a scar where you had your appendix took out."

"I'll have you know there's not a scar nor blemish on my body."

"Yeah," Doc agreed appreciately, "I can see that."

"You can, like hell."

Doc grinned. "You sure are taking the name of Satan's favorite pokey in vain tonight, sugar, which don't sound a bit purty on your young, innocent lips." Jerry flounced. Again Doc yawned and raised his voice. "Jack, what you aim to do, sit up with the unconscious and the dead all night? Fact is, it's mornin'. "

Jack rose and came across the room. "Holliday's come out of his shock; sleeping normally under the effects of the shot the doctor gave him." He looked at Jerry's brooding face. "You can go back to bed. You've had a pretty rugged evening for a typewriter jockey."

Jerry's face flushed. "You're damned right I will." She whirled angrily and whipped open the door. "A typewriter jockey, he says," she muttered bitterly. Lieutenant Holmes's two minions hovered anxiously in the hallway. Jerry's voice arose viciously, "Get out of my way, you two apes, before I claw you to shreds." The door slammed behind her.

"And she's just in the mood to do it, too," Doc grinned approvingly.

"What's biting *her?*" Jack's interest already was wandering.

"And you call yourself a detective," Doc said derisively. Jack regarded him inquiringly.

"Little girl comes into your bedroom in a pure nude outfit—a givin' of her all—and you don't even see her." Jack stared. "Practically throws herself at you and all you do is call her a typewriter jockey! Honest to goodness, Jack, sometimes I wonder if you hadn't ought to go and get a double shot of somethin' in your adrenalin glands."

Jack shrugged and turned to look down at the still unconscious lieutenant.

Doc shrugged. "Okay, okay, so you're still eleven years old and little girls is still a nuisance. Someday you'll grow up *maybe,* and discover girls is . . . "

"Why don't you go to bed." Jack didn't even turn his head.

"Why, thank you, son. That's just what I was aimin' to do. And what about you?"

"Somebody's got to sit on this until Police Chief Jordan and the FBI check in. They'll be along any minute. You go ahead. Oh yes, if Holmes's two goons outside are getting itchy, tell them the lieutenant and I are talking over a deal. I tipped off Chief Jordan to pick them up when he comes in."

Doc hesitated, "You really mean you're a gonna give all that two hundred fifty thousand back to Hilly Holliday, which I rightfully won fair and square over the poker table?"

Jack turned and looked at Doc with a glint of amusement. "Fair and square?"

" 'Course it was fair and square," Doc insisted doggedly, "I was playin' accordin' to the house rules, which was as crooked as Lilly Montrose's little heart, so anything I done was fair and square. Blame Skip Sullivan and his boys if I was just cuter and fancier than them."

"Yes, I see your point," agreed Jack.

"You do?" Doc's voice was hopeful.

"Except you were playing with the hot money from the Chicago bank robbery, while Hilly's hatbox of money was cashed away in Lilly's and Lieutenant Holmes's hidey-hole. Naturally you wouldn't expect to keep holdup loot."

"And who's a gonna know which money we was a playin' with?"

Jack shrugged, "You and I."

"Well, now, ain't we just the pure, lily white, come-to-prayer-meetin' boys. I swear, Jack, sometimes I wonder if you ain't too good to be true."

Jack looked at his partner, highly amused. "Okay, Doc, you tell me how deep you would dig into Hilly's hatbox, if you were handling this by yourself."

"Why, I'd— " Doc hesitated.

"You'd what?"

"Why, I'd," Doc finished lamely, "why I reckon I'd point out to Hilly that him not bein' our client and me savin' him two hundred fifty thousand dollars, I'd leave it up to him to dish out a suitable reward."

"Fair enough," Jack agreed. "Why don't you do just that—but," he added, "just in case he feels generous, remember anything he doles out belongs to the Triple A."

"But I won it, personal!"

"While performing a job for the agency."

"Well, if *that* ain't a typical piece of Jack Packard snidery. Okay, I *will* go to bed." He walked to the door. "And I hope I have nightmares about you sunk up to your Adam's apple in quicksand, and I just walk away, leavin' you beggin' for mercy."

15

It was 8:00 in the morning when a feminine but firm knock on the door roused Doc from three hours of exhausted slumber.

"They ain't nobody in here, go away," he yelled wrathfully, taking his head from under the pillow and rising on one elbow.

The knock became more insistent.

"You're awakenin' the dead!" he yelled.

"Ain't you got no respect for the defunct? Stop a wakin' up the dead."

The knocking continued ruthlessly; determined and spitefully louder. Doc groaned and pulled himself out of bed. He sat on the edge for a moment shaking his head, then raised himself and walked to the door in his wrinkled purple pajamas, splotched with orange suns.

"This better be an emergency like fire and floods and the earth a breakin' apart, or the management's a gonna find a corpse in the hallway." He yanked open the door. "Why, hello, honey." His voice became soft and seductive, a sort of masculine cooing. Actually, all he saw through sleep-bleared eyes was a beautiful girl. "I hope you brought your nighty on account this is a bedroom and I ain't half-through sleepin'—" Suddenly his eyes and brains cleared and he exclaimed, "Linda Holliday! What *you* a doin' in Las Vegas?"

"I came to keep the date you broke in Stone Canyon. Remember?" The petite, neat, expensive-looking twin sister of Hilly Holliday pushed past Doc into the room and banged the door shut, her voice suddenly heavy with reproach, "And for the love of all that's decent, *where* on God's green earth did you get those pajamas? Take them *off.*"

Doc looked startled. "Now look-a-here, Miss Holliday, they ain't *nothin'* I can't stand less than aggressive females —'specially in love makin'. If I take off my pajamas, I say 'take 'em off,' and when I take 'em off I do it for my own purpose or else I do it in private. Besides, I ain't ready to take 'em off on account I ain't barely had three hours sleep."

"I'm not interested in where or when or how you take them off. The point is I just got off a plane, I've had no breakfast, and those ghastly things turn my stomach."

"And you'd rather see me nekkid?" Doc was shocked.

"Good heavens, no. Don't you have something else?"

"Well, there is another pair in my bag," Doc said uncertainly.

The young woman marched to the bag and began scattering Doc's personal effects.

"Now wait a minute—"

Linda Holliday dragged out a second pair of pajamas only to squeal and drop them to the floor. They were a cerise pink with large green toads and purple dragonflies.

"Heeey, treat them gently," pleaded Doc, gathering them up with loving hands from where Linda had kicked them across the room. "Them's my special Sunday pajamas, specially bought in Bogota when me, Jack and Reggie was down there."

"Well, bury them. They give me the willies."

Doc carefully replaced them in his bag.

"And if that's all you have, either get dressed or get back in bed. Those orange splotches are making me dizzy."

Doc climbed back in bed and pulled up the covers. "Only," he said, "it don't seem very hospitable, especially when I got two pillows on the bed."

"That's the damnedest way of talking a girl into a seduction I ever heard," Miss Holliday said tartly, pulling up a chair beside the bed and making herself comfortable. "Aren't you even going to call downstairs and get me a double order of coffee?"

"Who's hungry at this time in the morning?"

"I am, damn it."

"And compromise you for bein' with a man in bed?"

"I'm not in bed."

"Maybe not, but I am."

"Well, a double scotch would keep me alive."

"The bar ain't open and I *never* keep a bottle in my room."

"Every other hotel in Las Vegas keeps open bar all night."

"That's on account they have casinos a workin'. I don't know why Jack had to sign us in here."

"The only respectable place in all Nevada and you'd have to find it," Linda said bitterly.

"I tell you, I didn't have nothin' — " He broke off. "Heeeey, looky, don't you have no room?"

"Of course I've got a room, but not here, thank you."

"Well, Miss Holliday, honey— "

"Do you have to be so formal, just because you're in bed?"

"Well, Linda, sugar, if you got a room, why don't you go along to it and get a little shut-eye. Then along about noon we'll all get together, Jack, you and me and Jerry, and put our irons in the fire. Ain't that a good idea?"

"No!"

"But I'm tuckered out, honey. You can't expect me to tell you all that's a been goin' on here now on account I'm too mealy-minded and besides it'd take hours."

"You don't have to tell me but one thing. An FBI man came out to my place in Bel Air and got me out of bed at three in the morning. He told me all I need to know, except where in hell is Hilly's quarter-million-dollar hatbox?"

"Oh, so *that's* how you knowed where he was."

"Yes. After that secretary of yours called and cancelled our appointment— "

"Uh-huh, little old Jerry Booker."

" —I tried a dozen times to reach the Triple A office and all I got was an answering service. Are all three of you boys here?" Miss Holliday's tone was not only accusing but biting. "And if you ask me, that's a fine way to treat a client who's given you the best years of her life— millionairess at that! I don't think you boys know which side your bread is buttered on."

"Sugar, I wanted to come." Doc's voice was placating. "Honest to goodness and hope to die a pitiful death if I didn't beg Jack with tears in my eyes to let me be by your side in your moment of despair. Only you know Jack. Mr. McCracken, the insurance investigator, wanted us to follow Hilly to Las Vegas and Jack wouldn't hear of nothin' else."

Out of the corner of his sleepy eyes Doc looked at the girl worth ten million dollars in her stocking feet and added softly, "Anyway, we all supposed it was about Hilly you was a callin' us, so's it seemed the right thing to get on his tail fast and furious, which is what we done."

"It wasn't Hilly at all," snapped Linda. "It was the two hundred fifty thousand the simple idiot was parading around in a hatbox. And I ask you again, where is it?"

"Honey, I'm surprised at you."

"*Miss* Honey to you, you Texas rat, unless you tell me where it is."

"I swear to goodness, I never hoped to see Miss Moneybags herself a fussin' over a measly two hundred fifty thousand. Money, money, money, that's all Jerry Booker ever thinks about, but you—*Miss* Honey, sugar, you sure are disillusionin' me by the minute. . . . I'm beginnin' to suspect that's all any female has in her head—a cash register."

Linda Holliday swore under her breath in a most unladylike manner.

Doc looked shocked. "Honest to Christmas, the things nice girls know about these days. Why, I can still remember the time when my mama washed my mouth out with lye soap until the skin come off for just one of them impolite words."

"Look, Doc, I'm serious." A new earnestness was in Miss Holliday's face and her eyes suddenly were dewy. "Hilly had no right to draw that money out of the bank. It was income tax money."

Doc looked interested. "You mean he stole it from the United States of America government?"

"In a sense he did. As you know, both Hilly and I draw a hundred twenty-five thousand a month, less taxes, from interest on the estate. Every month the bank executors send us each a check, minus the tax bite, which they put in our mutual tax-fund account.

"And that's the two-fifty Hilly took?"

"Damned right, and I want it put back. Otherwise, come income tax day, I'm going to have to make it up."

"But if Hilly's gettin' a hundred twenty-five G's a month—"

"He's up to his ears in debt."

Doc's eyes grew big. "On a hundred twenty-five thousand United States minted greenbacks—"

Linda snapped her fingers. "It goes through his fingers like that! Now, then, where's that hatbox?"

Doc hesitated, "Well, to tell you the absolute truth, Miss Holliday, Hilly and I sat in a floatin' poker game last night with the Skip Sullivan gang and I won every scrap of that hatbox full of big green right down to bottom of the box."

The diamond ring the girl had been slipping on and off her finger during the conversation, leaped from her hand and rolled under the bed. "You mean the hatbox is right here in this room?" In her excitement and relief her eyes darted about the bedroom, oblivious of the dropped ring.

"No, it ain't in this room. Jack said it was Triple-A loot and he took charge of it," Doc said, stretching his gangling length over the far side of the bed and peering under it in search of the ring.

"I don't believe you," Linda stated, rising to her feet and crossing to the closet. It was empty. She rushed into the bathroom, looked in the clothes hamper, tore aside the shower curtain, stalked out again. Seeing Doc half in, half out of bed, peering underneath, her eyes blazed. "Oh, so it's under the bed." She moved quickly to the far side and dropped to her knees.

"Yeah," Doc grunted, "about halfway under, I can see the gleam."

Linda dropped to her knees and peered under. She sat back on her feet. "You're lying, there's no hatbox under there."

" 'Course they ain't, I told you that. I'm a talkin' about the ring. And, lady, I wisht you wouldn't cast off diamonds in my presence. It smacks of 'castin' pearls before swine' which gives me an awful inferiority complex."

Linda looked at her vacant finger in surprise, and peered back under the bed. "I don't see it."

"It's under there, okay." Doc assured her, "See up yonder toward the head of the bed. You're a gonna have to wriggle under on your belly to reach it."

"Damn," muttered the girl.

"That is," Doc added, "unless you can bear the sight of me, in which case I'll wriggle under on *my* belly."

"Would you, please, Doc?"

"Why sure," Doc leapt off the bed with alacrity and slid under the bed. Linda bent low, watching him anxiously.

At that moment a key turned in the lock. In one swift motion the hall door was thrown wide open.

16

Jerry Booker stood in the doorway in her fetching gauze robe and pajamas. She paused, startled at the empty bed and apparently empty room. Doc and the petite Linda froze.

"All right, come out, wherever you are," Jerry called uncertainly. "The fun and games are over."

"Jerry Booker," fumed Doc from under the bed, "where'd you get a key to my private room?"

"Oh, under the bed, huh?" Jerry jeered, "*that* must be cozy." She closed the door and bent down. "What's the matter? The mattress too bouncy?"

Doc slid out from under the bed and scrambled to his feet. Linda Holliday popped up but remained on her knees.

"Now, looky, honey, don't get no wrong ideas," Doc defended himself, pulling down his pajama tops, which had slid up to his armpits. "The little lady accidentally dropped her diamond ring and it rolled under the bed." He handed the bauble to Miss Holliday. "And there's the ring to prove it."

"Cute," muttered Jerry, unappeased.

"And I still want to know what you're a doin' with a key to my bedroom," Doc demanded belligerently. "A member of the Triple A agency's got about as much privacy as a germ under a microscope."

"Well, if it'll make you feel any better I bribed a bell-hop, when I saw your girlfriend sneak in here."

"Spyin', huh? Why wasn't you asleep?"

"With her pounding on your door fit to raise corpses deader than me? Ha!" Jerry looked closely at the kneeling girl for the first time. "Say," she exclaimed, "aren't you Linda Holliday?"

Linda started to get to her feet and Doc helped her. " 'Course she's Miss Holliday," he said scathingly.

"Oh, brother," breathed Jerry, "first the male and now the female."

"And just remember, Miss Booker," said Linda tartly, "the female is deadlier than the male."

"You're telling *me,* sister."

Doc protested, "Jerry, that just plain ain't no way to talk to a millionairess."

"Well, pardon my lifted pinky." Jerry's eyes flashed. "Next you'll be telling me 'three's a crowd' and here all I've done was break my beauty sleep to rescue you from a fate worse than death."

"Miss Booker!" Linda's voice was sharp and authoritative. "I came here to find the hatbox with the two hundred fifty thousand. Perhaps you'll be kind enough to tell me where it is?"

Jerry shot a quick glance at Doc and received a nod. She shrugged, "The last time I saw it, it was in Jack's possession."

"But if Doc's telling the truth and won it in a poker game—"

"It's just like I said, Miss Holliday," Doc broke in, "Jack said any profits I made while on a case belonged to the Triple A."

Linda gave him a look fit for a loathsome insect. Jerry's eyes widened. "Y—you heard him!" she gulped.

"Well, in that case," said Miss Linda Holliday in a casual voice, which belied the determined expression in her eyes, "we'll go pound on Mr. Packard's room and see what that gets us."

"Jack ain't a gonna like it."

"Then he can lump it. What's his room number?"

Doc and Jerry looked at each other silently.

"Oh hell," exclaimed Linda, crossing to the phone, "I'll get it from the desk."

"Never mind," sighed Doc wearily, "he's right next to me, yonder." Then as an afterthought, "But Jerry better call him on the phone and wake him up before you tear the door off the hinges."

"Oh no, not me." Jerry took a step backwards. She grabbed Doc's bathrobe and thrust it at him. "For pete's sake, Doc, put this on before those pajamas blind me."

"Women," muttered Doc, shrugging into the robe. "No taste for color in a carload." Then, aggressively, "Now looky, Jerry, as my secretary I order you to call Jack."

"As your secretary I tell you to go take a jump at yourself. I've had my head bitten off too often—"

Doc picked up the phone and gave Jack's room number. As he waited he looked balefully at Jerry. "For insubordination beyond the call of duty I'm a gonna recommend no Christmas bonus for a certain—" He broke off as a rasping voice grunted into the phone. "Heey Jack, it's me, Doc —Doc *Long*—" He jerked the phone from his ear and put his hand over the earpiece for a count of ten, then put it back to his ear again. "Yeah, I know what time it is, fella. And we're still a comin' in."

17

"I've had exactly one-half hour of sleep," Jack said, eyeing the trio at his bed with the malevolence of a trapped animal. "This room's already been invaded by three goons, one murder, one attempted murder, one seizure, one house doctor, two hundred fifty thousand in hot money, and another two hundred fifty thousand in Holliday money, the homicide squad, the chief of police, and the FBI." He took a deep breath and glared at Doc, "And just when I get to sleep, I get a call from you, you silly, long-eared, red-headed Texas misfit of a jackass— "

"Sure, son," agreed Doc, "I *told* Miss Holliday, here, it was an invasion of privacy."

"You told her," snapped Jack balefully, "but you let her bully you into having her own way. If you don't stop letting pretty women lead you around by the nose— "

"Doc couldn't do anything about it, Jack," Jerry protested. "Miss Holliday was coming here to claw her way into your room, with or without us."

Jack's eyes rested on the Triple A's secretary without mercy. "It seems to me I haven't seen you in anything but slightly veiled nudity since we arrived in Las Vegas." Shocked surprise, smoldering quickly into resentment, widened Jerry's eyes as she unconsciously pulled her filmy robe closer about her. "And," Jack continued relentlessly,

126

"it always has been my conception that one of the principal duties of a secretary is to guard her employer's privacy, not to give aid and comfort to the enemy!"

"Nuts!" snapped Jerry.

"Jack, son, you should ought to have your mouth washed out with cayenne pepper for a talkin' to Jerry like you been. I swear to pieces, if I was Jerry I'd take the first plane back to Hollywood, leaving you and me to stew in our own smelly juices."

"Oh, no, you don't." A stubborn defiance now crept into Jerry's voice. "You're not going to get rid of me that easy."

"That might be a good idea," Jack nodded thoughtfully.

"You go to hell," Jerry's eyes darkened and her chin went up. "If you think I'm going to leave you two unprotected infants in the claws of Las Vegas's birds of prey *and* Miss Linda Holliday, you don't know me."

Jack uttered a half groan, half sigh, and turned his bloodshot eyes resentfully on Linda Holliday, who had been an interested and amused listener at the "family" squabble.

"Internal dissension in the mighty Triple A?" asked the young heiress politely.

" 'Course there's dissension!" Doc picked it up aggressively. "Ever'body just naturally hates ever'body, includin' you, sister, at 8:00 in the mornin'. That's human nature."

"You have a reason for being in Las Vegas, of course?" Jack said offensively.

Miss Holliday colored and said tartly, "If I didn't, I wouldn't be here. I want that two hundred fifty thousand dollars Hilly drew out of the bank in Los Angeles. Where is it?"

"You came in here at this time of morning to ask me that?" Jack demanded in an incensed voice. "You came here and woke me up . . . "

"She sure did, son," Doc agreed cheerfully. "She says it's money Hilly lifted out of their mutual income-tax reserve. She's searched my room and she's a gonna search yours, and when she don't find it here, she's probably gonna want to search Jerry's room."

"Over my dead body," Jerry muttered elegantly.

"Well, you can relax," Jack told Linda, now watching her with interest, "because Chief of Police Jordan took the hatbox of Hilly's money along with the hatbox of hot money. They're both locked up in the vault down at the station by this time."

"Yeah, only you meant *my* money, not Hilly's," Doc explained quickly, "on account I mentioned to Miss Holliday how I won it from Skip Sullivan in a poker game after he won it from Hilly. Only you say it's the Triple A's money because I won it while on a job."

Jack eyed Doc thoughtfully. Finally he nodded. "Yes," he agreed, "that's about how it is."

"We'll see about that," Miss Holliday murmured softly, but there was a dangerous expression in her eyes. "Nevertheless I'd still like to search this room and, as Doc suggested, the room of your secretary."

"Doc and his big mouth!" snorted Jerry.

"Wouldn't it be simpler to call down to the police station and verify the fact that the money's there?" Jack suggested, reaching to his bedside table. Before he could lift the receiver the phone rang shrilly. He made a face and lifted the receiver. "Yeah," he said wearily, "this is Packard. What's the matter, doesn't this town ever go to bed? . . . Oh," he grunted, still without interest, "morning, Chief Jordan, what's on your mind that couldn't have kept until our appointment this afternoon?"

A harsh, sibilant voice filled the receiver with splutter and violence. Jack listened with interest for a full minute. "But why call me?" he protested. "What gives you the idea I'm glad to get Las Vegas's criminal news firsthand . . . "

Again the voice over the receiver broke into a violent series of short, sharp expletives. A look of resignation came over Jack's countenance. "All right, all right, we'll dress and be with you. Give us an hour to pull ourselves together and get some coffee." Then as an afterthought, "Before you hang up, chief, I've got Miss Linda Holliday here in my room. She flew in from Los Angeles sometime last night. She wants to know where is the quarter-million her brother Hilly brought from L.A. Will you tell her personally, and get her out of my hair?" He handed the receiver to the girl.

Miss Holliday took it reluctantly, spoke briefly, then listened. Then she banged down the receiver. "I don't like this a bit," she said in a temper. "Not one little bit."

"Well, actually, I'm not very interested in what you like or don't like, Miss Holliday," Jack said sitting up in bed and stretching.

"A fine pair of detectives— "

"You seem to forget we're not representing you this time, Miss Holliday— "

"If you're employed by my brother—"

"We're not, we came over here for McCracken of the Home and Farm Insurance group." Jack flung back the covers. "Now, if you'll go crawl back into your hole, so I can get my clothes on—"

"You're a gonna get *up?*" Doc said in disbelief. "What the heck did Chief Jordan tell you anyway?"

"He wants us all to meet him at Morrison Hospital in an hour."

Jerry looked interested. "Isn't that where they took Lilly Montrose and Hilly Holliday?"

"That's right," Jack nodded. "About three hours ago somebody got by the police guard on Lilly's room, clubbed her over the head and then held a pillow over her face."

"Lilly's dead?" Doc was shocked.

"Completely."

"Aaaw, that's a durned shame. Who'd do a thing like that?"

"That's what Chief Jordan wants to know," Jack said dryly.

Jerry and Linda Holliday stared at Jack in silence. Jerry's eyes rejected the whole idea of murder. Linda's facial expression was blank, but her eyes were hooded pools of suspicion.

"This Lilly Montrose," Linda Holliday's eyes went from face to face, "you know her?"

"I thought you said you knowed everything about Hilly's shenanigans," Doc accused. "She's the girl that come to Las Vegas with Hilly; Skip Sullivan's girl. She double-crossed Skip to play footsie with Lieutenant Holmes, Mr. Big in this here dry gulch."

"And who Doc won from Sullivan in the poker game," Jerry murmured.

Doc looked indignant. "Yeah, I oughta be pretty mad at somebody a tamperin' with my chattels. Blame it all, I *am* mad! Smotherin' helpless girls under pillows! You'd think pretty little females was a dime a dozen, the way they get used up in this town."

"Okay, Doc. Take your indignation into your own room and put some clothes on it." Jack swung his pajamed legs out of bed, "Jerry, likewise. We'll meet downstairs and hope the coffee shop's open in fifteen minutes. You going, Miss Holliday?"

Jerry turned at the door.

"No."

"Oh, yes, you are." Jerry walked determinedly to the heiress's side. "I wrestled one dame to a nasty fall last night and I'm not above doing it again."

Linda Holliday was an inch short of Jerry's five foot four, but gave the impression of six inches taller as she coolly drew herself up and gave Jerry a down-the-nose 'empress to slave girl' stare.

Jerry was shaken but held her ground. "Damn it, Miss Holliday, can't you see just to look at him that Jack is in no condition to be taken advantage of at this time in the morning?"

From the doorway Doc grinned, "Yeah, Miss Holliday, honey, Jack's a mighty poor little frayed-out chromosome at any time, but he ain't worth a nickel at this hour in the a.m."

Linda Holliday looked at the heavy-eyed, tousled-headed, unshaven Jack slumped on the edge of the bed, elbow on knee, head in hand. She smiled for an instant. "He doesn't look very appetizing," she murmured.

"Positively revolting," Jerry agreed.

Jack raised his head and glared. "Out of here, all of you, before I come to life and throw you out."

"Not before I ask one question." Linda's face had lost its humor. "If Hilly has been associating with this Lilly Montrose and he is in the same hospital with her, is it possible my brother is being accused of her murder?"

The three stared at her in surprise.

"Because," she continued, "if such is the case, I wish to hire the Triple A to extricate him."

"You think he murdered Lilly?" Jack asked curiously.

"I think nothing . . . I'm only saying—"

"Does Hilly go into those fainting fits often?" Jack interrupted.

"Only occasionally . . . He has done so since childhood . . . they are harmless—"

"Is it a taint in the blood?" Linda's eyes blazed, but Jack continued, "I mean were either of your parents or grandparents similarly affected?"

Bright spots burned in Miss Holliday's cheeks. "I know nothing about my family's medical history, and if you want my opinion, you have a hell of a nerve to bring up the subject. As I said, the doctors have told me Hilly's is a harmless nervous affliction—"

"The affliction may be harmless to Hilly, but is he harmless when he comes out of one of these seizures?"

"If you're trying to implicate my brother in the murder of this Lilly creature—"

Jack shook his head, interrupting her blazing anger. "No," he said, "only I like a little background before we accept a commission."

"You've got Hilly out of trouble before."

"Girl trouble, yes," Jack agreed, "murder's something else again."

"Well, if you don't want the job—" Suddenly the girl's fire died out. "But I was depending on you," she said, her face now strained and troubled.

"Think nothin' of it," Doc said, his native Texas gallantry, dedicated to all helpless females, welling up. "'Course we're committed to helpin' Hilly. We done it before and we'll do it again."

Linda blinked at Doc gratefully, but Jack stared at him in disgust.

"Well, doggone it, Jack," Doc defended, "what is man put in the world *for*, if not to come to the rescue of poor, little weak females?"

Jerry Booker snorted. "Brother Packard will now lead us in prayer while Brother Doc plays soft tremolo music on his sobbing violin."

18

Lois Pallaski, alias Lilly Montrose, was not a pleasant sight. Victims of strangulation seldom are. When Chief Jordan pulled down the sheet, Jerry turned away hastily. Linda Holliday stared a moment longer, her eyes widening with fascinated horror.

Doc touched her arm. "Honey, you don't have to look at that," and turned her away.

"It's obviously a revenge killin' by one of Skip Sullivan's boys," Doc observed.

"It's not obvious at all," snapped Chief Jordan.

"Well, after all, Lilly *was* Skip's girl and she double-crossed him to play footsie with Lieutenant Holmes. And Lieutenant Holmes did kill Skip. I seen that with my own eyes. Why wouldn't one of Skip's boys want revenge?"

"I didn't say they didn't want revenge. I simply say— " Chief Jordan bit off a hunk of Star plug tobacco and chewed morosely, "I simply say it's not obvious, because, with the exception of Silver Logan, we hauled in all of Sullivan's known henchmen last night after the poker fracas. They were under lock and key at the time of Lilly's murder."

"Why isn't Logan in jail?" Jack wanted to know.

"Because we can't find him. But we will." Jordan crossed to the window and spat expertly. "Anyway," he said, returning, "Logan's not the killer type. But we still want him for questioning."

"Who's Logan?" Doc wanted to know, then he remembered. "Heeey, you mean that card sharp with the ciffy-cat white streak in his hair? Why, that hombre is mean enough to cut his own grandma's gullet from ear to ear."

"He's tough and mean all right, at the card table," Jordan admitted, "but he's been around Vegas for years and has no police record."

"But, Jack, you put Logan to sleep and tied him up. How come the cops never found him when they raided the place?"

"That's an interesting question. Remember, it was Lieutenant Holmes and his boys who did the raiding." Jack looked at the chief with speculation. "Looks like there's two possibilities. Either Holmes finished Logan off right then and there and ditched the body out in the sand dunes, or maybe Logan was actually one of the lieutenant's undercover boys in Skip Sullivan's inner circle and was released during the raid."

The chief scowled. "If Holmes killed Logan, why didn't he kill Sullivan at the same time? Why wait until he got Sullivan up in your hotel room?"

Jack agreed. "The killing seems to have been an afterthought when Holmes found himself cornered. So Logan must have been turned loose."

"But then it couldn't have been Logan that smothered Lilly, if he was on Lilly's side and double-crossin' Sullivan along with her."

"Which gets us right back to the fact that it wasn't a revenge killing by the Sullivan boys." The chief glanced over his shoulder at Jerry and Linda Holliday, now standing at the window with their backs to the death bed. He lowered his voice, "So who else had an interest in Lilly's double-cross?"

"You're thinking of Hilly Holliday?"

The chief nodded. "He was here in the hospital. He lost two hundred fifty thousand dollars. Lilly was the lure that brought him to Las Vegas, and finally, that fainting fit could have been a fake just to get him in here close to Lilly."

"But you had a guard on Lilly's door," Jack pointed out.

Chief Jordan scowled. "Why do you suppose I'm handling this case personally instead of turning it over to the homicide squad?"

"You mean you don't trust *anybody* in the department?" Doc looked shocked. "You mean maybe the guard was in on the deal and just plain walked away and let somebody get at Lilly?"

"The officer swears he was on the job all night, but until I know how deep Lieutenant Holmes's tentacles got into the department, I don't believe anybody." A black thundercloud of a scowl sat menacingly on Chief Jordan's face. "And that's why I'm asking you boys to take a hand in this. You solve this murder for me and Las Vegas is your town as long as I'm chief of police here."

"Why sure, Mr. Jordan— " Doc began.

"Shut up, Doc." Jack's voice was full of authority and no nonsense. Doc opened his mouth but shut it again.

"Under one condition," Jack eyed Chief Jordan pointedly, "if you're willing to go under the assumption that Hilly Holliday is innocent."

The chief's eyes popped. "But I just told you—"

"I know you did. But I still don't think Hilly did it. And the only reason I have for thinking so is that Hilly is the Triple A's client."

Chief Jordan glared. "That's a hell of a proposition."

"Actually I have another reason, but it won't mean anything to you." Jack waited until Jordan brushed by the girls for another expectoration out the window. When he returned Jack continued, "The Triple A has got Hilly out of several other jams so I've known him for a number of years. As you say about Logan, Hilly is just not the killer type."

Jordan strode over and looked down at the small, girlish figure lying under the sheet. After a moment he came back. "All right," he growled. "I can't say I like it, but you handle all the other angles and I'll handle Holliday myself. But I warn you, I think I've got the right man, and you're going to have one hell of a time finding anybody else. Lilly was killed because of the double-cross and for no other reason and who else have we got but Holliday?"

"Logan, maybe," Doc murmured.

The chief snorted. His reply, which Doc felt would not have been too complimentary anyway, was interrupted by an authoritative rap and the abrupt entry of a buxom, apple-cheeked nurse in a starched uniform which added breadth and width to her ample figure, but unfortunately no height.

"Chief Jordan," she stated categorically, "it is the rule of the hospital to remove the deceased with the minimum of fuss and while the other patients are still sleeping or occupied with breakfast. The morning routine begins at eight," she looked at her wristwatch pointedly. "Already it is 8:47."

"Sorry, Miss Westover," Jordan sounded apologetic but adamant. "But this room is out of your jurisdiction for the time being. The body is not to be removed until I say so."

Miss Westover's prominent eyes bulged slightly, "Nonsense," she snapped, "whoever heard of such a thing!"

Chief Jordan grinned. "You're hearing it now, Miss Westover." He turned to Jack and Doc, "This is Superintendent of Nurses and Day Supervisor Miss Westover . . . Jack Packard and Doc Long. I wish to have your full cooperation, Miss Westover, in their investigation of this case. I'll give you an official memorandum later. You've kept the night supervisor and the two night nurses on this floor?"

Miss Westover cast a jaundiced eye over Jack and Doc and was not impressed. Her eyes strayed to Jerry Booker and Miss Holliday at the window. "Female investigators?" she asked, disapproving of the two girls.

"I'm sorry," Chief Jordan said hastily. "Miss Booker, Jack and Doc's secretary, and Miss Linda Holliday, sister of one of your patients brought in last night, Hilliard Holliday."

"May I see my brother before I leave?" asked Linda, acknowledging the introduction with a slight nod.

"Visiting hours—"

Supervisor Westover's routine reply was broken off by the chief. "Yes, of course she may. Now, then, Miss

Westover," he continued, ignoring the head nurse's heightening color and tightening lips, "you have detained the night supervisor and the nurses?"

"I have," Miss Westover said shortly, "and they don't like it. They've had a bad night and—"

"Well, Jack and Doc'll want to have a word with them," the chief said breezily, "and then they can go. We'll have the girl's body out of here before noon. But first I want to bring Lieutenant Holmes over here from the jail. A good look at what happened to one of his pals may unseal his lips a little."

Supervisor Westover gave the chief a grim, disapproving stare and turned to the door. "The nurses will be in my office for another half-hour. After that I shall let them go." She walked out.

Doc grinned, "You ast me, Miss Westover don't like you much, chief."

"She's a stickler for routine. She's all right. She doesn't like it, but she'll cooperate." He turned to Linda Holliday. "If you want to see your brother, he's just down the hall in 338."

"Is he under police guard?"

Chief Jordan looked in surprise at the girl. "No, why? Should he be?"

Linda stared. "No, I just thought—" she shrugged and moved to the door.

"You might as well run along too, Jerry," Jack said. "Doc and I'll be busy here another fifteen minutes. We'll meet you back at the hotel. If we're held up, call the chief's office. Somebody there'll know where we are."

"Thanks, pal," Jerry said dryly, "what do I do, walk?"

"There's a taxi stand out front," the chief told her.

Jerry nodded and followed Linda out the door.

"What do you expect to get out of bringing Lieutenant Holmes over here?" Jack turned to the chief.

"Could be he has some idea who did this," he nodded at the bed. "He hasn't heard about Lilly's death. As I say, at least it might shake him up a little."

"If your department is as mixed up with Holmes as you seem to think, isn't it likely someone already has told him?"

Jordan frowned. "I'll take care of the leaks in my department. You take care of your end." He stalked out, spoke under his breath to the uniformed officer on guard outside the door and departed.

19

"Break my leg and call me Limpy!" exclaimed Doc, his raucous Texas voice as smooth and dulcet as whipped butter on melting hot griddle cakes. "I swear to goodness, Miss Martha, honey, if you ain't the spittin' image of Winnie May, my female cousin on my mama's side, down in Swamp Water, Texas. She growed up to be a nurse her ownself. You *are* a Texas gal, Miss Martha, ma'am?"

Nurse Martha Rodin, a tall, gangling girl in her late twenties, with wisps of brindle hair straggling from under her nurse's cap, colored faintly, her tight lips relaxing and a light of curiosity displacing the hostility in her grey-green eyes. "Oklahoma," she murmured.

"I knowed it," enthused Doc, "another one of our families stole out of her Texas cradle when she was diaper wet and transported over into Oklahoma. That's how Oklahoma get all their pretty women; a stealin' our Texas gals." Nurse Grace Parker gurgled suppressed laughter and Night Supervisor Mrs. Holden's eyes sparkled with fun. Encouraged, Doc enlarged. "Why, I'd a knowed you was Texas born and bred just as sure as I could spot Miss Grace, here, was a Nevada product. Right, Miss Grace?"

"Right," nodded nurse Parker.

"Sure," agreed Doc, "and they sure do grow some dainty little cubes of sugar here in Nevada." Doc's eyes rested on the youngest of the trio of nurses in a manner to cause nurse Parker to flush and the smile in the night supervisor's eyes to fade. Doc saw instantly he had made a misplay and turned admiring eyes upon Mrs. Holden.

"Mrs. Holden, ma'am, I sure do hope you have a strict and watchful husband, on account if you don't and I stay in Las Vegas long—"

Night Supervisor Holden bit him off sharply. "My husband is a Lieutenant Commander in the Navy and I'm quite capable of taking care of his interests while he's away."

"I just bet you are at that," nodded Doc agreeably. "After all, a night supervisor who had her nurse's trainin' in Hollywood with all life's temptations at her fingertips—"

"How do you know that?" Supervisor Holden demanded.

"Why, Mrs. Holden, ma'am, how can I *miss*?" Doc protested, "why, shuckens, Hollywood's written all over you. There's somethin' neat and crisp and *finished* about a Hollywood girl. How come the movies didn't get you?"

Supervisor Holden didn't exactly melt, but the frozen atmosphere into which Jack and Doc had stepped when they entered the hospital office had dissipated. Mrs. Holden's lips had pursed into an amused smile. "You're something of a psychologist in the matter of women, aren't you, Mr. Long?"

"They've been my lifelong study, Mrs. Holden, ma'am. They are my very favorite people."

"Obviously," she said dryly, turning to Jack, who had been silently observing Doc's five-minute warmup. "However, I think we'd better get on with the interview and let the girls get home. They've had a long, strenuous night."

Jack nodded. "We'll be as quick as possible. You've had instructions from your head supervisor and Chief Jordan to cooperate?"

The night supervisor nodded.

"Good!" Jack looked at the three. "I know, Mrs. Holden, that you were in charge and that nurse Rodin and nurse Parker were on duty on the floor where Lilly Montrose was killed." He looked at the two nurses, "Were either of you especially assigned to Lilly's room?"

"No." It was Mrs. Holden who spoke. "If the night light went on, whichever nurse was not busy at the moment answered."

"And did the light come on at any time?"

Nurse Rodin spoke up. "The charts will show that Miss Montrose put on her light twice. Once at 10:00 and once at 11:35." Jack nodded for her to go on. "I answered the first call. Miss Montrose was restless, feverish and thirsty. I gave her a sleeping capsule and a glass of water and stayed with her until she dozed off."

Jack nodded. "And the second time?"

Nurse Rodin looked at nurse Parker, who nodded. "Yes, I answered the second light. Miss Montrose complained that the medication was too light and, after consulting with Supervisor Holden, I gave her an injection, which put her to sleep in about ten minutes."

Mrs. Holden nodded agreement. "I came up from the office and checked on the patient myself."

"And so as far as you know, she slept from then on; in fact, was asleep when she was hit on the head and then smothered?"

All three nurses winced, and nurse Parker's hands clenched in her lap. After a moment Mrs. Holden nodded, "Yes." Then after a second she looked at Martha Rodin. "I believe nurse Rodin went into the room at 2:15 to check and found the patient resting quietly."

The tall, gangling girl nodded miserably.

"And which one of you found Lilly dead at 4:30? You, nurse Rodin?" Again the girl nodded, her face flushed.

"Why," asked Jack, "did you go in the second time?"

"It was our last check on the rooms before making out our report in anticipation of the day staff which comes on at six. I was checking that side of the hallway, and Miss Parker the other. It was just chance I found her."

"I see. Which definitely establishes that Lilly was murdered sometime between 2:15 and 4:30," Jack said thoughtfully. "Now, then, I want you to answer a question which might get someone in trouble." He looked at all three anxious faces carefully. "During that period between 2:15 and 4:30 did officer Mike Stern, who was on guard outside Lilly's room, leave his post outside her door?"

There was a moment of uncomfortable silence. Finally, Supervisor Holden said flatly, "That is a question nurse Rodin and nurse Parker will have to answer. I was not on the floor at that time."

Jack looked at the two nurses. Nurse Rodin stared at Jack. Nurse Parker stared at the clenched hands in her lap.

"You see," said Jack quietly, "officer Stern swears he never left the door unguarded, but if that were true, how would anyone have gotten into the room?"

The breathless voice of nurse Parker burst out, the words tumbling from her lips, "At no time did officer Stern leave his post, I am sure of it!"

Nurse Rodin gave her a startled look, her mouth open as though to comment. She closed it abruptly, but after a moment she nodded. "To the best of my knowledge that is true . . . " A savage pink had spread over her cheeks, not in the least compatible with the brindle red of her hair. Nurse Parker's eyes raised from her lap to cast an instant look of shocked surprise and gratitude, only to look down again.

Doc looked from the two girls to the supervisor, whose own face was flushed and not a little grim. "Why, shame on you two honeypots for a sittin' there tellin' whoppers with your bare faces a hangin' out showin' guilty knowledge— " Jack stopped him. "But Jack— " Doc protested.

"Let it go, Doc," Jack growled, "it's obvious the door was not guarded at all times. Why, is a matter that can come later." He turned to the supervisor, but before he could speak, she asserted: "Leave this matter to me. Either I'll get an explanation or we'll go to the head supervisor."

"Thank you," Jack said, "but leaving that for the time being, let's turn to Hilliard Holliday's room for a moment. It is three doors further along the corridor and on the opposite side from Lilly's room. Did any unusual occurrence take place there? Anything, no matter how small?"

"Oh, no," nurse Parker's eyes raised in surprise. "As you know, he was brought into the hospital unconscious, under a heavy sedative. He was still asleep at the 4:30 check-out . . . "

Jack looked at nurse Rodin. She nodded without a shadow of hesitancy. "Nothing at all."

Jack turned back to Mrs. Holden. "One more question and I think we're finished." He hesitated, frowned, and then asked, "Between two and four in the morning, is it possible for someone from outside the hospital to walk in and get to the third floor without being noticed and stopped?"

"I would have thought not," Mrs. Holden said reluctantly, "but it appears that they not only could, but did. I mean," she went on, "the night staff is at a minimum. The front receiving desk is closed, but my office opens on the main corridor and I should have noticed anyone coming in."

"That's the only possible entrance at night?"

The supervisor nodded. "I would have heard the elevator if it had been used. I thought I would have heard any footsteps on the stairs."

"Probably not, if the person was being careful," Jack said thoughtfully. "And there are two nurses on each floor?"

"Two," the supervisor nodded.

"Anyone else on duty in the hospital at night?"

"One medical and one laboratory intern sleep in for emergency cases. They and the other nurses were questioned by Chief Jordan. The two interns were in bed between two and four. None of the nurses saw anyone enter or leave."

Jack glanced inquiringly at nurses Rodin and Parker.

"No one," said Rodin positively.

"At least we *saw* no one," modified Parker.

"Either there was an outsider or this hospital's a housin' a murderer, *that's* for sure," Doc muttered, dissatisfied. "Now, looky, Jack," he glared at his partner, "I'm all for pretty, female girls, especially in nurse's uniforms and *double* especially if they're in trouble, but I just plain can't stomach a barefaced prevaricator." He turned to the two nurses, his washed-out blue eyes cold and unfriendly. "I'm against girls tellin' lie-tales *any*time, but I can't stand a little female who out-and-out whoppers to us and shows in her face she's playin' you for a poor fish."

Nurse Parker's eyes were back on her clenched hands in her lap, her face flushed and her lips trembling. Nurse Rodin's eyes were fastened on Doc, her lips grimly sealed.

"Doc, Supervisor Holden said— " Jack interposed, but the Texan interrupted doggedly. "I *know* she did, but the point is, Chief Jordan's police department is so whamperjawed and gogglin' from the Lieutenant Holmes ruckus, even the chief don't know the *good* cops from the *bad*. And why ain't it reasonable to s'pose this here officer Mike Stern, who was a guardin' Lilly, was one of the lieutenant's henchmen? We know Holmes tried to kill Lilly before our eyes at the hotel. So maybe this Mike Stern finished up the job for him."

Nurse Parker's eyes had suddenly come up, indignant horror blazing through dewdrops of tears. "That's a terrible, unforgivable lie." Her voice trembled with emotion. "Mike is a fine, loyal law officer who is simply devoted to Chief Jordan."

Doc shrugged, "We don't *know* that," he stated dogmatically. "And you and Miss Martha, here, a keepin' stuff to yourselves, sure don't make him look very wholesome."

"All right," cried the younger nurse desperately, "I'll tell you. It wasn't anything like that at all. Mike and I are engaged to be married— "

Supervisor Holden's inarticulate exclamation of disbelief brought nurse Parker's eyes to her. "Of course you didn't know about it, Mrs. Holden. We've been going together for about a year, but we didn't become engaged until last night." The look of stern disapproval in the supervisor's face caused the girl to add, "I know it's against the hospital rules, and I know I'll be disciplined. That's why we tried to keep it a secret." She cast a quick glance at her fellow nurse. "Thank you, Martha, for trying to help." Then she swung back to Doc. "Don't you see?" she pleaded, "Mike couldn't have done what you suggest. Yes, Mike was away from in front of Miss Montrose's room for about ten minutes. We were in empty 306 not more than ten minutes, maybe less, and Martha promised to keep her eye on Miss Montrose's room while we were away."

"And I did, too," asserted nurse Rodin, "every second."

"Well," said Doc cheerfully, friendly again, "now don't you two feel better to get that off your chests?"

The two nurses looked at the night supervisor's grim visage doubtfully.

Doc followed their gaze. "Aw, now, Mrs. Holden, honey," he said with soft persuasiveness, "You couldn't be mad at a little female girl for being in love and just gettin' herself engaged. And besides, looky how they've helped out in our investigation."

"I hope you're not presuming to tell this hospital how to maintain discipline." The supervisor eyed him coldly.

"Oh no, ma'am, only—"

Mrs. Holden cut him off. "Thank you," she snapped.

Doc looked at Jack unhappily.

"It's like this, Mrs. Holden," Jack said gently. "The newspapers are going to be full of Lieutenant Holmes's activities, as well as the murders of Skip Sullivan and Lilly Montrose. Naturally that's going to involve the hospital. But think of the added reflection on the hospital if it was to become known the police guard was lured away from his post by one of the hospital nurses."

Nurse Grace Parker gasped, "I did not lure him away."

Jack shrugged. "That wouldn't keep the press from saying so."

The supervisor's face was a thundercloud.

Jack continued: "However, if you do nothing to discipline nurse Parker, I don't see why any of this should ever get outside this room. You forget her quite forgivable slip of discipline and we'll forget what we've heard in here."

Supervisor Holden wrestled with her conscience for several seconds. All eyes were upon her, waiting. Finally she nodded reluctantly. "I've never done anything like this before in my entire career," she said with dissatisfaction, and then to the nurses, "and don't take it as a precedent; and don't think you'll not pay for it."

"Well, now, that's more like it— " Doc's cheerful relief was cut off abruptly by the vicious bark of a revolver shot just outside the open window.

Jack kicked over his chair getting to the window and Doc was one step behind. A melee of shouts, curses and loud, confused exclamations greeted their ears.

20

The body of a manacled man lay on the sidewalk in front of the hospital. Chief Jordan stood over him staring at a second-floor window, his voice pouring forth commands intermingled with vituperative invectives. A uniformed officer, to whom the body was manacled, knelt on the sidewalk working frantically to get his keys from his pocket. Three other uniformed men scattered on the run to cover all hospital exits.

Mrs. Holden and the two nurses were crowding to the window, when Jack turned abruptly, cut across the room and raced for the stairs, Doc at his heels. Without pausing Jack yelled over his shoulder, "Watch the elevator, Doc. If anyone comes down, hold him."

"Okay, son, him or her." He swerved from the stairs to the elevator and punched the button frantically.

All was confusion on the second floor. Jack grabbed the arm of a nurse. "Where did that shot come from?"

The nurse jerked her arm free. "We couldn't be sure. One of those rooms." She pointed vaguely.

One of the rooms which she indicated was marked Women, another Men, and the others seemed to be private hospital rooms.

"Did you see anyone come out of any of them?"

"I didn't, but I heard someone scream . . . "

"It was one of the nurses," exclaimed an elderly gouty patient, whirling toward them in a wheelchair. "I heard her yell and saw her bust out of the Ladies room and rush down the hall. She was scared as hell. The gunman must still be hiding in there. She's the only one to come out."

The nurse looked startled, opened her mouth, closed it suddenly and turned away. It was then Jack saw Supervisor Holden looking at the nurse with a sharp, warning glance.

"Which way did she go?" Jack snapped.

The wheelchair patient pointed down the corridor. "Running like the very devil was after her."

The elevator door opened and Chief Jordan stepped out, followed by Doc. Jordan's eyes were blazing. "Shooting a prisoner under my very eyes," he stormed. "Let me get my hands on the— " He looked at Jack with blood-shot eyes. "Where is he?"

"Everybody thinks he's in the Women's room," Jack snapped. "No one's come out but a panic-stricken nurse, who must have been in there when the shot was fired, according to the patient in the wheelchair. He witnessed— " Jack turned. The wheelchair was gone and so was Mrs. Holden.

The chief already had drawn his gun and was starting toward the door.

Doc tried to follow but Jack grabbed his arm. "Doc, I want you to come with me."

"Huh, and leave the chief alone with the killer?" Doc sounded aggrieved.

"Shut up and come on." Jack took off down the corridor.

"Where we a goin'?"

Jack grunted, taking the stairs to the third floor two at a time. In the upper corridor, he strode down to the receiving desk, where five or six nurses were congregated, talking in low, excited voices. At the men's approach they broke off, eyeing them uneasily.

"Which one of you nurses just ran up from the second floor?" Jack questioned. They eyed him in more surprise.

"They lost their voices," Doc grinned. "Now, ain't *that* a fine howdydo. Four, five, six pretty female women and not one of 'em's got a voice."

A middleaged nurse eyed Doc severely. "That's a ridiculous question. These girls belong on the third floor and have no business on the second floor. Furthermore, they've all been right here under my eye for the last half hour. Now, you tell us, who are *you*?"

"This is Jack Packard and I'm Doc Long, working with Chief of Police Jordan. They's just been a murder . . . "

The nurses gasped, their varied reactions of excitement, fear and distaste showing distinctly on their faces.

"This is enough time wasted," Jack growled. "If you all were here, then one or more of you must have seen a nurse from the second floor run up the back stairs."

There was a general disclaimer silenced by the older nurse. "I was the only one at the desk when the shot was fired—"

"Oh, you heard it?" Jack's voice sounded dubious.

"Of course not. But nurse McKay heard it. She was attending a patient toward the front of the hospital. She looked out the window and heard voices but could see nothing. She came out to tell me. Also nurses Willowby and Jenkins heard it, more faintly, and they came out. The other two girls were working in the rooms on the other side and only knew about it when they came to the desk."

"So at the time of the shot, you alone were here at the desk?" Jack brought her back to the point at issue.

"I have said so."

"Then you must have seen the nurse who ran up the back stairs."

"I did not," the nurse said severely. "I was in the back office making up the patients' charts."

"What's above the third floor?"

"The roof."

Jack was interrupted by the elevator, out of which stepped Chief Jordan and the head supervisor.

"Did you get him?" Doc asked.

Chief Jordan scowled. "Who?"

"He wasn't in the Ladies restroom?"

"He wasn't anywhere on the second floor. The head supervisor and I have covered every nook and cranny, and now we're going to take the third floor."

"What about the first floor, chief?" Jack asked.

"I've got five men on the first floor and in the basement. What I want is not only the killer but that fool of a screaming runaway nurse."

"I want to get hold of her myself," said the head supervisor grimly. "What a way for a nurse to behave."

"Well, apparently all the nurses are accounted for on this floor," Jack looked at the older nurse, who nodded emphatically.

"And all are accounted for on the second floor," the chief grumbled. "There's nothing on the first floor but offices and laboratories. We're checking on the female laboratory assistants, and if it wasn't one of them, then we know damned well the killer was a man dressed in a nurse's uniform."

"In that case you'd better be looking for an abandoned uniform as well as the man who was in it," Jack suggested.

"Heey, in that case," Doc's eyes widened, "the nurse the old feller in the kiddie-car saw pop out of the Ladies room could have been the killer, himself."

Chief Jordan scowled. "Well, he's still in the hospital. All the exits were covered ten seconds after the shooting." He turned on his heel, "Now, then, Miss Westover, let's get down to business! Every—"

"Yes, I know," murmured the buxom head supervisor resignedly, but without reluctance, "Every nook and cranny of the third floor. Shall we begin with the late Lilly Montrose's room?"

"That's the last place to look. I have a police guard inside with the body. Or I should have." He strode abruptly down the hall to the dead girl's room and flung open the door. He staggered as though buffeted by a heavy wind and then recovered. Even the back of his neck grew fiery red and his bull voice proclaimed his dissatisfaction in full range. "Officer Macey, what the hell do you think you're doing? Goddamn it, sitting there sound asleep with a comic book over your face! I don't know which I hate worse—a smart dishonest cop or a dumb illiterate sonofabitch . . . Get up off your dead ass . . . " The door slammed and the chief's voice became only a volcanic rumble.

The nurses stood rigid, their eyes on Head Supervisor Westover, one or two bursting with inner laughter, the older nurse's eyes popping with indignation.

"My, my," Doc grinned. "Policeman Macey probably ain't a gonna get no bones broke but he's a gettin' his feelin's chewed up and spit out somethin' marvelous."

"You nurses get back to your duties," snapped Supervisor Westover. "Move, when I speak to you! This is still a hospital, not an insane asylum!"

The nurses fled.

Doc approved, "They sure ain't no poverty in your voice, Miss Westover! When you speak up, folks *listen*."

Before she could reply, Chief Jordan reappeared. Still choked with disgruntlement, he growled, "All right, Miss Westover, we'll search now." They moved off.

Throughout the clamor, Jack had been standing at the desk jotting down notations in a small black book. He snapped a rubber band about it and stuck it in his breast pocket. "Come on, I want to talk to Hilly Holliday."

"Yeah, how about him, anyway?" Sudden realization came to Doc as he followed down the corridor. "If he's alert and back to normal, you'd a thought with all the ruckus up and down the halls, he'd at least of stuck his nose out the door."

Jack paused before Room 338 and listened. After a moment he knocked.

"Sure is quiet in there." Doc's voice was uneasy.

21

Jack tentatively pushed open the door, Doc peering over his shoulder.

"Holy jumpin' catfish!— " Before the words were out of Doc's mouth, Jack pushed the door wide and the two entered. "Heey, Jack, Miss Holliday, a lyin' alongside Hilly, naked as a jaybird, and will you looky at her clothes, ripped and tored by a maniac. And looky at them finger scratches on her shoulders and chest. You think Hilly'd do that to his own sister?"

Jack was bending over Holliday. "Hilly didn't do anything to his sister," he said grimly, "he's dead."

"Hilly's dead?"

"What about Linda?" Jack moved around the end of the bed to the girl's side, pushing Doc aside.

"She's a breathin', but not very good." Doc looked about anxiously, then his eyes returned to the bed. "Hilly under the covers, dead! Linda on top the covers, stripped nude-naked and unconscious."

Jack raised up from his examination. "Call Chief Jordan and the head supervisor, quick, Doc."

"You bet you!"

In thirty seconds Doc was back with the chief and Miss Westover. The plump matron gave one horrified exclamation, pushed past the chief's outraged "Goddamn it," and was an efficient hospital attendant.

"Holliday's gone, Miss Westover," Jack said. "It's the girl who may still have a chance."

The supervisor made certain of Hilly and then moved swiftly to Linda. Her first act was to flip a blanket over the girl.

"Leave things as they are, damn it," roared the chief, "until I get pictures of this shambles, and my homicide crew's been over the room."

"A girl in this state's got to be kept warm," Miss Westover said in an absent, matter-of-fact voice without raising her eyes from her cursory examination.

The chief reached for the bedside telephone, but Miss Westover snatched it from his hand. "Doctors before detectives," she said firmly in reply to the chief's glare, lifting the receiver. She spoke quickly but quietly into the phone, put up the receiver and handed it to Jordan.

In his turn he gave a number, but spoke neither quietly nor quickly, leaving little doubt the third floor of the hospital soon would be overrun with Las Vegas's finest.

Jack, who had been prowling the room, suddenly went to his knees, snatched a tissue from a box on the bedside table and reached under the bed. He came up with an injection syringe, the needle still in place and the glass tube nearly empty. "This could be the answer," he said, holding it out to the supervisor. "Can you tell whether this is from your hospital equipment?"

As Miss Westover reached for it, Jordan exploded, "Don't touch that! If there are fingerprints, I want them."

Miss Westover jerked back her hand, but shook her head at Jack. "That doesn't belong to the hospital. We use only disposable injection needles." Then on second thought. "Wait a minute, it might have come from our laboratory, at that. They still have need for them and it looks like standard equipment."

"You had any report from your men in the laboratory, chief?" Jack asked.

Jordan scowled. "Yes, nothing down there, but if this came from there, somebody's going to sweat or my name's not Jeff Jordan."

"Yeah, if, like you say, you can't trust *nobody* in your department," Doc agreed from the floor, where he was examining Linda Holliday's disheveled garments.

"What the hell do you think you're doing?" yelled the chief.

Doc looked up, surprised, "Why, I'm a lookin' over— Heeey, looky at this dress," he said, holding it up. "Most of the hooks and eyes tore off the back and the waist split down the front from neck to belt line."

"Damn it, Long, I want things left as they are!"

"I'm a puttin' 'em back the way they was," Doc said unconcerned. "And will you look at this brassiere. Looks like the band's been cut with a knife. And these here panties! The waistband busted and then just plain tore off the girl."

The chief's mouth opened, but snapped shut again as the door opened and a graying doctor in a white coat stepped in, followed by two nurses with a hospital gurney. From the street below came the trite, routine police siren whining to a halt before the hospital.

"Goddamn it," yelled Jordan, "get that cart out of here."

The startled nurses looked at their chief supervisor, who nodded slightly. They backed out self-consciously, but held the door open. The medic had paused to eye the police chief with disapproval and then went into a momentary conclave with Miss Westover. Next he bent to examine the unconscious girl.

As he worked, Miss Westover murmered, "We've found an injection needle which should be sent down to the laboratory for a test, doctor. Perhaps you can identify it."

The doctor straightened, eyeing the supervisor sharply. "Why hasn't it already been sent down?"

"Because I've got it," the chief said aggressively, "and I'm not letting it out of my hands until my fingerprint man gets here."

"May I see it?"

The chief held it out reluctantly. The doctor looked at it and frowned, then took the chief's wrist and brought the needle down to his nose. He shook his head. "It'll have to be analyzed, and quickly, if I'm to do anything for the girl."

A flurry of heavy footsteps, a gruff word of inquiry, another of command, and the homicide squad arrived en masse, headed by a sour, grizzled Lieutenant Houlihan and trailed by a cameraman, the fingerprint expert, and a short, paunchy, redfaced individual from the coroner's office. Another, a plainclothes officer, took up his stance just outside the door, eyeing the two nurses beside the gurney with an appreciative grin.

Chief Jordan had thrown the blanket back from Linda and the cameraman snapped a picture of the bed as originally discovered—the deceased Hilly beneath the covers, the unconscious Linda alongside. The fingerprint man was at work on the syringe the chief had given him.

"All right now, Caton," the chief commanded, "a close-up of the scratches on the girl's neck and shoulders. Step on it, the doc wants to get to work on her." He turned to the grizzled lieutenant who now had the syringe. "Well, what about it?"

Lieutenant Houlihan shook his head. "No soap!"

"No sign of any kind of fingerprints?" the chief looked at his fingerprint man in disgust.

The expert shrugged, "Sorry, chief."

"All right, doctor, the syringe is yours. And so is the girl. You can take her out of here now."

Supervisor Westover nodded to the nurses in the hallway. The brunette brushed by the guard, guiding the wheeled table through the doorway.

Quickly and efficiently Supervisor Westover and the two nurses wrapped Linda in a sheet and blanket and slipped her onto the table. Taking the syringe from the doctor's hand, the supervisor handed it to the little blonde. "Take this down to the laboratory. We want an emergency report on the content. I'll help Miss Chisholm out with the patient."

The blonde nurse slipped quickly out the door, and the gurney followed, Westover bringing up the rear.

Jack, who had been in the bathroom, came out thoughtfully. "There's no nurse's uniform hidden in this room, unless it's shoved down under the covers with Holliday."

Jordan eyed him with interest. "Why, did you expect to find one in here?" He yanked the covering off the still body, and stared. What remained of Hilly Holliday was fully clothed, including shoes. "Now what the hell!"

"I'd say Hilly'd been well enough to get up and dress hisself, before the killer come along," Doc suggested.

"How soon can you have an autopsy?" Jack asked.

The chief looked at the coroner's assistant, who shrugged. "Within a couple of hours after you release the body."

"Take him, then."

"Well, you won't need Doc and me here any longer. Everything else is routine and you can do that better than we can."

"You mean you just don't want to spend the next twenty-four hours questioning every blessed man, woman and patient in this place?" the chief growled, exasperated. "All two hundred and forty-seven of them."

Jack grinned. "Don't worry, we'll try a couple of other angles. When you've finished here we'll meet and put our pieces together. See what we've got."

"If I don't come out of here with the murderer and the evidence, we're licked," growled the chief stubbornly. "I know he's still in the place and so is the gun that killed Lieutenant Holmes. You agree to that, don't you?"

Jack nodded. "Could be," he said, but his voice didn't carry any real conviction.

"Goddamn it, he's *got* to be. I had every exit covered ten seconds after the shot was fired. He couldn't possibly have got out."

"Unless," murmered Doc softly, "your force is as riddled with Lieutenant Holmes's henchmen . . . "

Every policeman in the room turned and stared at Doc with loathing resentment. Lieutenant Houlihan stepped up to him with his fist doubled. "Were you speaking of me, perhaps?" he said, a glitter of pure homicidal mania in his yellow eyes.

"Why, no, son, I wasn't," said Doc softly. "I swear to my grandma on my mama's side, you folks is the touchiest police department I ever *did* see."

"You want to make anything of it?" The grizzled officer still was not satisfied.

Doc shrugged. "Only if somebody watchin' the exits just happened to let the killer through. Why then, sure, I'd be glad to make somethin' of it."

The lieutenant's fist tightened. "I've been wanting to slug some nosy outsider with a big mouth ever since this business broke," he said bitterly, "and maybe you're the baby I've been looking for."

"Let him alone, Houlihan," the chief said with authority. "Maybe he's got a point, although I don't think so. I picked the men I brought over here with me from the old-timers, and I don't think Holmes ever got to them. But I don't know for sure. And neither do you."

22

When Jack and Doc stepped outside the air-conditioned hospital, the glare of the desert sun hurt their eyes and the roasting oven heat enveloped them.

"Well, fry me for a egg," Doc gasped, stripping off his coat and loosening his tie, "and cook me brown around the edges. If this ain't the very place my mama warned me against ever since I was old enough to tell lies. Only thing that's lackin' is the little imps of Satan in long red underwear and the old boy with horns and cloven hooves."

Jack, with his coat over his arm, headed for the taxi stand, preoccupied with his own thoughts. Doc clamored in after him and slammed the door as the driver turned to them for instructions.

"Heeey," exclaimed Doc happily, "looky who we got. The same dried-up old sage rooster who took us out to the floatin' poker game last night."

"Yep," agreed the dusty, shriveled old driver, grinning through yellow, broken teeth. "But if you're looking for more of the same . . . "

"Nope," Doc said, "take us to a nice cool place where the drinks are long and cold and—"

"Never mind that," Jack broke in, "take us to our hotel, the Regal Spa."

"Aw, now, Jack, we ain't in *that* much of a hurry. Couldn't we— "

Jack interrupted, "The Regal Spa, driver. I want a shower and change and then I've got some telephone calls to make. While I'm doing that, you can pick up Jerry at the hotel and go get your drink. I'll join you later."

"Why Jerry?" objected Doc. "I thought I might call up one of the nurses we was interviewing . . . I got her number and— "

"I got the message," Jack said dryly. "That's why I suggested Jerry. Besides, we've left her at the hotel all morning and she's probably feeling neglected."

Moments later, the old man wrenched the ancient taxi violently into the Regal Spa driveway and slammed on the brakes. He rang down the register flag and yanked off the receipt as Doc clamored out and reached into his pocket, ignored the receipt held out to him and handed the old man a five-dollar bill.

"This here," he said, "is because it's so hot I'm lightheaded and don't know what I'm a doin', plus on account of because we're gonna need you later."

"And," continued Doc, "if you should happen to be around in fifteen or twenty minutes, I might be needin' a taxi after I've showered and changed my wet wash which I'm a wearin' now." He followed Jack into the lobby.

"You sure are puttin' on the Sphinx act, son," he said looking at Jack disapprovingly. "If you're a thinkin' as hard as you look to be, don't it hurt your head?"

"You go to the desk and see whether there are any messages before you come up," Jack answered absently. "I'll be in my room on long distance."

"Yeah, to where?" But Jack already had headed for the elevator. "My, my," muttered Doc, "ain't we just *too* incommunicado for words this a.m." He wandered over to the desk. The prissy, elderly clerk of the night before with the same wing collar, Adam's apple, store teeth and, Doc suspected, dirty mind, was on duty again. Doc looked about, and sure enough, also among the three or four bell-hops was the young man, but in an impeccable fresh uniform. He grinned and moved up to the desk. "Anything I can do for you, Mr. Long?"

"What goes on here?" Doc eyed first the hop and then the clerk. "Can't the Regal Spa afford enough help, or are you and daddy-o here chained to your jobs night and day out of pure love of service to your public?"

The boy grinned. "We have a revolving work schedule," he explained, "One week, night duty; one week, day. We're just shifting to day work."

Doc nodded. "Is Miss Booker up in her room, you happen to know?"

"No, I put her in a taxi about an hour ago." The bell-hop shook his head admiringly. "If I ever get to the place where I can afford a secretary, I'm going to get a duplicate copy of her."

"But can she type?" The elderly clerk chortled salaciously.

Doc's light blue eyes fastened on the clerk's face. "Now, ain't you ashamed," he said. "A old man like you a thinkin' thoughts like that about a girl young enough to be your great-granddaughter."

The clerk's long bony hands fluttered for a second, then he turned to the letter boxes and turned back with a slip of paper.

"Miss Booker left a note for Mr. Packard," he said primly. "Do you wish to take it up to him?"

Doc received the folded paper and opened it. "Dear Jack: When I left Miss Holliday at the hospital she asked me to meet her in her room at the Desert Palace. She gave me her key, Room 416, saying I might get there ahead of her. Didn't say why, but I suspect she wants to pump me. Don't worry, my pump handle's broken and my well's dry. Be back in an hour. Jerry."

Doc looked at the kid. "You say she's been gone an hour?"

The boy shrugged, "Maybe hour and a quarter or hour and a half."

Doc stood puzzling for a moment, then made up his mind. He turned to the clerk. "If Jack wants to know what's become of me, tell him I went to the Desert Palace to meet Miss Booker."

"If you'd care to call Mr. Packard's room—"

"Just do what I ask, you mind?"

The clerk's lips sealed closed in a straight line. His fish-like eyes glinted, but he nodded.

23

The lobby of the Desert Palace was as different from the austere Regal Spa as a country village main street is from Grand Central station. Just off the lobby was a casino equipped with a bar, gaming tables, a hectic, heated mass of tourist gamblers, cut-glass chandeliers, and a rash of all shades of blondes, brunettes and redheads in net tights, bare midriffs and abbreviated brassieres. Doc's tender heart went out in all directions: First, to the silly amateur gamblers apparently with full pocketbooks and empty heads (if there was one thing Doc disapproved of it was commercial legalized gambling); second, to the beautiful bevy of busts and limbs so enticingly mouthwatering until you got a glimpse of their avaricious mouths and hard, glittering eyes. And, thirdly, his heart went out to the rich, ice-tinkling bar, for he was a hot and thirsty man. He hesitated, but after a moment of indecision heroically decided, against every instinct, to wait until he'd collected Jerry.

He pushed through the lobby crowd of new arrivals and milling melee of cautious sightseers, all of whose eyes were turned longingly toward the casino. He was one of ten in the self-service elevator, but he alone got off at the fourth floor.

Four-sixteen had not the slightest sign of being inhabited. Doc put his ear to the panel door—nothing. He barely touched the knob; locked. He squatted on his long shanks, squinted at the lock, and cussed under his breath colorfully but without obscenity. "I just plain hate these modern palaces of sin with no decent keyhole for a preliminary gander into the immediate future. And, with all this modern air conditionin', " he muttered, rising up and looking above the door, "no transom." He sighed, taking a sliver of flexible steel from a tiny slit in his belt. He glanced casually over his shoulder. The portion of the corridor in view was empty. Quickly, with breathless, taut diaphragm and incredibly nimble fingers, he took thirty seconds to release first the night latch and then the normal day lock. As the door moved open the smallest crack, the telephone rang. He waited. It rang a second time.

"Well, move," a masculine, burned-out voice rasped.

"You want me to answer it?" That was Jerry Booker's voice sounding surprised.

"Answer it, but watch what you say," the rasping voice warned, "I've never killed anybody in my life, but I may just be about to."

The receiver was snatched up just as the phone began a third ring.

"Hello?" A slight pause, then Jerry's voice again, "No, Miss Holliday isn't here just now. She gave me her key and asked me to wait . . . " Another pause; Jerry sounded annoyed. "This is Jerry Booker, if it's any of your nosy business. Who should I say called?" Again a pause, then Jerry still annoyed, saying "All right, Santa Claus, call around again about next Christmas. Goodbye!" But the receiver didn't slam down. Instead Jerry said three more words with intervals between: "What? . . . Yes! . . . No! . . . " and hung up.

"What was that last all about?" asked the voice suspiciously.

"If Miss Holliday wasn't in, was *I* engaged for the afternoon and evening," Jerry sounded bored. From outside Doc heard the barest rustle of skirts as she flung herself into a chair. "I said 'yes.' Then he asked if I couldn't break the date. I said 'no.' "

It'd been Jack on the other end of the line who had said, "Are you in danger? Is there someone with you in the room?" He got a yes answer. Then, "Hasn't Doc arrived yet?" and got a no answer.

The telephone bit gave Doc an idea. He closed the door gently, waited a second, and then tapped on the panel. There was a momentary pause, and then Jerry's voice, "Yes, who is it?"

"Telegram for Miss Linda Holliday," Doc called out in a bored singsong voice. Another pause and then the night latch slipped back and the door opened.

Jerry's eyes widened for a second and then slid sideways in a warning that the raspy voice was just around the door jamb. "Well, where's the telegram?"

"Yes, Madam, but you'll have to sign." Doc's Texas imitation of a bellhop caused a brief glitter of horrified amusement in Jerry's eyes. She held out her hand through the doorway. In an instant Doc had grabbed her wrist and yanked her through the door, landing her in a heap in the corridor behind him. In the same instant he flailed around the door jamb with his coat. There was a single pistol shot, and then Doc followed the coat around the jamb.

"Why, you two-tailed ciffy cat!" he complained indignantly, coming down on the gunman's pistol hand with the edge of his own hand, sending the weapon spinning across the room. "I'll teach you to go shootin' holes in my imported Italian sport coat." He stuck his fist into the paunch of the retreating figure, and then delivered a second

short murderous blow to the man's Adam's apple. The gunman coughed, stumbled and sank to the floor.

"Well, well, and *well*," Doc said happily, pleased with
the results, "will you looky what we got! Mr. Silver Logan, alias Max hisself, white streak in his curly locks and
all." He turned to the corridor where Jerry was shakily picking herself up from the carpet. "You all right, Jerry, honey?"

"You're a hell of a knight in shining armor on a white
horse," she gasped, leaning against the wall and rubbing
a bruised elbow.

"Always complainin'," said Doc cheerfully, pocketing
Logan's weapon and turning the gambler's face up with
the toe of his shoe. "You're rescued, ain't you?"

"Oh, I'm rescued, all right," agreed Jerry bitterly, "but
why did you have to let your white horse kick me in the
stomach?"

"Yeah," Doc said, "it's always a shock to a little female girl to be rescued from a fate worse than death. Kinda like comin' up out of deep water. What you need is a
decompression chamber."

"What I need is a drink, damn it."

"Now you're a talkin', sugar! Get on the phone and
order a couple of long, wet mint juleps and after that call
Jack—"

"That was Jack on the phone. He's on his way over."

"Well, whoooeeee, make it three mint juleps then and
tell 'em we're out in the middle of the Sahara Desert and
step on it."

On the way to the phone, Jerry paused before a mirror and cursed softly under her breath at what Doc's rescue methods had done to a perfectly good thirty-dollar coiffure. She pinned up a few straggling hairs, then picked up the receiver.

The mint juleps and Jack arrived at the same instant. He looked at the tray of drinks; at the reclining Silver Logan; at the disheveled Jerry; and finally he looked at Doc with disapproval. "Where," he asked accusingly, "is Logan's drink?"

Doc grinned. "Why, now, I never thought of Mister Logan," he admitted, "on account I just figured he'd had too much already." He skinned off ten one-dollar bills from a dwindling roll and put them on the waiter's tray.

The waiter had been looking at Logan with a worried expression and seemed relieved with Doc's explanation. He handed around the drinks, shaking his head. "I don't understand people," he said to no one in particular. "They come all the way to Las Vegas for a good time and then they get blotto and stay blotto the whole time they're here."

Doc followed him to the door, "Why, son, that's how some folks enjoy theirselves," he said soothingly, closing the door on the disapproving waiter.

Jack bent over Logan. "He's coming around, but slowly."

"I can help that," Doc said, going to the bathroom for a glass of water.

Jack looked up at Jerry. "How did you get tangled up with Logan?"

Jerry shrugged, "I came over here to Miss Holliday's room, as she asked me to. When I opened the door, there he was, sitting in a chair with the gun pointing at my middle."

"Why?"

Again Jerry shrugged, "Waiting for Miss Holliday."

"Did he say why?"

Jerry shook her head, "Just said we'd wait for her together." Then as an afterthought, "Heeeey, she's sure a long time getting here? Was she still with Hilly at the hospital when you left?"

"She sure was," answered Doc, coming from the bathroom, "a lyin' unconscious on the bed beside her dead brother."

Jerry's eyes opened, "Hilly's dead?"

Doc dashed the water in Logan's face, bringing a gasp from the supine card shark. "Deader'n an iced mackerel. And there was Linda, a lyin' beside him outside the covers stripped naked as a jaybird."

Jerry looked scathingly at first Doc, then Jack. "You mean she didn't have *anything* on?"

"Not even a beauty patch. And is she ever stacked," he added.

"And I suppose you two just stood there and gawked."

"Well, I don't think I missed anything before the head nurse come in and throwed a blanket over her."

"That's the trouble with these rich dames," muttered Jerry viciously, "There isn't anything they won't do to get attention. And what's more, they get away with it."

"But she didn't do it on purpose," protested Doc, "She was unconscious."

"I'll bet."

"Yeah, with her clothes a layin' on the floor ripped and tore. Some sex-mad fiend musta been loose in the hospital, and I wouldn't be surprised if we got him right here."

"How'd he get out of the hospital?" Jack grunted.

Suddenly Logan opened his eyes and was torn by a paroxysm of coughing. Jack turned him face down and hit him between the shoulderblades, then took him under the arms and dragged him to a chair.

"Feeling better?" Jack asked.

Logan looked up at Jack with a sullen stare.

"Yes, sir," Doc said with satisfaction, "won't Chief Jordan be glad to get his hands on this baby. A real life-sized triple murderer—Lilly Montrose, Lieutenant Holmes, and Hilly Holliday. Not to mention the fiendish attack on *Miss* Holliday."

Indignation suffused Logan's face. His mouth opened and his lips moved, but no words came. A spasm of surprise flashed in his eyes.

"You'll have to talk louder'n *that*," Doc admonished.

Apparently Logan said, "I can't," but no sound came. Panic seized him and he tried to rise, but Jack pushed him back.

"If you're faking—" Jack warned, but Logan shook his head desperately.

"He was talkin' plain enough when he had Jerry in the room alone," Doc commented suspiciously. "Maybe he is just a playin' sick."

Logan glared balefully at Doc and then, his eyes resting on Jack, he pointed at his throat. Jack bent over him for a moment and then turned slowly to Doc. "I don't suppose some redheaded Texas idiot smashed Logan on the Adam's apple by any chance."

Doc's eyes opened innocently. "You mean a little tap like that unsettled his talk box?"

"Oh, great!" Jack looked at Logan in disgust. "He'll be lucky if he's talking a month from now."

"But hittin' a man on the chin's dangerous, Jack," Doc protested. "A hombre could bust a knuckle doin' that. Here," he said, taking a pad and pencil from his coat and thrusting them in Logan's hand, "a sore throat ain't a gonna keep you from writin'. "

Logan looked at the paper in his hand and then up at Doc, shaking his head.

"Watcha mean, *no,*" Doc said belligerently, "write somethin'. "

Logan shrugged, and painfully, with great deliberation, wrote "Silver Logan" in big round childish letters.

"Okay, okay, we know you're Logan, now write why you was a holed up in Linda Holliday's room waitin' for her with a gun?"

Logan's eyes appealed to Jack and again he shook his head.

"Fine," Jack's disgust was scorching, "you dislocate a man's larynx who just barely can write his own name."

"Aaaw, he's just a woofin' us." Doc's disbelief lacked conviction. "How come a card slicker that can read a poker deck *front and back* can't write?" He looked at Logan balefully, "You sure you can't write?"

Logan nodded.

"Well, maybe you just got phlegm in your throat. Maybe a good shot of liquor'll open up your gullet." He looked about.

Jack and Jerry hastily picked up their mint juleps, by this time nicely frosted.

"That's a good idea, Doc," Jack agreed, "hand over your glass."

"Now, wait a minute," Doc protested, "the liquor's too diluted in a mint julep. What he needs is a straight shot."

"No, the cold, frosty liquid'll probably do his throat as much good as the alcohol." Jack lifted Doc's glass from his hand and gave it to Logan.

"Now, looky here, Jack— " Doc's protest broke off as Logan eagerly lifted the long glass to his lips and without pause drained it down to the last mint leaf and cube of ice. "There you are," the Texan exclaimed sourly, "if he's still got that big hole a goin' *down* his throat, why ain't he got room enough for words to come *out?*" He turned threateningly on the seated man, "All right, now, Logan, talk!"

Logan's eyes had brightened and there was the appearance of a man fully recovered. He opened his mouth and his lips formed words, but still no sound came.

"That's just plain nauseatin'," Doc complained plaintively, "Mint juleps at two-and-a-half a throw and me so thirsty I'm a sweatin' my life's juices, and he still ain't a talkin'."

"Here, Doc," Jerry held out what was left in her glass, "you paid for the drinks. You should get something."

Doc rejected it. "No, dad-blame it, if I'm a gonna be a martyr, I'm a gonna be a full-fledged martyr complete with a wailin' wall."

"Well," murmured Jerry, gratefully sipping from the glass, "What do we do now?"

Jack picked up the receiver and gave a number. "Hello," he said after a moment, "will you tell Chief Jordan that Jack Packard is on the line with information about the Lieutenant Holmes case."

Almost instantaneously the chief's gruff voice answered. "Well, what you got?"

"Silver Logan."

"What!" yelled Jordan, "Where?"

"He was waiting in Linda Holliday's hotel room with a gun."

"The gun that killed Holmes?" The chief's voice was eager with relief.

"Now, how would I know that?" Jack wanted to know. "You've got a ballistics man down at the station, haven't you?"

"Of course it's the gun."

"I don't know," Jack said doubtfully. "How did he get out of the hospital and over here to Miss Holliday's room, when you had all the exits plugged up? Unless, of course, one of your guards was a Holmes man and let him slip by."

"Yeah, naturally that's what happened," Doc put in.

A few well-chosen unprintable words tortured the line which must have seared the eardrums of any snooping telephone operator.

"The only thing, chief," Jack pointed out, "if Logan was responsible for Hilly Holliday's murder and the attack on Linda, why was he waiting with a gun over here for Linda to come back to her room?"

Suddenly Logan was on his feet, waving his arms wildly. Doc grabbed him and threw him back in the chair. He was violently protesting something. Sweat stood out on his forehead and again he made a desperate effort to rise, but again Doc tossed him back in the chair.

24

"Now sit still, you dad-bloomed ciffy cat, before I *really* smack you," Doc threatened, picking up a lamp base and holding it over Logan's head.

Jack had been watching Logan's reaction, missing the chief's last remarks.

"Hello, hello! Packard, you still there?" came frantically over the wire.

"Sorry, chief, Logan seems to be unhappy about something."

"What about? What's he saying?"

"Nothing," Jack advised him. "He can't talk."

"Can't talk?"

"He got a little bruise on his Adam's apple and he's lost his voice. If you want to send a car over for him, I suggest you take him into the emergency room."

Jordan snarled, "Never mind emergency, I want some answers fast. He can write it."

Jack said softly, "You'll be disappointed about that, too. He can't write."

"What are you talking about?"

"We tried it," Jack assured him. "He just barely can sign his own name. I still suggest getting him to a doctor."

There was a vicious expletive and then a pause. In the background Jack could hear Jordan shouting orders furiously. Then he came back on the phone.

"If Logan can't talk or write, how the hell are we going to sweat him?"

"I'd gather," Jack surmised, "from your unfriendly attitude that you didn't have much success searching the hospital."

"Oh, you'd gather that would you?" snarled Jordan.

"Nothing at all?" Jack wanted to know. "Nobody hiding in the basement or on the roof? No murder gun? No guilty nurse or nurse's uniform?"

"Yeah, we got the uniform. So what?"

"Oh? Where was it?"

"At the bottom of the laundry chute mixed with other dirty laundry. Different style and make from anything worn at the hospital."

"Well, that's something. If you can run that down— "

"Damn it, that could take days or weeks. I've got a man going around Las Vegas stores, but you've got the man I want up there in the Desert Palace."

"I thought you told me Logan wasn't the killer type," Jack protested.

"How the hell do *I* know who's the killer type?"

"What about Linda Holliday? She going to make it?"

Jordan grunted, "Out of danger. Actually, never was in danger."

"Oh?"

"The killer gave her brother such an almighty dose, he had only enough left to put the girl to sleep. We found the empty bottle in the bed when we removed Holliday's body."

"What was it?" Jack asked with interest.

"Never heard of it. I've got it written down somewhere. If you're interested, call the hospital laboratory. The bottle had a prescription number on it, a San Francisco doctor's name, the name of the pharmacy, and Holliday's name."

"You call the pharmacy?"

"The lab did. It was a prescription which had to be renewed by the doctor each time. Contained a heavy opiate and was to be given in doses of one cc by injection whenever Holliday came down with one of his epileptic fits."

"Could he give it to himself?"

"I suppose so, it was his needle. We found the box in his coat pocket."

"You make anything of it?"

"Such as what?" There was reserve in Jordan's voice.

"Well, either the killer knew he carried the stuff or else he'd intended killing him in another manner and chose the opiate at the last moment. Maybe saw it lying on the bedside table. It would be quieter than a gun."

"And what was Holliday doing all this time? Rolling up his sleeve for the murderer? And what was Miss Holliday doing when she came into the room and the needle was held out to her?"

"You've got a nice question there," agreed Jack.

"Unless he bashed them over the head before the injection."

"You don't bash people over the head and not leave a mark," Jordan said sourly.

"No marks, huh?"

There was an abrupt knock on the corridor door. As Jerry crossed to open it, Jack finished quickly. "Your men are here for Logan. I'll be in touch with you later."

He hung up as two piano-moving-type plainclothes men barreled into the room. The older and uglier of the two, with heavy seams of dissipation about his mouth and dark bags under his eyes, walked over to Logan's chair and stared at him with mean, deliberate, bloodshot eyes. The other, thick in the shoulders, bull-necked but with a foolish, moronic grin on a hairless, baby-smooth face, fished out a pair of handcuffs and dangled them on a stubby forefinger.

"Hi, Silver," he greeted, "long time no see."

Silver Logan looked at them in stark terror. A heavy sickroom stench popped out of his pores in beads of sweat. His hopeless despair transferred pleadingly to Jack and Doc.

"Yes, sir," said the grinning one, "you've been mighty hard to come by. But you sure left your mark around. A strangled Lilly, a poisoned playboy, and Lieutenant Holmes himself, shot smack through the heart and while he was handcuffed to me with these very manacles. But aren't you ashamed of yourself for only halfway killing the millionairess and then ripping off her clothes? That makes you some kind of a sex maniac."

Logan shook his head in violent protest, opening his mouth and moving his lips in agonized silence.

"Oh, you won't talk, huh?" the one with the baby-smooth skin said softly, but it was the older man whose big ham hand suddenly swung back and slapped Logan with an open palm. Even so, Logan's head spun and snapped against the back of the chair.

Jerry Booker cried out a protest as though she had been struck. Jack picked up the phone and muttered a number into it. The heads of the two plainclothes officers swung mechanically toward him, questioningly, their eyes blank, waiting.

Doc had moved over beside Logan's chair. His face was peaceful and friendly, but his pale blue eyes were suddenly the color of bleak, gray slate. "Ain't you boys a bein' a little rough," he said softly, "on account Mister Logan here really can't talk." The two men's eyes turned to him. "It's on account he accidentally got hit on the Adam's apple and lost his voice."

The smoothfaced man suddenly blossomed out with his moronic grin and looked at his partner. "Did you ever know it not to happen?" he said, as though enjoying it. "Always the Hollywood or L.A. shamus coming over here to our playground and start telling us our business. Sometimes you'd get the impression these private operators think they run the whole shebang."

Jack had turned his back and was speaking softly into the mouthpiece. Suddenly he turned and held out the receiver. "Which one of you is Lundgren? Chief Jordan wants to speak to you."

The older officer made a grimace and stalked to the phone. "Yeah?" he grunted into the mouthpiece. After a moment another grunt, then finally a third, whereupon he slammed down the receiver and stalked back to Logan. He grabbed him by the coat collar and yanked him to his feet and swung him about. The other gathered Logan's arms behind him and snapped on the cuffs, then stepped back and looked at the oler man for instructions.

"Chief wants this baby delivered to the emergency room. He'll meet us there." Then without so much as a glance at Jack or Doc, "Seems as if we're running a taxi service. Our two heroes and the heroine want to ride with us."

The expression of relief in Logan's eyes was that of a man receiving a reprieve. The baby-skinned officer turned his moronic grin on Jack, but his eyes were malevolent. "Kinda attached to our killer, seems like. Maybe you folks are playing footsie with the Skip Sullivan crowd. Maybe the boys on the force would like to know why you're interested in our boy here who killed Lieutenant Holmes."

Jack looked interested. "I'm sure Chief Jordan will be highly elated to know you men are so concerned over Holmes's death. He's been looking for Holmes's pals in the department."

An opaque film hooded all expression in the other's eyes, but his moronic grin remained fixed. The older officer spat viciously on the soft hotel carpet and yanked Logan toward the door.

25

Jordan was waiting at the emergency door which was at the rear of the basement of Morrison Hospital. He received his two subordinates sourly, muttered something and ordered them back to headquarters. He eyed the hand-cuffed Logan morosely and nodded him into the waiting room. There a uniformed officer took him in tow and led him into an examination cubicle, where a young intern and a pretty redheaded nurse were waiting.

When the door had closed, the chief turned on Jack grumpily. "Now maybe you'll tell me why in God's name you're so sure Lundgren and Keefer are two of Lieutenant Holmes's gang and that Logan would never had arrived here alive without you in the police car?"

"It was obvious Logan knew them and was in a panic. I know that's not proof but why take a chance when Logan's testimony may be the key to the real killer."

"I sure do love a witness who can neither talk nor write," the chief muttered bitterly. "I'll bet half the state of Nevada that silly Texas partner of yours slugged him in the throat. It's an old Texas trick."

"I wasn't present," Jack said, "so all I have is Doc and Jerry's version. As I get it, Doc knocked the gun out of his hand and slugged him. His throat struck the edge of a table when he fell."

"Like hell!" But the chief was somewhat mollified when Jack handed him Logan's gun. He nodded with satisfaction. "It's the right caliber. We'll see what ballistics has to say about the slug."

"Do you still have the hospital under guard?"

Jordan looked at him hard, "I not only have it guarded, but we're still using a fine-tooth comb on it. And more than that, I've had every man on the hot seat who was at the exits when and if the killer escaped, and I'm satisfied none of them are Holmes's henchmen."

"Then the killer must still be inside and that lets Logan off the hook," Jack pointed out.

"Maybe," Jordan said with reservation, "or maybe Logan knew of some escape hole we haven't discovered."

"Has Miss Holliday recovered consciousness?"

The chief nodded gloomily. "But all she does is upchuck and spin like a top. Doc Henry says she may not get rid of the nausea and dizziness for another twelve hours. He gave her something to put her back to sleep."

"You didn't get anything out of her?"

"Every time she started to speak she gagged. Oh sure, we got plenty out of her, but nothing that would interest a judge or jury."

Jack hesitated a moment, "As you know, she's our client." The chief grunted and started to speak, but Jack continued, "Oh sure, I told you the Home and Farm Insurance Company was our client and it still is, but Linda asked us for help the minute she arrived in Vegas. Now that Hilly's dead, there's no conflict of interest and I think it's only right that we help the girl."

Jordan grunted, "You could be representing the murderer."

Jack nodded, "I've wondered about that. I've wondered about it a lot. For instance, there's the sudden death in L.A. of the man who originally set up the deal for Hilly to bring the hatbox of money to Las Vegas. Then Linda's sudden arrival here, and right on top of that the Lilly Montrose murder.

"Linda could have come here to the hospital right after she left the plane, before she came to our hotel. Again, Lieutenant Holmes was shot from the second floor Women's rest room while she was in the hospital.

"Then comes Holliday's death from poisoning—an overdose of his own medicine. Who would know better about the stuff than Holliday's sister? She could even have given herself a small shot to put herself out, after ripping off her own clothes to give it an air of criminal attack by a man. By the way, was she examined? Was she physically molested?"

"If you mean was she raped why don't you say so?" Jordan took a plug of tobacco from his shirt pocket and bit off a hunk. "Yes," he said around the plug, "she was examined. No, she wasn't raped."

Jack nodded. "Which adds to the possibility that Linda set up the attack angle for herself."

The chief nodded.

"Of course, if she isn't the killer—and I'm playing it that she's not—then the man who is guilty could have set up the ripped clothes and naked-girl scene just to throw us off the scent and get the police looking for a sex maniac."

"You make an awful good case against the girl," the chief growled. He went to the outer door and spat. "Heeey," he exclaimed, coming back, "what's become of Doc and your secretary?"

"I sent them to check out a couple of things."

"What?" The chief's eyes narrowed.

"Just a couple of details we overlooked when we were here this morning." Jack changed the subject. "Getting back to Linda Holliday, I was suspicious enough of her that I made a couple of telephone calls to Los Angeles. Three, in fact. The last to our Hollywood office to get Reggie York to check back through the newspaper morgue files on the Hollidays. At no time has Linda ever been linked with any Las Vegas man or men of unsavory character. I know for certain she has never been connected with her brother's funny business. In fact his troubles until now have always been of the playboy type—women; married and single. Never anything with money or mobs."

"That proves nothing," asserted Jordan, "just because she was smart enough to keep out of the papers."

"Right," agreed Jack, "but that was a whale of a good shot from that bathroom window with a revolver. A good sixty feet, shooting down and through the heart."

"Proving what?"

"That unless Linda Holliday is an expert shot, she couldn't possibly have done it, even on a fluke. So I had Reggie call the president of a crack pistol team in Beverly Hills. He knew her name but he'd never heard of her as a crack shot. Then Reggie called a close friend, who the Triple A once got out of a bad jam with Hilly. She said Linda was afraid of guns—even refused to have one in the house—and to her knowledge had never fired so much as a water pistol."

"Do you take it from that, she's pure as a lily?"

Jack shrugged. "So far as Lieutenant Holmes's murder is concerned. And I think Lilly Montrose and Hilly were killed by the same hand."

"Why?—I mean, why all three murders?" Jordan said stubbornly.

"I'm beginning to wonder."

"What?"

"Whether Lieutenant Holmes *was* Mr. Big in the game he was playing here in Las Vegas. Perhaps he was the real Mr. Big's righthand man. If that is true and the game was up with the arrest of Holmes, maybe it became necessary for the *real* big man to close the mouths of those who knew who he was."

Jordan looked interested. "Now that's a big idea with a knot in its tail." He was thoughtful for a moment, walked to the door and spat. Coming back, he said, "Only thing is, you'd think as chief of police I'd have some idea who he is."

"You didn't know Lieutenant Holmes was playing fast and loose, using your own department as a blind," Jack pointed out. The chief's bronze face reddened slightly. "And if that's a fact, then it's also possible that you wouldn't have heard of the man at the top."

The inner cubicle opened abruptly and the young intern came out, shaking his head. "I'm sorry, chief, but his throat's so swollen even an x-ray doesn't show the true damage." He looked anxiously at the clouded face of Jack. "It's a tough one," he apologized. "We're doing everything we can to reduce the swelling, but it will be at least another twenty-four hours before he can speak, even if nothing else is wrong."

"Well, talk or no talk, I'm holding him as a material witness. We'll take him down, lock him up and bring him back tomorrow," Jordan said.

"It would be better if we could keep him here, under guard, of course, and keep his throat packed." The intern spoke uncertainly, but it was obvious he disapproved of Logan's removal to a jail cell.

Jordan hesitated. "Well, all right, but goddamn it, you've had three murders connected with this hospital already, so if anything happens to Logan I'm going to raise hell and put a rock under it."

26

The blazing sun, which had crossed the Nevada desert much too close to the earth's surface all day long—to the extreme discomfort of native and transient alike—now stood deep in the far west, a malignant red eye.

Long, heavy black shadows still smoldered on the hot paving and desert stones. Even the waters of the multitude of swimming pools, filled with brief trunks and bikini nudity, under the last hissing rays created a macabre fantasy of boiling pots of lobsters.

It was 6:45 when Jerry Booker shucked off her brief street attire and sank her hundred and nine pounds of feminine symmetry into the tiled tub. At 7:20 she tapped at Jack's door dressed in a crisp, cool linen dress, smelling of something outrageously expensive and enticing.

"Whooeee," approved Doc, as the door closed behind her, "will you looky what we got this time, Jack—Little Miss Powder Puff in person, risin' out of sea-green foam. Jerry, honey, you just *got* to be livin' a life of sin. The Triple A agency sure can't afford to support you in the manner to which you aspire."

"All right, pull yourself together, Texas," Jerry eyed the tomato and bacon sandwich Doc was dribbling on his fingers and relishing, along with a tall, beady glass of milk.

"And thanks for waiting for a starving girl. Is there anything left?"

Doc waved his hand to a well-laden buffet across the room. "All laid out in stacks. He'p yourself, sugar."

Jerry walked over to the table just as Jack came out of the bathroom, a cheese and ham sandwich in one hand and a large, refreshing glass with ice, mint and sugar topping it in the other.

"You, too!" she flung over her shoulder, dipping into a large silver platter of sandwiches and picking up a glass similar to Jack's. "Not a gentleman in the place."

"I told you to be here at seven o'clock," Jack informed her, "it is now thirty minutes after."

"It takes a girl—" she protested.

"It sure does, honey," Doc agreed. "But the results are worth it."

Jerry looked at Jack for confirmation, but he had settled himself in a chair, studying a small black notebook overflowing with neat cryptic notations. She made a face and curled up in a chair facing him.

"All right, Doc," he said, not looking up, "I assume from your shaved, showered and slicked-up appearance that you made contact."

"Now ain't that a silly question!" The disgust in Doc's voice was somewhat minimized as he licked a gob of mayonnaise off his fingers and returned to the buffet for another sandwich. "Me and Miss Oklahoma, namely, Miss Martha Rodin, R.N., is a gonna break bread and dance our shoes off in the Well of Plenty Cabaret Room beginnin' at 8:30 on the nose."

Jerry eyed Doc's sleek appearance without enthusiasm and then noted Jack's casual appearance. "I haven't been out on the town once since we arrived." She fixed her eyes on Jack pointedly.

"Yeah, Jack," Doc encouraged, "give the little girl a big night once in her life."

Jack raised his eyes briefly, frowning. "Listen, you fuzzyheaded Texas lamebrain, keep your mind on the business at hand. Do you know what you're going to say to nurse Rodin?"

"Do I know what I'm gonna say to a girl?" Doc looked at his partner with derision. "Son, I *always* know what I'm a gonna say to a female."

"And you always get the same answer, 'no,' I hope," Jerry muttered, still piqued.

"Now ain't that a little bit of dirt out of a unchaste mind," Doc said indignantly.

"Will you two idiots shut up," Jack said impatiently. "Doc, three murders in a respectable hospital simply don't make sense. Not unless there's something rotten among the personnel. You're going to make Martha Rodin talk."

"Well, naturally," agreed Doc in an injured tone, "but you don't make a girl, and especially a nurse, say anything important until you get her eatin' out of your hand."

"Well, cut the monkeyshines and get down to business. It could mean the difference between life and death to at least two more people; and I mean tonight."

Jerry's eyes grew big. Doc stopped a sandwich on the way to his mouth. "Heeey, you mean that?"

"I do." Jack abruptly turned to Jerry. "You get in to see Linda?"

"Just for a minute," she nodded. "She's asleep, all right."

"What room?"

"Three-forty!"

"Back on the third floor, huh," Jack muttered. "You were able to stick around until they brought Silver Logan up from emergency?"

Again Jerry nodded, "Three thirty-nine. Just across the hall from Miss Holliday."

Jack nodded. "It's beginning to be a pattern." He raised his eyes to the buffet and handed Doc his glass. "Pour another bourbon over the ice and give me a chicken sandwich."

Doc looked at his partner, frowning for a moment, then took the glass, saying to Jerry, "The Sphinx has spoke, but what he says don't make no pattern to me." He poured bourbon into the glass, picked up the tray and returned. Jerry snatched a sandwich for herself as the tray went by. As Doc returned the platter to the buffet, a sharp rap sounded at the door.

Both Jerry and Doc looked at Jack. He waited. Again the authoritative rap. Jack put down his drink and sandwich and went to answer. Doc followed, leaning against the wall out of sight, to the right of the door.

Jack opened the door a crack with his foot braced against the bottom. Then it swung wide.

"Joe Denton," he welcomed with pleased surprise. "Come on in."

Denton stepped in, followed by a second and third man, noting with a glint of humor Doc's position beside the door and then let his eyes rest approvingly on Jerry.

"This is Miss Booker, the Triple A's house mother," Jack said, closing the door. "You know Doc Long."

Denton nodded. He turned to the tall, spare man with the imprint of the legal mind stamped upon him, and identified him as Lawrence M. Lambert, Nevada's state's attorney. The smaller, worried-looking man he identified as Dr. Charles Willard.

Jack had been looking curiously at the state's attorney, but swung to Dr. Willard with questioning eyes.

"You've had an interview with Silver Logan?"

"I've seen him," said the little doctor dryly. "I've been reading lips for years. His lips move, but they make no sense."

Jack frowned thoughtfully.

Doc put in, "You mean he's out of his head or he's been doped up or something?"

The doctor looked at Doc with approval. "I made sure about that. No, he's sensible enough and he's had no medication, except normal for his throat condition."

"Then he's just plain bein' ornery and playin' dead?"

The doctor nodded, "I suspect so."

"Who was present during the interview?" Jack asked, looking from Dr. Willard to Denton to the state's attorney.

"The first time a Miss Westover, Chief Jordan, and a hospital staff man, Dr. Corrigan, I believe. The second time, Jordan, Mr. Lambert," he nodded at the state's attorney, "and Mr. Denton."

Jack looked at Denton curiously. "The Feds are still interested, even though you've got the bank robbery funds back?"

"Have we?" Denton said dryly. "Oh, by the way, I've been wanting to tell you when we counted the money in Hilliard Holliday's hatbox, there was twenty-seven hundred fifty dollars over the two hundred fifty thousand."

"Heey," exclaimed Doc excited, "that must of been some of Skip Sullivan's money I won at the poker game."

"That's what we figured."

"Why, looky at me, Jack, I'm finally on my way to bein' a millionaire."

"That's Triple A money," snapped Jerry.

Everyone turned to stare at the girl.

"Well, doggone it, it is," she persisted, "Doc got the money doing a job for the agency while on a salary. There-fore, any profits go into the agency's bank account."

"Did you ever see such a money-grabbin' female?" Doc snorted in disgust, "I swear to goodness— "

"Never mind that now," Jack turned back to Denton. "I said you have the bank funds. What do you mean by saying 'have we?' "

Denton crossed and sat on the bed.

"Heeey," apolgized Doc, "everybody grab a chair. We're a great bunch of hosts."

The state's attorney Lambert chose the best chair in the room, which had been Jack's. Dr. Willard chose a straight back.

"And another thing, you folks hungry or thirsty? Jerry, where's your instinct for makin' folks happy? Especially men?" Each shook his head. "Well, I'm thirsty. Milk and sandwiches laid a nice foundation, but it don't soothe the shock of just makin' and losin' twenty-seven hundred dollars in less than thirty seconds." He stomped over to the buffet.

Denton and Lambert followed him with amused eyes. Then Denton turned serious eyes on Jack.

"An interesting thing has happened down at police headquarters," he said in a dry, matter-of-fact voice. "Mr. Lambert, here, and I, along with Chief Jordan and the police property clerk, opened the safe, only to discover that both hatboxes with contents had been removed."

Doc dropped the ice tongs. "The police station's been robbed?" he cried in a panic. "My twenty-seven hundred dollars is missin'?"

Jack's eyes hardened. "A half a million dollars!" he said softly, looking from Lambert to Denton. "You gentlemen don't seem much perturbed."

Lambert's eyebrows raised. Denton grinned. "Oh, there's plenty of activity down at headquarters, both in my department and Jordan's. In Reno, too, I imagine." Denton looked at the state's attorney with a twinkle in his eye. "Mr. Lambert's telephoned for half a dozen state investigators.

I've asked our Los Angeles office for a little help, and Jordan showed his indignation by throwing the police property lieutenant into solitary."

"You think he's the guilty man?" Jack looked doubtful.

"Well, he's the only man with a set of keys," Denton shrugged, "but, of course, the keys were available to the assistant property man and to Jordan."

Jack's questioning look brought another shrug. "The assistant is only on night duty and apparently was home in bed at the only possible hours for the hijack. At least, according to his story and his wife's. Jordan was over at the hospital most of the day."

"Has the property lieutenant been been questioned?" Jack sat down on the bed beside Denton.

Denton grimaced, "Wrung out dry. He maintains astonishment and shock. Says he's been property man for seventeen years and nothing ever has been missing from the safe before. He has great faith in his assistant and anyway, to his knowledge, the keys have never been out of his possession."

"Except when in the hands of his assistant," Doc put in.

Denton nodded. "Until we can break his alibi or maybe find someone who saw him in the vicinity of police headquarters during the day . . . " Denton left it up in the air with a shrug.

Lambert suddenly entered the conversation, breaking a long spell of watching and listening. "What about the murders?"

Jack glanced at his wristwatch. "Doc," he warned, "you and Jerry are going to miss your date."

Doc stared, his face clouding, "Son, ain't you just a little—"

Jerry's own startled glance changed abruptly. She bounced to her feet and grabbed Doc's arm, digging her nails into the thin Italian fabric. "No, he's not," she said, "and fascinating as this conference is, I still haven't seen Las Vegas by night and you promised this was my night to toss my bushy tail over my shoulder and howl."

She had moved the reluctant Doc to the door before she turned to Lambert and Denton. "Excuse us, gentlemen, but come the call, and the lame and halt and blind shall be made well and the dead shall rise to fill the night hour with cheer, the click of chips and dice, and the shuffling of feet in all the whoopee houses." She looked at Jack, "See you later, boss, wearing a sign on my chest, 'Room 3107 Regal Spa Inn' just in case of blackout and I lose our Texas boy here."

She turned Doc to the door, then back again. "Aren't you going to say good night to the gentlemen, Doc?"

Doc grinned. "She ain't really tetched in the head," he said, patting Jerry's hand on his arm tolerantly, "it's just that she's free of her mama's apron strings and it makes her a little dizzy."

"Good night," Jerry blew Lambert a kiss and the door closed behind them.

"Heey, what's goin' on here?" muttered Doc, jerking his arm free of Jerry. "I got me a date with nurse Rodin, so how come you're a hornin' in?"

"Thanks, pal," murmured Jerry in an undertone, "and keep your voice down, at least until we get to the elevator. Apparently Jack didn't want Lambert and Denton to know you were dating the Oklahoma nurse and wanted to get you on your way before you spilled it."

"Then you ain't a goin' with me?"

"No, didn't you hear me tell Jack I'd see him in my room, later."

Doc grunted, "So that was what you was a gettin' at?"

Jerry pressed the elevator button and looked at her number-two boss candidly. "I'm beginning to believe you when you say your brains are in your fists and finger tips —all of them."

"Secretaries should be seen and not heard," Doc commented without rancor, eyeing himself with satisfaction in the mirror on the elevator door, "and the cuter they are— " The elevator door moved silently open.

Jerry shoved him in with a final, "I think Jack's insane to trust you with that Rodin dame without me along to protect you."

The door slid shut on Doc's happy-go-lucky grin.

27

When the door closed on Doc and Jerry, both Joe Denton and Lambert continued to stare at it, Denton with a frown of concentration on his face. Lambert's eyes were hard with suspicion.

"You were asking about the murders," Jack said smoothly. Two sets of eyes turned to him. "I haven't had a chance to talk to Denton. In fact, I thought he no longer was interested after we recovered the money. I've gone over our case with Jordan, but that was this morning before I knew the hatboxes were missing."

"You think there's a connection between the two?" Lambert's eyes still were cold and suspicious.

"Don't you?"

"I'm asking *you*, Mr. Packard, and if you do think so, why?"

"I thought it was obvious," Jack shrugged. "It began with Lieutenant Holmes killing Skip Sullivan here in this room, after wounding Lilly Montrose. Once the murders began, they followed one after another at the hospital. Lilly first was finished off, then Lieutenant Holmes and then Hilly Holliday. So far as Lilly is concerned, one of Holmes's lieutenants simply finished what Holmes had bungled. Holliday had to go because, once Holmes's gang rule was uncovered, he, like Lilly, knew too much of the inner workings."

"And you think Holmes's own man killed him?"

Jack said cautiously, "It could have been either way. Yes, maybe Holmes was killed either to prevent him from talking or to give someone else leadership of the Holmes gang. Or Holmes could have been a revenge killing by someone close to Skip Sullivan whom we haven't spotted."

Lambert said shortly, "Jordan tells me the Sullivan gang was under detention."

"With the exception of Silver Logan," Denton put in.

"Did ballistics come through with a check on the gun we took from him?" Jack asked.

Denton nodded. "It didn't fire the bullet taken from Holmes."

Jack nodded. "I didn't think so." He looked at Dr. Willard who had moved into the background. "You think perhaps Logan might make his lips talk sense so you could read them, if I could arrange it for just you and me to see him?"

Lambert cleared his throat sharply and looked suddenly at Denton, who said quietly, "I doubt if you could arrange it. Jordan seems to want to be present if there's any break in the case."

Jack nodded, still looking at Dr. Willard, "I was just asking."

"I think he could make himself understood to me, if he so desired. Whether he will or not . . . " The doctor shrugged.

Jack turned to Denton. "I got the impression from something you said that you may be personally checking all the hospital personnel? Find anything there?"

"The patients, too," Denton agreed, but shook his head, "I've got a man on it. Nothing so far."

"I've a few, two or three, names I'd suggest you give special attention," Jack took out his black notebook and turned several pages. "Miss Westover, the chief supervisor; Night Supervisor Holden; and nurse Grace Parker, who is engaged to officer Stern, who was supposed to be guarding Lilly Montrose at the time she was killed. Stern himself, although Jordan has already put him through the ropes, and finally the doctor or intern who was on call duty last night. I haven't been able to get his name."

Both Lambert and Denton were staring at Jack.

"You sound as though you thought the Morrison Hospital was a den of homicidal maniacs instead of a respectable institution," Lambert snapped disagreeably. "What in God's name would nurses have to do with a Las Vegas gang fight?"

"Nothing to do with the actual murders perhaps," Jack commented agreeably, "but someone on the hospital staff might very well be covering the killer. After all, if Jordan is right, the man must still be in the hospital. Everyone going and coming is being doublechecked by his guards."

"And I think he's right," stated Lambert flatly. "And you know what else I think? I think with Jordan that the best possibility is your own client, Linda Holliday. I think further that you are asking the chief and Denton here to put on a wild goose chase for a phantom killer to take the heat off the Holliday woman."

Jack looked at Lambert thoughtfully. "You feel that way even after the reasonable proof I gave Jordan that she couldn't have done it."

"You told him she was afraid of guns and couldn't possibly have shot Holmes through the heart from the second floor; that it would have taken an expert shot at that angle and distance. And how do we know she is afraid of guns and that she's not a crack shot? Your evidence is hearsay and pretty damned flimsy."

"I'll go along with you," Jack said mildly. "Naturally she's not ruled out, but she's a safe enough bet, in my mind, to keep her as a client."

"I should think you would," Lambert's antagonism was more apparent now. "I would, too, if I were running an unethical private detective agency and had a client with all the millions she has."

"I doubt if you know anything about the ethics of the Triple A agency," Jack answered mildly, "but you might ask Denton, here. He's known us for a number of years. And you might remember that Jordan personally asked us to get into the case."

"Not that you wouldn't have anyway with an heiress for a client," Lambert snorted.

"Not that we wouldn't have, anyway," agreed Jack.

"Well, Jordan was an ass to invite you in," Lambert asserted, "And I'm inviting you out."

Denton was watching with interest. Dr. Willard coughed and moved uneasily in his chair.

Jack shook his head. "Oh, no, Mr. Lambert, not at this stage of the game."

"Are you questioning my right?"

"Not at all, except I don't think you want to do it."

"I do want to do it," Lambert snapped. "I have done it."

Jack said softly, "It will make a pretty queer story for the Los Angeles newspapers that just at the stickiest point in the case, with a solution in sight, the men with the answers were taken off the case."

"Answers?" Lambert's face flushed, his eyes bulging. "If you've got answers, why the hell haven't you said so? What are they?"

Jack shook his head. "I'll just give them to the papers with proof, if we're off the case."

"Give me the answers with proof and I'll forget what I said," Lambert's body moved to the edge of his chair, crouched. "Who's the killer and I want evidence that'll stand up in court."

Jack shook his head. "I want twelve hours more."

Lambert's body relaxed. "You haven't any more idea than I have," he said sourly. "Just a cheap private eye trying to play smart."

"That's for you to decide." Jack's voice was cold.

"You guarantee the killer with evidence that will put him before the firing squad in twelve hours?"

"You'll either get your man or we'll pull out and go back to Hollywood," Jack said, "that is, provided we take Linda Holliday with us."

Lambert nodded, not in agreement, but as though Jack had just made an important point against himself. "You see where that puts you!" he said, no longer emotional, but in a dry matter-of-fact legal voice. "Your interest is limited to one person, Linda Holliday. My interest is the integrity and reputation of an entire city and the state of Nevada."

"Yes, I'm glad you explained that," Jack was now the aggressive one. "I was wondering what brought the state's attorney rushing down here and by what authority. After all, a couple of local murders and a matter of a missing half million dollars . . . "

Lambert's eyes grew hard. "The state of Nevada has a major interest in keeping Las Vegas safe. Tourists and their pocketbooks come by the hundreds of thousands, and legalized gambling is the state's best source of income. We have no intention of frightening away potential contributors to our wealth with sensational headlines of senseless murders, thefts of large sums, and corruption within the police department."

Dr. Willard, who had been only half listening with bored disinterest, moved restlessly in his straight-backed chair. "I'm sure this conference is important and necessary," he said mildly, "but I do not see how I am involved and it's getting on past my dinner hour."

Denton agreed. "Why don't we break it up? Now that it's agreed Packard will produce our killer and, I hope, the missing money within the next twelve hours— " He looked at Lambert. "You did agree, didn't you?"

Lambert hesitated, then nodded.

"Good!" Denton got to his feet. "Then nothing more can be accomplished here and I have a couple of errands— "

Jack broke in as Dr. Willard and Lambert arose, "Just one thing more. Was this visit of the state's attorney and the local federal man made with or without the knowledge of Jordan? And if the latter, why?"

Denton, his back to Lambert, grinned and winked at Jack, "That's a damned good question, Packard."

"It may be a good question," Lambert said stiffly, 'but I believe it falls within the category of private interdepartment business and does not concern you."

Dr. Willard in the lead, opened the door and was first out. Lambert turned and was at his heels. As Denton followed closing the door behind him, he said lightly, "See you soon, Jack," and a packet of matches slipped from his hand to the carpet.

The front cover of the matchbook was an advertisement for Herman Lee Fong's Bratwurst and Chow Mein Rathskeller. Jack turned the packet over thoughtfully. The advertisement was repeated. He opened the book. Noted in ink were two bits of information. "Best hour 8:30 P.M." and below, "Mrs. W's integrity not to be questioned. On duty at all hours tonight." Jack tore off the top flap, ripped it into small bits and flushed it down the toilet. His watch said 8:10.

28

Jerry Booker sat in her room staring out the window at the vivid green lawns of the enclosed Regal Spa gardens which were heavily shadowed by the tall white-barked poplars, all drinking thirstily under the glistening shower from the rain-bird sprinklers. Immediately under her window was the fabulous sea green pool washed by ten thousand candlepower of soft amber lighting.

For a moment she was thoroughly fed up with Las Vegas and wished vehemently for the familiar streets of Hollywood. She even thought of the evening plane back to Los Angeles, which would be taking off in another hour.

"No, damn it, not without my two goons," she muttered, "they might be Triple A Number One detectives, but without the woman's touch—" No, she had to stand by to see that Doc didn't talk Jack out of that twenty-seven hundred gambling profit, if and when they laid hands on it.

In the midst of her commiseration the telephone rang. It rang a second time before she came to and realized that someone still knew of her existence. She bounced out of her chair, snapped the receiver from the cradle, and said in her most lush, bedroom, come-on voice, "Yes? This is Jerry Booker speaking."

A grunt came over the line, then Jack spoke. "What's the matter, you have a sore throat?" Chagrined, Jerry flared. "You must have the wrong number."

"I doubt it," Jack said dryly. "I'll pick you up in five minutes. We're having dinner with Joe Denton at the Herman Lee Fong Bratwurst and Chow Mein Rathskeller."

"The what?"

"Never mind, just get ready."

"Ready for what?"

"Five minutes." The receiver clicked.

Jerry slammed down her own receiver viciously. "Bratwurst and Chow Mein Rathskeller! A mixture of German and Chinese garbage. And it'll smell like it, too," she grumbled. "The things a girl does to keep food in her mouth and a roof over her head . . ."

29

Jerry got the shock of her life. The short-order Chinese chop house, which she had envisioned as smelling of boiled cabbage, sauerkraut and soy sauce, did not materialize. Instead, Herman Lee Fong's Rathskeller (in a cellar, naturally) began with an exterior Oriental garden of lush grass, fountains, jacaranda and monkey pod trees in full bloom, and an overhead display of colorful paper Chinese lanterns.

The descent to the lower levels of exotic splendor was made via an escalator with mirrored steps edged in silver. The walls and ceiling were chinese red with gold trim.

The ceiling of the waiting room at the foot of the escalator was onyx, upon which subtle red and blue flames played, from an unknown source, in everchanging moving patterns, sometimes fascinating, sometimes sinister, but always with the puckish, perverse humor of the imps of Satan romping in the flickering coals of hell fire. A fountain played in the center of the lounge, featuring a slim, white, nude marble figure of an Oriental girl bathing deliciously beneath the fountain spray.

Jerry had clasped Jack's arm descending the escalator and now continued to cling, her eyes wide, her lips parted. At the moment she looked extremely young and naive. Perhaps it was the lighting. Perhaps she was indulging in a moment of that childish delight which sometimes rises in even the most sophisticated of us.

"Holy cow," she murmured, "I don't know whether this represents the Oriental conception of heaven or hell."

Jack grinned. "What's Hollywood got that Las Vegas hasn't?" He nodded at a large black scroll upon which was printed in silver letters:

We invite you to choose our
main Chinese dining room
or
the Tahitian room
or
the Japanese Hanging Garden room
or
the Singapore room
or
the German beer hall.

As they approached the open archway, the main dining room came into view displaying a wide expanse of gleaming linen and silver. At the far end was a small dance floor and beyond that a stage. Among the tables, Oriental busboys in scarlet coats and tight black silk pants moved about their affairs. Not a waiter in sight.

Jerry protested, "Hey, we must be early." She sounded disappointed. "No musicians, no waiters, no diners."

"But," Jack consoled her, "here comes the maitre d'."

Approaching them was a slim, medium-height figure in full dress, his patent-leather hair immaculate, his upper lip adorned with a small spike mustache. His English was perfect and his manner gracious, but his eyebrows raised questioningly in polite disdain. Obviously people with stomachs demanding food at this early hour were painfully beyond the pale.

Jerry shriveled under his lifted eyebrows, but Jack was amused. "I think you have a Mr. Denton expecting us."

The Oriental eyes darkened, the disdain faded, and a marked cordiality transfigured him. "Ah, yes, the Tahitian room. This way, please."

Trailing behind, Jerry muttered, "How about bringing me here some night at a more suitable hour, when the place is bouncing?"

"Business before pleasure."

Jerry snorted and made an uncouth remark, but her eyes were missing nothing. Apparently the secondary dining areas were alcoves of fair proportion circling the main dining room. They passed the Singapore room and what obviously was the German beer hall, and across the way she saw the Japanese garden room.

As they entered the Tahitian room, Joe Denton rose from a table. He seated Jerry between himself and Jack, then spoke a few words in undertone to the maitre d', who departed quickly.

"I've ordered drinks and the dinner," he murmured apologetically. "I'm sure you'll be pleased, but even so, we have to eat and run."

Jerry said with dissatisfaction, "I never eat and run. It gives me indigestion. If we're in such a hurry, why didn't we stop at a drive-in?"

Denton looked at Jack and grinned. Then to Jerry, "It's unforgivable, I know. But I've got things to say and then work to do. Some other time I'll do right by you, if you'll permit it."

"That's a date," Jerry said promptly, "and I've got a memory like an elephant."

"And an appetite," Jack added. "The secretary of the Triple A-One Detective Agency makes up on free meals for the meager pickings she gets at the ofice."

Denton laughed, then his face sobered. As he opened his lips, a luscious Tahitian girl in a short Chinese jacket and tight silk trousers brought the drinks, smiled companionably at all and was gone.

"Mmm, yummy," murmured Jerry soulfully, "Now I know all!" She raised her glass to Denton and sipped her drink. "Wowee! She ran a very pink tongue over very red lips, "Why did my mother never put this in my nursing bottle?"

Denton nodded and grinned. "One to a customer, so make it last,' he warned. Then his face settled into grimmer lines as he said to Jack, "My men from L.A. arrived a couple of hours ago. They could only spare three. I've got one on that night supervisor Holden, another on the tail of Chief Jordan, and the third one planted on the first floor of the hospital."

Jack's eyes were amused. "I hope Jordan doesn't catch on."

"He won't," Denton assured him.

"But if Jordan is involved, as you apparently think," Jack frowned, "why did he bring us in to investigate?"

"If I'm right, he's smart and sure of himself. Makes him look good to call for outside help and he feels he has everything nailed down."

Jerry stared. "You mean Lieutenant Holmes was really only a front man for Jordan? That the chief himself is Mr. Big?"

Jack returned to his original question. "I still say he made a mistake bringing us into the picture, especially with you Fed boys nosing around. I just can't believe the chief would ask for that much trouble, no matter how cocky he feels."

"The big mistake was heisting that hot bank money from the police vault. Once that bank loot had been recovered, we were out of it. The Feds would never touch these local killings unless we were specifically invited in. But with the bank loot gone again, we're in to the finish."

"But I don't think Jordan would make that kind of a mistake."

Denton shrugged. "All crooks are greedy. Even the smart ones. The bank loot, plus Holliday's two hundred fifty thousand, was just too much gravy to pass up." Denton looked at Jack with amusement. "Anything else we don't agree on?"

Jack nodded, "I think you're wasting a man on Supervisor Holden. At best, she's just a pawn."

"Who would you have him on?"

"Our friend, State's Attorney Lambert."

Denton stared. "Why?"

Jack shrugged, "I just can't swallow that a man of Lambert's caliber would rush down here from Reno over a couple of local killings, or even for a fouled-up police department."

"Aren't you forgetting how sensitive the Nevada official family is to any scandal in Reno or Las Vegas? Any trouble that is liable to scare off tourists is dynamite. It's Nevada's bread and butter."

"Maybe," Jack said doubtfully, "but you can't tell me that the chain of gangster personnel, which starts way down with the Lilly Montrose girl and goes up through Lieutenant Holmes and, if you're right, Jordan, doesn't reach somebody higher up. And the fact that Lambert came rushing down here so fast suggests he's got some interest beyond his official duties."

Denton nodded thoughtfully. "That does fit in with something that's been gnawing at the back of my mind; Lambert's eagerness to work with me, his sending north for men out of his own office to come down here and clean up the police department, and his conferences with me, *excluding* Jordan. He's certainly bent over backwards in the name of clean government, and throwing suspicion on Jordan. Yet all the time I've had a stinking feeling he's not telling everything he knows."

Jack nodded. "What do you make of Dr. Willard's not being able to make sense out of Silver Logan's lip movement?"

"I'd say Logan's deliberately playing dead because Jordan has insisted on being present. What he might be able to tell us could be signing Jordan's death warrant."

"Or could it be Lambert and the fact he brought Dr. Willard from Reno with him?"

Denton shook his head. "I don't think anyone of Logan's caliber would know the chain of command beyond Jordan—if it goes any further, which would need some careful investigating."

Jack grinned. "Well, I can see you like Jordan for the villain. I'll take Lambert, myself. Or, I'll put it this way. This dust-up down here is worrying somebody in Reno and either Lambert is the man or he was sent down here by the real Mr. Big. By the way, where is Lambert?"

Denton looked at his watch. "Just about now he and Jordan are leaving for the airport to meet the 9:20 plane from the north. It was Lambert's idea that Jordan should meet his men and be able to identify them and instruct them before they got into town."

"I don't get it," Jack frowned. "If Lambert is suspicious of Jordan, why have his men cozy with him?"

"I suspect it's a ruse to give the chief confidence that Lambert doesn't suspect him. But," Denton nodded, "I don't see what use the men will be if Jordan knows them and they're put under his command."

Jerry had been sipping and listening. "Maybe Lambert's men already have their instructions and they'll just pretend to be pally with Jordan."

Both Jack and Denton looked at her.

"Well?" she said defensively, "why not?"

Denton grinned, "I'll buy that." He looked at Jerry. "Smart cooky. I could use you."

"Don't be fooled," Jack admonished, "it's only the alcohol splashing around in the vacuum."

Jerry looked at him morosely. "I've been waiting for a good reason to cut your salary," she said. "This is it."

Exotic aromas of strange and wonderful foods wafted into the Tahitian room, followed by two South Sea maidens in sarongs with a well-laden wagon. For the next five minutes business was laid aside while the table was heaped with fragrant food and flowers, and a handsome lei was placed about Jerry's shoulders.

When the serving girls had departed on sturdy bare feet, the varied dishes where tasted and exclaimed over, and the flowers duly appreciated. The three then settled in to satisfy their appetites.

"As I'd mentioned," Denton picked up the conversation, "Supervisor Westover is our girl. She's been here almost three years. She's a natural for anything that may happen in Las Vegas. Already she secretly has had Silver Logan and the Holliday girl moved to another part of the hospital which will be under her special care for the night."

"Suitable dummies have been arranged in the beds of their former rooms?" Jack looked amused.

"How was she able to do that?" Jerry demanded. "Aren't the police guards on duty outside the doors?"

Denton chuckled. "Our Miss Westover is a very capable woman. She carried Miss Holliday through the bathroom to the adjoining room, put her on a gurney and wheeled her out under the nose of the guard and into the operating room down the hall, then out a second door and into a private room."

"Linda's still out?" Jerry asked.

"From sedatives." Denton nodded. "She's completely recovered from the poison. By morning she'll be able to talk, but," he added gloomily, "I doubt whether she'll have much to talk about. Silver Logan was able to walk to an adjoining room and climb on the gurney. I don't know how she gained his confidence and got him to cooperate, but he did, willingly."

Jack looked at his wristwatch. "Do you know where we can get hold of Dr. Willard? I'd like to go with him to see Logan while Jordan and Lambert are at the airport. Maybe Logan will talk straight for once. Or how about taking Miss Westover along? If she has his confidence, maybe he'd talk for her."

Denton shook his head. "Willard's staying at the St. Martin Hotel. He may possibly be there. Otherwise, all I know is that Lambert told him to report to the hospital at 9:00 tomorrow morning."

Jack started to rise.

"Hold your horses." Denton clapped his hands. A young and beautiful girl in a sarong appeared almost instantly.

"Will you bring a phone to the table, please," Denton ordered, "and have your operator get the St. Martin Hotel." The girl bowed and departed.

"I don't think we'll come here again, Jack," Jerry said petulantly. "I'm getting an inferiority complex. Besides, this is too rich for the blood of a growing girl." She looked at Denton balefully.

"You might come to a worse end. Now pipe down and listen. It's been arranged for you to take over the hospital switchboard at 10:00," Jack said, looking at Jerry.

"For how long?" Jerry objected.

"Maybe all night. We'll see."

Jerry groaned.

"You're to listen in on every conversation until you know definitely it's an authentic hospital call. The moment anything suspicious presents itself, you're to put either Denton, Miss Westover or me on the line."

"I'll be up to my armpits in switchboard cords, you know that," Jerry grumbled.

"On you, they'll look good," Jack told her.

30

It was ten minutes after eleven, three bars and two nightclubs before the tawny locks began to fall down over the Oklahoma nurse's eyes, and the friendly, easy smile had softened with intimacy.

The Las Palmas's chic, sleek, Mexican marimba band had taken five, and the ripple of the little steel ball on the wheels, the click of dice, and the soft voices of the girls at the blackjack tables could be heard across the dining room through the archway to the casino.

With sorrowful Texas sentimentality, Doc looked across his bourbon and water and Martha Rodin's half-consumed martini into her provocative cat's eyes. "Yes, ma'am, Miss Oklahoma, honey, if you ain't the identical twin image of my cousin Winnie May, I'll buy you champagne for our nuptial breakfast in the morning."

Nurse Rodin's cheeks grew pinker and she slipped her hand under Doc's arm. "You're a darling, darling," she murmured, rubbing her cheek on his shoulder affectionately, "but if nuptial means what I think it does, the answer's uh-uh."

"You mean you're butterin' me up with one hand and turnin' me down flat with the other?" Doc asked indignantly.

"I'm filled right up to here with husbands," she said, raising her hand to her epiglottis, missing it the first time, "Men, yes, husbands, uh-uh!"

The band filtered back and struck up a samba beat as the tables around them emptied and the dance floor overflowed.

"You want to dance?" Doc proposed. Martha giggled. "Huh?" she inquired. "In my stocking feet?"

Doc peered under the crisp tablecloth. "Heey, sugar, you a startin' to undress already?"

"I'm used to nurse's flat shoes. High heels make my," she looked at Doc archly, "you-know-what ache." A little liquid giggle escaped. Then she bent closer to Doc and asked, "You know what, Doc? I was on night duty last night. How'd you know I wouldn't be on night duty tonight?"

"On account," Doc assured her, "I keep track of my women."

"Women?" Martha frowned with playful severity. "How many you got?"

"Only one in Las Vegas, honey, namely you."

"I bet."

"Cross my heart." Doc did.

Martha sighed, "What time is it?"

Doc looked at his watch. "The evening's still in its rompers."

The girl brushed back another dangling strand that kept getting between her eyes and her martini glass. "That means eighteen hours and forty-five minutes before I'm on duty back at the hospital, and you know something? I'm glad."

Doc showed interest. "You don't like it there?"

"I don't mind people dying naturally in a hospital, but murder gives me the willies."

Doc agreed, "Yeah, especially with one of the victims your own special patient." Martha looked at him, her eyes perfectly sober for the moment, but Doc continued on, "You ast me, there's something wrong in that hospital."

"You're telling me!" Martha said morosely, taking a large gulp from her martini glass. "What I could tell you . . . " She didn't finish, nodding her head owlishly.

Doc raised his eyes and caught their waiter watching Martha intently from three tables away. His eyes shifted at once to Doc and a saturnine face faded to gracious attentiveness as he moved in to hover over them.

"Dinner now, perhaps?"

Were the waiter's eyes fixed with too purposeful politeness on Martha? From where he sat, Doc couldn't be sure.

"Heeey, how about that, sugar," he said. "You hungry?"

"I always eat at midnight. Is it midnight?" If the waiter had anything to signal to the girl, it wasn't getting across.

"Not yet."

"Then I'm not hungry."

Doc waved at the glasses. "The same."

The waiter hesitated, shrugged and departed.

"You're trying to change the subject," Martha accused. Doc shook his head in protest.

"What were we talking about?" Martha's hand wandered as she reached for her glass.

"Why all the things you know about the hospital that I don't know." Then Doc added encouragingly, "And I sure did admire you this morning, the way you covered up for your nurse pal, Miss Parker. You're okay, number one, for my money."

Martha shrugged. "She's a nice kid. Nothing wrong with Grace, except she's madly in love with Mike Stern. But I ask you, who wants to get married, especially to a Las Vegas policeman? I've tried to tell her, but she won't listen. But there's nothing wrong with Gracie Parker, even if she is the niece of Chief Jordan."

"Niece of Jordan, huh?" Doc murmered. "And what's wrong with Jordan?"

Martha stared, outraged, "He's the chief of police, isn't he? What more do you want?"

"Is that something against him?"

"Maybe you think Lieutenant Holmes was the first police officer who died suddenly. Maybe you believe the newspaper stories about officer Clyde Smith getting shot to death in a gun battle with robbers last year; and Sergeant Luke Bowman being run down and crushed to death under the wheels of an escaping holdup car. Ha! Maybe you don't know as much about the Las Vegas police department as you think you do."

"Maybe I don't," Doc finished off his bourbon and water as the waiter returned to replace their glasses.

"Ouch! Heeey!" The unladylike yelp brought Martha half out of her chair, jarring the waiter's arm with the suspended martini and sending a wave of the chilled liquid down the front of her low bodice.

"Madame, it is unforgivable." The pained expression on the waiter's face seemed genuine.

"You're damned right it is," Martha glared, mopping her front. "First you massage my ever-aching hummels with your number elevens and then I get a public gin bath."

"My most humble apologies," murmered the waiter, handing her a fresh napkin and bending over her with still another. In a moment he stood straight. "You will send me the bill for having the dress cleaned. I am Charles, waiter number eight. I will also bring you a fresh martini immediately."

Doc had been leaning with both elbows on the table watching the tableau with a nonchalant, what-the-hell, all-in-a-night's-work grin on his lips, but with a glint in his pale, blue eyes. He didn't miss the puzzled, resentful stare on Martha's face as her eyes followed the departing waiter. Then she looked at Doc, her eyes beginning to blaze. "Now what the hell did he mean by that?"

"He said he'd pay for—"

"That's not all he said."

"Oh?" Doc was interested.

"When he bent over me he said, 'Lady, you're drunk. Your tongue's running at both ends. Go home.'"

"Well, well, and *well*!" Doc turned toward the bar. The waiter was not in his range of view, but shadowed by a pillar, and leaning against the bar was a vague, dark face attached to a short, thick-shouldered body. As Doc stared the face turned away, lost in shadow.

"Excuse me a minute, honey." Doc rose as the marimba band finished with a flourish and the dancers flocked back to their tables. When Doc arrived at the bar there was no short, thick-shouldered man among the drinkers. He returned to the table to find Martha's spilled martini had been replenished and the waiter gone.

"He say anything when he brought you the drink?" Doc sat down casually, holding his bourbon up to the light before sipping it.

"No," Martha said sullenly. "Just looked at me." She looked at Doc defiantly. "Who the hell does he think he is, telling me I'm drunk?"

Doc agreed, "No gentleman— 'specially a waiter— should ever tell a lady she's drunk."

"And even if I wanted to go home, I wouldn't go now," Martha announced belligerently. "I've never been thrown out of a place yet and this is not the night for it."

"You know," Doc said thoughtfully, "it might not be a bad idea at that."

"To hell with it."

Doc grinned. "The real old Texas fight, huh?"

"Oklahoma."

"Okay, Miss Oklahoma, you're a settin' the pace tonight."

Miss Rodin took a healthy gulp of her martini. "And another thing, my frien', you may be a Hollywood detective but you don't know anything about Las Vegas police."

"Honey, maybe we'd better save the rest of that for some other time."

"Oh, you don't want to hear it, huh?"

"Sugar, they ain't nothin' I want to hear more, only— "

"Well, get this," Martha yawned and her eyes glazed slightly, "get this," she repeated solemnly, "officer Clyde Smith was shot six times with a police revolver."

Doc looked about him, suddenly wary. No one near-by seemed interested. Neither the waiter nor the vague face which had vanished from the bar was anywhere in sight.

"And," continued Martha, lifting her glass "Sergeant Bowman was not run over *once,* but three or four times. Just to make sure."

Doc took a deep breath. "Sure would be interesting to know who shot Lieutenant Holmes from the second-story Women's washroom."

"You know what I think? I think— " Martha giggled for a second, "and, brother, would Holden have kittens if she heard me talking, but a girl's got to talk to somebody, especially when she's fed up to here!" She aimed for her throat, but couldn't find it, and gave up with a shrug.

"Who's Holden?"

"Night Supervisor Holden, who else?"

"Oh yeah, yeah, sure," Doc agreed. "Forget her. All I'm interested in is what *you* think."

"About what?" Martha asked vaguely.

"What you think about who killed Lieutenant Holmes."

"Why, I think that homicide detective, Perry Faber, killed him."

"Huh? Who's he? Was he in the hospital?" Doc's eyes gleamed. "How'd he get into the picture?"

"He was disguised as old man Peterson and went around the corridors all last night and this morning in a wheelchair."

Doc looked confused. "Heeey, wait a minute. Who is old man Peterson?"

"The wheelchair patient in 264. He has the gout."

"And this police detective, Perry Faber, took his place? Who knew about it? And why did he pretend to be Peterson?"

"He came into the hospital right after that Lilly Montrose was brought in. He told Supervisor Holden that Chief Jordan not only wanted a regular policeman on guard outside Lilly's door, but a disguised second guard on duty, because Lilly was an important state's witness and was in deadly danger."

"So Supervisor Holden helped him rig up the Peterson disguise?"

"Yes, and they took old man Peterson up to the isolation ward for the night, telling him something about having to fumigate his room, and he could have his room and wheelchair back this morning."

"But I saw the old man in the wheelchair this afternoon when I was over there. You mean this Detective Perry Faber's still there?"

"No, that was old man Peterson." The girl frowned. "Some time this morning—I was off duty down in the supervisor's office talking to you and Mr. Packard and then went home—anyway, sometime after Lieutenant Holmes was shot, old man Peterson was brought down from isolation and this homicide detective got back into his own clothes and just walked naturally out through the police lines, on account he was a policeman."

"And you think this Faber not only killed Lilly, but Lieutenant Holmes?"

Martha nodded blearily. "*And* the Holliday young man, and doped up Miss Linda Holliday." She took a deep breath. "You know, it's getting awfully hot and stuffy in here." She yawned and giggled. "You don't suppose I'm getting a little drunkee?"

"But why didn't Supervisor Holden tell us; that is, if she was in the clear?"

Miss Martha Rodin sighed and suddenly dropped her head in her arms on the table, tipping over the remains of her martini.

Doc patted her shoulder gently. "That's the ticket, honey. Nothin' better for red-eye than a little shut-eye." Then he went back to his deduction problem. Either Supervisor Holden was in on the whole hospital business or she had been threatened by Faber or maybe she, like Martha, knew too much about the whole police department and was afraid to speak out.

He had meant to ask Martha how she knew so much about the two policemen who'd been murdered earlier.

Also, who knew about Faber replacing old Peterson besides the supervisor and herself. He shrugged. Maybe the whole nursing staff on duty was in on it. Maybe even the chief supervisor. What was her name? . . . Oh yeah, Miss Westover.

As Doc got to his feet, he saw their waiter watching their table with a sour expression. He waved. The sour look was changed to a reticent, stiff expression of disapproval as he approached, then changed again to gratitude as Doc fished out a twenty-dollar bill.

"I reckon you was right, son, about the young lady havin' a nose full," Doc acknowledged cheerfully. Hostility and reserve tensed the muscles of the waiter's face and neck. Doc ignored it. He handed the bill to the waiter. "Think a little of Uncle Sam's minted lettuce'll make it worth your while to keep an eye on sleeping beauty here, while I make a phone call?"

The waiter relaxed and bowed, but refused to smile.

"Oh yeah," Doc turned back, "I just had a thought. You ain't by any chance one of them, whatchacallit—lip readers, are you?"

The waiter's face froze. Again Doc paid no heed, continuing cheerfully, "On account if you are, I might have a job for you in a little while that might pay off in some real sugar."

The waiter relaxed slightly. He glanced carefully about him and said cautiously, "Mister, if you have any regard for your own or this girl's skin, please get out of here."

"Now that's interestin'," Doc said with a friendly nod. "Only thing is I got an important phone call to put through. Think five or ten minutes is a gonna make too much difference? I mean, after all, if you're worried about us, ain't we safer here with all these folks millin' around than maybe out on the street or in a private home?"

The waiter shrugged.

"And about that lip readin' stunt? Yes or no?"

There was a long, hesitant pause. Then, "My wife neither speaks nor hears. We communicate by lip reading."

Doc grinned and nodded. "I'll be back right quick. And don't give Miss Oklahoma here any more martinis." Doc's taut, lanky figure moved without haste through the milling crowd.

31

Doc brushed lightly against a customer, turning with a word of apology only to look down into an aggressive dark face with small mean eyes and a cruel evil mouth. The man turned abruptly away with an under-the-breath expletive. Doc's blue eyes frosted over. Under other circumstances he would have made something of it, but he couldn't delay the phone call just for the pleasure of a brawl. Something about the unpleasant character nagged at the back of his mind as he continued on his way, trying to retain every detail of Martha's story. Later he was to remember both the face and the thick shoulders, and make a key witness for the prosecution.

He spent ten minutes in the phone booth running down Jack and another ten minutes pouring out his story.

Jack's only comment was "Uh-huh! Now get rid of the girl and get over here to the hospital, fast."

Doc came out of the fogged-up booth, sweating and in a bad mood. "Now ain't *that* a show of gratitude for practically solving three murders singlehanded," he muttered. "And I swear to goodness if that hospital operator didn't sound like Jerry . . . " He shrugged and pushed his way back to his table as the band struck up a rumba and the aisles crowded with dancers.

Martha Rodin was as he had left her, head in her arms, except that someone had thrown her light wrap over her shoulders, but in such a way it made her look hump-backed. Doc saw their waiter half a dozen tables away and waved to him. As the waiter approached, Doc lifted the lemon yellow coat from the sleeping girl's shoulders as the first step toward getting her to her feet. As suddenly as he raised the cloak he dropped it back. His light blue eyes now paled to a frosted white, stared reproachfully at the waiter, who had reached his side now at his elbow.

"You keep an eye on my girlfriend here, like I ast you?"

The waiter blinked in surprise. "Every minute, sir, with the exception of a few moments when I filled a bar order for the next table. Why? Is anything wrong?"

Doc looked at the two couples at the next table, the two men, graying sixty in sedate dinner jackets, and the two girls, slightly exhilarated with champagne and cling-ingly companionable. Secretaries and their bosses. Doc's summation was instinctive and instant. He turned back to the waiter. "Keep watchin'," he said shortly. "I got me another phone call to make."

This time he had Jack in a matter of seconds, sure now it was Jerry at the switchboard. "Looky, Jack," he said plaintively. At that instant, out of the corner of his eye he caught the stealthy movement of the Men's room door across the hallway and the sudden projection of a man-sized revolver in a deliberately steady hand. He sank to the floor of the booth an instant before the gun's detonations shocked the eardrums of the diners.

From the floor of the phone booth Doc murmured into the phone mouthpiece, "The sound you just heard was a police automatic pointed in my direction. The phone company ain't a gonna like what happened to its booth.

Huh? Oh, I'm a sittin' on the floor and folks is a millin' around outside like Sandy Claus Lane in Hollywood. But before they bust the door down, what I really called to tell you is that while I was a reachin' you a few minutes ago, somebody planted a huntin' knife between nurse Rodin's shoulderblades. So what am I s'posed to do now?"

Jack grunted a question. Doc added this and that, listened a second, grunted and hung up, then painfully got to his feet. In his hand was a sizable gun of his own, fitting into his big sensitive fingers with familiar ease. He looked slowly around at the startled faces outside the booth, noting the neatly drilled holes in the glass to the left and to the right of him, and grinned sheepishly. Then he opened the door and stepped out. " 'Scuse me, folks," he said in an abashed voice, "I was just plain stupid, havin' my shootin' pistol and a playin' with it whilst I was on the phone. Naturally, with a hair-trigger like I got, what was bound to happen, happened."

There was momentary reaction of relief mixed with jeering laughter. Two burly bouncers were pushing through the crowd. One of them said grimly, "You dropped to the bottom of the booth when your own gun went off?"

"Why sure, son." Doc admitted, "first thing I thought of was somebody was a shootin' at me. And I reckon I ain't as brave as some of you Las Vegas boys."

The second bouncer held out his hand. "Let me see your gun for a minute."

Doc shook his head good-naturedly. "Sorry, friend, but I just plain don't never pass my gun around. Why?"

"I just wanted to see what kind of a gun shoots two ways at once." He nodded at the holes in each side of the glass booth.

"Yeah," agreed Doc, "ain't that a humdinger of a gun?"

The crowd laughed.

"You want to leave it that way?" the older bouncer asked.

"Suits me if it suits you," Doc said agreeably, "and if there's any more questions, my name's Doc Long and I'm a stayin' at the Regal Spa. Okay?"

The older bouncer looked at his partner, shrugged, and nodded. "But you'll have to leave. Guns are not allowed."

Doc grinned, "Yeah, I can understand that now. Oh, by the way," he added casually, "I come in here a lookin' for police detective Perry Faber. You know him?"

Again the bouncers exchanged glances. The older nodded, "Yes, we know him."

"He been here tonight?"

Another hesitation and another nod. "He just left about three minutes ago."

"Aaw," said Doc, "he missed me. Durn it, anyway, he won't like that."

Doc followed the bouncers through the now amused crowd toward the door and was surprised to see his waiter with a bill on a silver tray.

" 'Scuse me a minute, fellers, I forgot to pay my bill." He swerved quickly to the waiter, fishing in his pocket. Under his breath he said, "Get out of here fast, Charlie. Miss Oklahoma's got a knife in her. Meet you at the Morrison Hospital soon as you can get there."

He dropped a twenty-dollar bill on the silver tray as the two bouncers approached. "Keep the change, feller. It was worth it." He nodded to the whitefaced, slackjawed waiter and followed the two men to the street door.

32

The telephone rang in room 264, which best surveyed the whole second floor corridor. Joe Denton picked up the bedside receiver, listened a moment and handed it to Jack. It was Jerry Booker from the hospital switchboard. "You wanted a report on all incoming calls and in-hospital communications every fifteen minutes."

"Well?"

"Nothing! Just friends and relatives inquiring about patients. Dr. Littleton said he'd be out for the evening and left his number in case of an emergency."

"Keep listening in," Jack ordered. "It's an outside bet, but something may come through."

As he hung up there was a shuffle at the door. Denton ducked into the bathroom. There was a sharp tap and Chief Supervisor Westover slipped into the room. She looked anxiously at Jack, who shook his head. "Nothing yet, it's too early." He raised his voice, "It's Mrs. Westover."

Denton came back into the room. "It's just that I've disappeared from the hospital scene; still here but unseen; alert eyes everywhere, but forgotten. This room is perfect."

Miss Westover nodded unhappily, checked her watch —it was 9:50—and turned to the door. "I've given the present night supervisor, Miss Coleman, strict instructions to report to me every half hour. I must get out where she can find me. And then I want to get back to Miss Holliday and Silver Logan."

Jack looked at Denton. "One of your men on guard while Miss Westover's been away?"

"He'd better be," Denton said grimly.

Miss Westover nodded. "Yes, inside the room."

Jack started. "The room? You mean, one room?"

"Why, yes," Miss Westover expressed surprise. "You wanted the Holliday girl and Logan hidden. How better draw attention to that wing of the hospital than to have a Fed patrolling a beat in the corridor? By doubling them up for the night, either Mr. Denton's man or I can keep out of sight in the one room with them."

"But have you forgotten that we caught Logan waiting for Linda in her hotel room with a gun?" Jack frowned. "And she's in a drugged sleep and there's nothing the matter with him but a sore throat."

"Good gracious!" The chief supervisor yanked open the door.

"Just a moment, Miss Westover," Denton stopped her. "Close the door please."

The door was closed reluctantly, but Miss Westover still remained poised for instant action.

Denton said, "My man is quite aware of the situation. He's been ordered to take any necessary measures in an emergency. Personally, I think you've arranged an ideal set-up."

The supervisor, relieved, looked at Jack questioningly.

"Furthermore," Denton continued, "with my man on the job, I suggest you don't keep checking on the Holliday-Logan room. It might arouse interest or suspicion."

Again she looked at Jack and then said uneasily, "I don't know, Mr. Denton, I'd feel better to check once in awhile. I've taken over the responsibility for those two patients. There's been too many murders in this hospital already. I intend to see there is not another."

Denton grinned and said gently, "Don't you think that should be left in the hands of law enforcement officers?"

She looked at Jack yet a third time, whose eyes rested thoughtfully on Denton.

"How about this?" Jack suggested, "you'll be making your rounds continually tonight in view of what happened last night. Naturally, you'll cover the room under guard along with the rest of the hospital. Just don't go there oftener than any place else."

Denton nodded readily. "I think that's the answer."

Miss Westover's face expressed satisfaction. "Very well." She glanced at her watch, saying, "I've got to go now," and moved quickly out the door as though fearful of being called back again.

Denton grinned at Jack. "The natural-born diplomat."

Jack was looking at his watch with a worried frown.

Denton sobered, nodding agreement. "I know," he said, "if the plane from Reno with Lambert's men arrived on schedule, why aren't they here?"

Jack turned to the phone. As he reached for it, the bell rang sharply under his hand. He jerked the receiver to his ear.

"That you, Jack?" Jerry's voice was breathless with excitement.

"Yes?" Jack felt Jerry's tension, then listened.

"Chief of police Jordan is down in Emergency. He was shot at the airport. He died on the way in."

Jack hung up the phone and turned to Denton. "I thought you said you had a man on Jordan's tail."

Denton nodded sharply. "What happened? Where is he?"

"Down in Emergency, dead."

Denton swore softly.

"Now maybe you think I was right about Lambert. Taking Jordan out to meet the plane was a set-up. His men got their instructions before they left Carson City."

"Is that what happened?"

"How do I know what happened?" Jack's face wasn't pleasant. "We'll probably never know the truth if we listen to Lambert's explanation."

The phone rang again. Jack picked up the receiver, listened for a moment, then held out the receiver. "For you. Somebody sounds as though he were talking from the bottom of a well."

Denton shot across the room and snatched the phone. His conversation was short, sharp and succinct. There was an ugly note in his voice as he slammed down the receiver. "That was the tail," he said in disgust. "Somebody sandbagged him in the airport parking area. He's just come around and picked up the information that Jordan was shot while he was out."

Jack grinned sympathetically, "Tough."

Denton snorted. "He can hop the next plane back to Los Angeles and take his headache with him."

Again Jack reached for the phone. "I'd better check Emergency."

33

On the first floor, Lambert was leaning heavily on the information desk, wiping his flushed face with a large white handkerchief. He was holding his pinch-nose glasses in his other hand, and at the moment looked more like an aged corpse in shock than the immaculate Machiavellian politician of the afternoon.

As Jack approached, Lambert straightened and returned his glasses to his bony nose. His hand shook. "A terrible thing has happened," he said, searching Jack's face with hooded eyes.

"Mr. Lambert, who murdered Jordan?"

"You know, then?"

Were his eyes for a moment evasive? Jack couldn't be sure. He nodded his answer.

"Where's Denton?" the state's attorney asked abruptly.

Jack shrugged. "He had business outside the hospital. You didn't answer my question. Who shot Jordan?"

"Young man," Lambert fixed Jack with baleful eyes, "if I knew that, I'd hound him to the full extent of the law. Hound him to his grave."

"You were there, weren't you?"

"I was not."

"Didn't you tell Denton that you and the chief would go to the airport to meet your men from the north?" Disbelief was in Jack's voice.

Lambert nodded. "And I wish I had. I might have prevented . . ." He paused and wet his dry lips with a pallid, less than pink tongue. "Unfortunately, at the last minute I was called by the capital. I sent Jordan on without me."

"That can be checked." Jack's attitude was uncompromising.

Lambert's eyes sparked, "Look here, young man, what are you implying?"

"Was I implying anything?"

"You'll take a different tone of voice." Some of Lambert's former self-assertiveness was taking over.

"Who brought Jordan's body in?"

Lambert looked surprised. "My men, naturally. Five of them. They're down in Emergency making statements."

"What are their statements?"

Again Lambert's eyes sparked with angry belligerence. He opened his mouth, then snapped it shut. Then in a cold, formal voice, he said, "The five men dismounted from the plane and met Jordan in the waiting room. He led them out to the parking lot and my five men and Jordan got into the police car. Jordan was at the wheel. He had just started the motor when a figure stepped out from behind a parked car, fired once and vanished. Jordan slumped over the wheel. Two of my men got him into the back seat and tried to administer first aid. The other three spread out over the parking lot. A car, without lights and some distance away, sped out of the parking lot and immediately was lost. My men got back into the police car, and raced into town, for Jordan was still breathing. He died on the way in."

"I suppose there were other witnesses?"

"That I do not know."

Jack turned to the phone. "Packard speaking. I'm at the information desk on the first floor. If either Denton or I are wanted, try here. If I've left, try the desk on the second floor." He hung up.

"Are you in charge here?" Lambert asked with a hint of disapproval.

"I am while Denton is out and now that the chief is dead."

"The police have a second-in-command, I should imagine," Lambert's voice was dry and aggressive.

"If so, he hasn't shown up. He's probably having kittens over Jordan's murder."

"It's just as well, because my men will be taking over as soon as they've finished downstairs. At that time we'll dispense with your services."

Jack took a slip of official note paper from his pocket and handed it to Lambert. "Jordan thought I should have this memorandum."

Lambert glanced at it. "Of course you understand this no longer carries any weight. In any event, my orders supersede a chief of police."

Jack nodded and fished in his pocket a second time, bringing out a gilt-edged card with an official stamp on it. "But as a special deputy sworn in this morning by Denton—"

"The Feds have no jurisdiction in a local murder case unless specifically called in," Lambert snapped.

"But all this ties in with the missing quarter-million dollars of bank loot, which is federal business."

Lambert's face became pinched and ruthless, but before he could speak, a uniformed policeman came in the front door with a blinking, sleepy-eyed Dr. Willard.

"This man says he is Dr. Willard, head of a state department in Reno. He says you asked him to come here, Mr. Lambert."

Lambert nodded and the officer withdrew.

"Sorry I'm late," the doctor appologized, without seeming particularly sorry, "but I was sleeping and the hotel didn't put through my call."

Lambert looked at him bleakly. "I suppose you've heard Jordan's been shot to death."

Dr. Willard's eyes came awake. "When did this happen?"

"Within the last hour."

The little doctor shook his head in bewilderment. "It's time somebody came down here from Carson City and straightened out this police department. What a mess." His voice was mildly disapproving and his gray, myopic eyes turned to Jack for confirmation. "No telling who did it, I suppose?"

"Yes. I think we know," Jack said softly.

Both men stared at him. Lambert snapped. "You smart private eyes make a big noise but do mighty little to show for it."

Dr. Willard moved uncomfortably from one foot to the other and murmured, "Well, I got out of bed to see whether we could read the lips of that fellow who lost his voice—what's his name, Logan?"

"You'll have to wait," Lambert said sourly. "Jordan's murder has upset everything." He turned to Jack. "You're sure you don't know where Joe Denton is?"

Jack shook his head. "Just out."

"We'll go talk to the night supervisor." His eyes sought the phone and then Jack. "Who is she and where do we find her?"

"First glassed-in cubicle down the hall across from the elevator." Jack jerked his head in the general direction. "She's Miss Coleman."

"Make yourself comfortable until we get around to you, doctor. Packard, you come with me." Lambert now, if not actually officious, definitely was giving the impression of taking over.

"Actually," murmured Jack, following him down the corridor, "Miss Coleman isn't in charge tonight."

Lambert swung around. "She was in charge last night, wasn't she?"

"No, that was Mrs. Holden. The 6:00 a.m. to 2:00 p.m. shift took over the graveyard shift. All the nurses on last night's shift are off until two tomorrow afternoon."

"You say Supervisor Coleman isn't in charge? Why?"

Jack shrugged. "Miss Westover, the chief supervisor, didn't like what went on here last night. She likewise is aware that both Linda Holliday and Silver Logan, patients here, are susceptible to the same virulent malady that took out Lilly Montrose and Miss Holliday's brother, and I imagine you could include Lieutenant Holmes."

Lambert frowned. "You're saying Miss Westover is on duty tonight?"

"Oh, I'd guess Miss Coleman's carrying on with the routine work of a night supervisor. Miss Westover's keeping an eye on the second and third floors for emergencies."

Lambert grunted, swung on his heel, and entered the night supervisor's office. A tall, handsome young woman in uniform and with a mass of jet black curly hair that defied confinement beneath her nurse's cap looked up from her paperwork. Her cool, guarded black eyes, in a face of pale olive complexion, measured her two guests with reserved inquiry.

"Miss Coleman," Lambert stated, "I'm state's attorney Lambert just down from Carson City. You know Mr. Packard."

"No, I don't," Miss Coleman said, eyeing Jack with interest, "however, I know about him . . . why he is here."

Lambert grunted. "I've brought five of my men from Carson City. I am having them relieve the local police guards at the hospital. I am told there are three entrances. The front door, one in the rear, and one through the basement emergency room."

Miss Coleman nodded. "At night, however, the rear door and the entrance from Emergency are kept locked."

"There's no other entrance from the outside? A fire door, laundry or garbage chute or windows?"

The young woman's lips curved in a touch of a smile. "The windows on the first floor all have iron grills." She nodded at her own. "The laundry and garbage chutes go to the rear of the basement. There is a door there, of course, for delivery and pickup service, but it is kept locked at night, and the door leading from that portion of the basement to the rest of the hospital is always locked."

Lambert nodded. "My men will take over. They'll be in the uniform of state police. One of my men and myself will be on the second and third floors."

"You'll find Miss Westover up there." Her eyes looked from Lambert to Jack with an increased flick of interest. She would know them again if she saw them, Jack surmised.

"May I use your phone?" Lambert picked up the receiver without waiting. He asked for Captain Fillmore in Emergency and spoke rapidly concerning the disposal of the state troops and the dismissal of the local police. Captain Fillmore was then to join him on the second floor.

Miss Coleman listened with her eyes on her paper work, except for one out-of-the-corner glance at Jack. It was an odd expression—a mixture of curiosity, humor, and something else which Jack found difficult to classify. It could have been instinctive impudence or a touch of feminine intelligence or something less personal—something she would like to say, but not in the presence of Lambert.

34

At 12:40 the corridors of the third floor of Morrison Hospital were dim, empty, and silent, save for the phantom, wispy whisk of the two nurses' starched uniforms as they moved from patient to patient—a mysterious sort of ethereal, ritual patrol duty by these spirits of mercy.

The second floor showed more lights and movement. In the second-floor hallway, besides the two nurses performing their midnight rites, there was a burly, shadowed figure of a captain of the state police in a straight-back chair, leaning against the wall. Behind the nurses' desk, the adjoining office was brilliantly lighted, showing through the half-open door the figures of the state's attorney, Miss Westover, a sleepy Dr. Willard, and Jack.

Lambert's face was flushed with exasperation. "We've waited over two hours for Silver Logan to wake up," he said angrily. "How much medication did you give the man? A normal sleeping pill is only effective for about two hours. I know. I've taken them."

"Oh, our hospital dosage under normal circumstances would keep a patient sleeping for four hours at least," Miss Westover said pleasantly. "It was an injection."

Lambert snorted. "This is gross interference in police matters, Miss Westover. If you didn't know it before, you'd better know it now. You've exceeded your authority."

Miss Westover's eyes widened. "Mr. Lambert," she said stiffly, "I am chief nursing supervisor in this hospital. There is no one who tells me what I should do, with the exception of the directors or a patient's private doctor."

Lambert's eyes stared in baleful frustration at the plump, friendly-faced woman. He turned abruptly to Dr. Willard. "What about it, Willard? Can't Logan be given some stimulant to snap him out of it?

Miss Westover's face stiffened. "I should hope Dr. Willard would recommend no such thing."

Lambert continued to look at Willard. The latter sat up a little straighter and opened his sleepy eyes, looking first at Lambert and then at Miss Westover. A faint whimsical smile lighted his face for a moment as he shook his head. "Over Miss Westover's dead body? No, I should think not."

Lambert's face hardened. He turned back to the chief supervisor. "Miss Westover, I think I shall put this matter into the hands of the district attorney. You've kept this Linda Holliday woman under sedation for over fourteen hours, and now Logan—either one of whom may lead us to the murderer if allowed to talk. This has some pretty serious implications."

"You will do as you wish, of course," Miss Westover said calmly. "As for Miss Holliday, she has been conscious twice, but each time was so ill from the poison in her system she was unable to talk."

Lambert arose abruptly. "I want to see these people for myself."

Miss Westover sat very still.

"Well?" demanded Lambert impatiently.

"You have a guard outside their doors. I have opened the doors a crack so that you were able to see the beds were occupied. If you insist on entering the rooms against doctor's orders, I shall have to take steps which both of us will regret."

"Such as what?"

"Call the interns and have you forcibly ejected from the hospital." Miss Westover's eyes were no longer friendly and there was little doubt she meant what she said.

"You realize I'm the state's attorney?" Lambert said harshly.

"And you realize I am the chief supervisor and have the final word of authority in this hospital." She had not moved, but suddenly she seemed to tower over Lambert.

Lambert hesitated a moment. Dr. Willard watched with sleepy cat's eyes. Finally Lambert said in a restrained voice, "Of course, you must realize what a senseless threat you have just made. I have five state troopers to back me up and I imagine I could recruit sufficient police if necessary."

"And you are aware, of course, what a perfectly beautiful political scandal such action would stir up for the newspapers?"

Dr. Willard chuckled. "She has something there, Mr. Lambert."

Lambert turned on his heel, walked out of the office and down the corridor to confer with Captain Fillmore. Miss Westover sat calmly watching his progress.

The little doctor twisted his head after him anxiously. "Isn't he liable simply to walk in on your patients?"

Miss Westover smiled grimly. "I think not. I had special locks put on those two doors this evening. I doubt if Mr. Lambert is a man of physical violence."

Dr. Willard turned to look at the supervisor with a curious expression in his eyes. All he said was, "You're a remarkable woman, Miss Westover—quite amazing, in fact."

35

Midway through Lambert's heated exchange with Westover, Jack had excused himself and drifted up to the second floor. Entering Denton's hide-away, he heard the Fed murmur.

"I feel like I was tied hand and foot and up to my neck in a grain sack in this fool lookout," Denton grumbled.

Jack grinned. "Well, you're getting away with it. Lambert's been asking after you all evening, but he's walked right by you at least twice. This is a real first class set-up."

Denton shifted impatiently. "Well, what's the news?"

"Lambert didn't go to the airport with Jordan. Said he had a conference call from Carson City which would have made him miss the plane, so Jordan went on alone."

"He could have planned it that way," Denton said thoughtfully.

"I thought you maintained Lambert wasn't our man," Jack reminded him.

"And you still think he is?"

"I don't know," Jack admitted. "I'm beginning to get a new picture. Something was said downstairs . . . "

Jack broke off as the phone rang, and he picked up the receiver.

"Jack, Doc's on the line." Jerry plugged in the outside call. For ten minutes Doc told his story and Jack listened. At its conclusion Jack asked again about the waiter who could read lips.

"Sure I'm sure, son," Doc insisted. "He wasn't never within hearin' distance of our table all the time nurse Rodin was a talkin' and yet he seemed to know too much and he was worried."

"Well, gather him up along with nurse Rodin and bring them here to the hospital."

Doc protested, "Seems kind of a shame to bring Martha in, pie-eyed like she is, for all the other nurses to see."

"Forget the sentiment. Bring her." Jack's voice sharpened. He hung up the receiver.

"Now what?" Denton demanded.

Jack ran his hand through his hair and grinned. "You weren't so dumb after all, putting a man on Supervisor Holden."

"What the hell are you talking about?"

"Last night police detective Perry Faber . . . You know him?" Jack broke off.

"I know him. He's a dangerous man." Denton's eyes grew hard. "Why?"

"Last night Detective Perry Faber came in and told Supervisor Holden to ditch old man Peterson so he could take over the wheelchair as a disguise. He said the chief wanted a double guard on Lilly Montrose. Nurse Martha Rodin was the only one besides Holden who knew of the switch. How she knew I don't know, but we'll find out when Doc gets her here."

Jack pulled out a chair, straddled it, facing the door which masked Denton. "It's pretty obvious, although not proven, that Faber scragged Lilly and filled Holliday and his sister full of Holliday's medicine, which was fatal in large doses. However, it's a certainty that he got up out of the wheelchair, went into the restroom and shot Lieutenant Holmes, and then dashed back to the wheelchair before anyone realized what was going on."

Denton frowned. "What about the nurse who screamed and ran down the corridor?"

Jack shrugged. "Who saw her but the man in the wheelchair? As for the scream, what about Supervisor Holden? She was in the office only a few steps from Faber's wheelchair when I dashed up the stairs."

"And the abandoned nurse's uniform found at the bottom of the laundry chute?"

Jack nodded. "That fits in with Martha Rodin's story that she thinks Holden was threatened by Faber. He may have told her to get a uniform and put it down the chute, making her believe that she now was an accessory in the murder of Holmes and maybe the other two."

"But why drag a mysterious nurse into the picture?"

Jack shrugged. "Everyone heard a woman scream. That had to be accounted for, and it took the pressure off Faber by sending everyone off on a wild goose chase. By the way, were you here when a police sergeant Bowman and police officer Clyde Smith were killed?"

Denton nodded watchfully. "Died in the line of duty."

"Martha Rodin doesn't think so. She thinks they were murdered and she has some pretty good evidence, if it can be proved."

There was a long thoughtful silence. Finally Denton glanced up and said, "I don't know what Doc Long did to get her to open up like this, but that young lady has signed her own death warrant, unless we close in on this bunch in a hurry."

Jack nodded. "Doc's on his way here with her. And he's found a waiter at the Las Palmas who can read lips. His wife is a deaf-mute."

"The hell you say," Denton said softly. "He's sure sticking out his neck to admit it. Who is he?"

"Doc didn't say. He's bringing him along."

Denton abruptly wheeled his chair towards the phone. "We'd better get word to Supervisor Holden, and I'd like to talk to my man on the job there, if I can reach him." As he reached for the phone, it rang sharply. He picked up the receiver and after a moment handed it to Jack. "Your girl on the switchboard wants you, fast."

Jack snatched the receiver from him.

"It's Doc again, Jack." Jack barked into the mouthpiece, "Doc, you crazy idiot, why aren't you on your way?"

"On account, son, when I went back to my table I found nurse Rodin with a huntin' knife up to the hilt in her back and her evenin' wrap drawed up over her so's not to excite the diners."

Suddenly Jack's eardrums were filled with an explosion. "Doc! Doc!" he yelled. "What was that?"

After a pause, a plaintive Texas voice murmered over the wire. "The sound you just heard was a police automatic pointed in my direction. The phone company ain't . . . "

"Are you all right?"

"Oh, sure. I'm a sittin' on the floor of the booth and folks is a millin' around outside like Sandy Claus Lane in Hollywood . . . "

"Did you see who shot at you?"

"No, but I can guess."

"Faber?"

"You want to bet?"

"Now, look, Doc, do you think you can get out of there by yourself or do you want to wait until I send somebody down . . . "

Doc snorted. "Looky, Jack, just because I let a nice girl like Miss Rodin slip through my fingers ain't no reason to insult me."

"Stop being funny—"

"I gotta go now. See you at the hospital." The receiver at the other end clicked up.

Jack turned to Denton. "The Rodin girl's been knifed. She's dead. Somebody took a shot at Doc. Probably Faber."

Denton nodded soberly. "One by one, the people with something to say are being eliminated."

36

When the two uniformed bouncers led Doc Long out the front doors of the Las Palmas and turned indifferent backs, leaving him spotlighted beneath the blatant neon-lighted marquee, he momentarily felt "as naked as a jay bird after a mob of crows' pluckin' party." He had time for an even more succinct simile in the instant before he faded into the deep shadows of the Las Palmas parking lot: "As naked as a party girl poppin' out of a men's smoker happy-birthday cake, only to discover she'd been delivered to the Ladies Aid Convention by mistake."

Doc had to admire how fast the mind works in an emergency; time to feel the cold wind of danger, despite the warm night breeze of a live and breathing desert; even time to note the sinister hunks of darkness to the right, to the left and before him, and the myriad brilliant lights of other resorts of fun and frolic interspersed along the strip. He even saw the salt-shaker glitter of diamond points clustered about a pale new moon high in the sky.

All this was instantaneous, for the time it took Doc from lighted marquee to inky shadows was one good shallow breath. If Detective Perry Faber with his too-handy shootin' pistol was waiting outside to evaluate the results of his shots into the phone booth, Doc wanted no part of him.

As Doc squatted on the still sun-scorched parking lot paving beside the brick facade of the Las Palmas, his pale blue eyes adjusted quickly to the darkness. With instinctive care to detail, he examined the cars along the curbing on both sides of the highway. There were three empty taxis directly in front of the Las Palmas, five slinky sports cars, a scattering of imports like infant shadows among mastadons, a Chrysler Imperial, three Cadillacs, and a Rolls Royce complete with uniformed chauffer. For the rest, there was a score or more sedans from shiny new to ancient vintage. It was one of these that caught his interest. Something or someone very still seemed to be hunched over the wheel. In the darkness it could be a sleeping tourist, full of happy juice, or merely a topcoat tossed over the wheel. Or it could be Mr. Trouble, himself.

Keeping in the shadows, he moved along toward the service door at the rear of the Las Palmas. If his lip-reading waiter was making an exit, it should have been by now. Suddenly from the rear of the parking lot came the grind of a starter, sharp and clear in the night desert air.

Doc raced down the shadows and then burst out under the stars as a pickup truck shot backwards out of a line, hiccoughed and died. A nervous driver, plus a truck badly in need of a tune-up, but it gave Doc the edge he needed. Again the starter ground and again the engine roared. The stinking fumes swathed Doc as he came up behind the truck, dodged the lurching machine as it completed its backing, and jumped into the bed. The truck bucked forward and caught hold, racing from the rear entrance of the lot with the speed of unleashed insanity. Fortunately for pedestrians and unwary drivers alike, the side street was empty. Fortunate, too, for Doc and the driver that the truck veered at the last minute, missing the concrete exit abutment by a breath, and that no cars were parked on the far side of the road to obstruct the wide two-wheel swing into the street away from the highway, but toward the heart of town and, in general, toward the hospital.

In Doc's estimation the man at the wheel might be a waiter, but what he knew about driving an automobile you could wad up in your eye and not feel it. That was, if he was the waiter! Doc crouched on the bed and raised his eyes above the sides. It was just too all-fired dark. Suddenly the truck swerved again and came onto a street with lights. One look was sufficient. Doc relaxed on the floor, content in the belief the hospital was the next stop.

For the first time now, since the discovery of Martha Rodin's murder, Doc had a moment to let his pent-up indignation rise and simmer in the forefront of his mind. He had two complaints he wished to take up with Faber personally, provided he was the guilty man. And for Doc's money, there was no second choice. First, it was against every Texan principle in his makeup to see anyone lay violent hands on a woman—especially a pretty one. It choked him with fury to have one beautiful creature eliminated from the world. It was depriving man of what he needed *more* of and it was such a damnable waste.

Secondly, and even more to the point, was Doc's outrage that a young woman temporarily in his charge should come to such a sticky end. If there was one thing Doc prided himself upon, it was his sworn duty to come to the aid of beauty in distress. Maybe Faber thought he could go sticking knives in Doc's female charges with impunity, but from this moment on Faber was a ciffy cat of the first water and Doc's sworn enemy.

Typical of Doc, he already had forgotten Faber had shot at him. That was all in a day's work. But killing women! That was the living end.

Some latent instinct snapped Doc out of his reverie. Headlights from behind had been hitting the back of the cab too persistently, and now they were growing brighter. Doc cautiously lifted himself up to his knees. He was fearful of giving himself away to the driver. Why he shouldn't let the waiter know he had a companion, he wasn't sure, but it was Doc's philosophy that on any case it was better to play a lone hand. And, anyhow, ignorance was bliss, especially for the wicked, until round-up time. Not that he suspected his waiter of wickedness, but just the same . . .

He peered over the side. Uh-huh, somebody was coming up—fast now. Doc slipped his gun from its underarm holster, just in case. If the waiter was conscious of the approaching car, he showed no sign.

It was a low-slung, foreign, righthand drive car with a monstrous hood that let the driver sit low, hidden until the last minute. Doc admired the resplendent chrome which gave the car the effect of the tail of a comet behind the blazing lights. The powerful hum of the motor reminded Doc of a plane clipped of its wings. It was a beauty.

And then in an instant it was beside the waiter's truck and riding neck and neck. The waiter glanced sideways for the first time, surprised that the powerful machine had not shot by him, and in that same instant an arm snaked out of the driver's seat with a gun. A panic jerk of the wheel sent the truck reeling at the moment two guns flashed in unison and two neatly drilled holes appeared as by magic in two windshields.

A momentary flash of two astonished eyes as the sports car driver's face turned in Doc's direction gave him a perfect second shot, except for the erratic convolutions of the truck, now off the road and pitching and tossing in the gravel. The sports car flashed away in a blur of light and chrome. The trucked skidded and ground to a halt.

"I swear to my grandma, fella," Doc said in an aggrieved voice, as he climbed over the side, "If you ain't the worst driver since the city feller put the old mare into the shafts wrong end to."

The voice completely undid the driver. The whites of frightened eyes in the pale, drawn face stared at Doc, gun still in hand.

"It's all right, son, it's only me," Doc reassured comfortingly, thrusting the gun back in its holster. "And a good thing, too, you ast me, on account you'd be pluckin' a harp by now if I hadn't hooked a ride."

"Who are you?" gasped a shaken voice.

"Oh, yeah, kinda hard to see in the dark, huh? I'm Doc Long, remember? We got a date at the hospital."

"No," the waiter cried out. "First I must go home. Before anything else happens, I must get home!"

Doc opened the door on the driver's side. "Look, friend, you ain't in no condition to drive. I'll take over."

"Not to the hospital. I must go home," insisted the waiter, his teeth clicking as though with ague.

"You *are* in a state," Doc said sympathetically, "but what's so all-fired important about gettin' home?"

"My sister-in-law's life is in danger."

"Sister-in-law? How'd she get into this?"

The waiter's jaws shut tight, he stared straight ahead, holding the wheel tightly.

"Okay, son," agreed Doc, "move over. To your place first and *then* the hospital."

Without a word the waiter moved and Doc clambered in under the wheel. "How far you live from here and where?"

"About a mile, straight ahead."

Under Doc's handling the truck behaved itself with sedate decorum, even permitting a generous fifty-five miles an hour. In less than two minutes the waiter said eagerly, "The next driveway on the left." But suddenly Doc stepped on the gas and shot by the driveway. The waiter's hand gripped his arm. "We've passed. Where are you taking me?"

Several hundred yards beyond the driveway Doc pulled the car up in the shadow of a sprawling pepper tree.

"What are you trying to do?" There was a note of belligerence in the waiter's voice.

"Son, where's your eyes?" Doc said guardedly. "Didn't you see the big chrome sports car parked under the trees just the other side of the driveway?"

"Oh, God," cried the waiter, throwing open the car door and leaping out.

Doc scrambled out and grabbed the man's arm as he started to run back up the road. "Easy, friend, easy."

"Don't you understand?" the waiter pleaded, trying to pull away. "My wife and sister-in-law are there alone. We'll be too late . . . "

A fusillade of shots riccocheted in the night and marred the driveway with spurts of fire. The waiter gasped and stood trembling.

"That was two guns. Our friend seems to have run into somethin'." Doc snatched his gun from its holster as the motor of the sports car started up, and in an instant the machine was streaking toward them. Suddenly, it was upon them, and Doc's automatic barked four times the instant it was abreast.

For a moment the machine held steady, wavered and then suddenly swerved violently, hit the gravel edge of the road, and then a ditch and rolled over and over.

"That's a durned shame to do a thing like that to such a handsome automobile," Doc muttered regretfully. "Well, shall we go see what's left of the pieces?"

37

Footsteps pounding down the paving turned Doc back toward the driveway. First the approaching figure was a mere shadow, then an outline, and finally a man with a gun. He stopped abruptly five paces away.

"Who are you?" he demanded warily, eyeing the gun in Doc's hand.

"Doc Long, Triple A Detective Agency," Doc said laconically. "Who are you?"

"Breedon. One of Joe Denton's men."

"Well, welcome to the party. This here's . . . " Doc paused, perplexed. "Heeey, what *is* your name?"

The waiter, still stunned by events, muttered huskily, "Charles O'Dell."

"Yeah," said Doc cheerfully, "Mr. Charles O'Dell, waiter at the Las Palmas. How come you was staked out in Mr. O'Dell's front yard?"

"That was nice shooting on that sports job. Hadn't we better go see what you got?" Breedon said noncomittally.

"Might as well, I reckon," Doc answered agreeably. "Only I don't think Detective Faber's in any condition to care much, one way or the other."

The three started the three hundred yards down the road to the overturned car. "Faber?" asked Breedon with interest. "You're sure?"

"No, I ain't and that's a fact," said Doc. "Only I'd lay a small wager of ten bucks that it is. By the way, Breedon, do you know him by sight?"

"No, I was just imported from L.A. on this job. Why? Don't you?"

"To my knowledge I never set eyes on the ciffy cat. How about you, Mr. O'Dell?"

The waiter nodded grimly. "Yes, I know him."

"Good!" Doc approached the wreckage tentatively from one side. Breedon took the other. "Wisht we had a flashlight." Breedon produced one. "My," Doc said admiringly, "you boys is equipped." The flashlight played on the interior of the sports car. The windshield, half collapsed, dug into the soft, sandy soil. "Yeah, he's in there all right. Reckon it was his seatbelt that kept him in when the car was a floppin' around." Doc reached down and got hold of the unconscious man's wrist. "He's still alive," he said after a moment, "but he don't look very comfortable. Don't suppose you got a hydraulic jack in your left rear pocket?"

"Afraid not." Breedon grinned.

"Don't have everything after all," Doc sounded regretful. "Somebody ought to speak to the U.S. government about it." Doc stood up. "Yep, he's alive all right." He turned to O'Dell. "How about you a scroochin' down so's you can get a peek? See if he's sure enough Faber."

O'Dell reluctantly got down on his knees beside Breedon with the flashlight and peered under. After a moment he straightened up, his face white and strained in the beam of the light. He nodded grimly. "It's officer Faber," he said between tight lips, "and I never thought I'd see the day when I would be glad to see a man in his condition."

"He sure must of been bad medicine for you," Doc said with interest.

"My family's been living in hell the past two days," O'Dell burst out passionately, "ever since Faber shot and killed Lieutenant Holmes from the hospital window, and my sister-in-law, Grace Holden, saw him come out of the restroom with the gun in his hand."

"Holy cow!" exclaimed Doc, "Holden's your sister-in-law?"

"That's why I was staked out in his front yard," nodded Breedon.

"Well, whoooeee," Doc said, pleased, "then we got the whole story right here in our pocket. Ain't we the ones, though!"

"All except the missing quarter-million holdup money," Breedon reminded. "Not to mention the Holliday hatbox of long green."

38

At half past one in the morning an average Las Vegas citizen would most likely neither have seen nor sensed anything untoward in the corridors of the Morrison Hospital, the patients' quarters, nor in the demeanor and efficient discipline of the hospital staff. True, one might have wondered at the several state troopers' uniforms, and possibly the unprofessional prowling of a medium, well-set figure with black curly hair and sharp sardonic eyes. Still and all, the wheels of normal activity were well greased and running smoothly to the unpracticed eye.

Not so for the initiate, from youngest student nurse through the ranks to elderly nurse Trouble (pronounced Tru-bull), whose sensitive nose caught the climactic tension without knowing why or where lightning might strike. True, it was unheard of for Chief Supervisor Westover to be on night duty, and who had heard of the door of a patient's room being locked? It is likewise true that everyone was aware that two patients had been murdered the night before and a third man shot down on the hospital steps. But what was expected tonight was a closed mystery. Still, it was evident that something was anticipated, and below the strict, calm hospital routine there were raw nerves and grim anxiety.

As Jack Packard slipped quietly around a corridor corner he passed the second-floor nurses' desk, and glancing briefly into the small room behind, he could see

Lambert sitting at the report desk, his tired, red-rimmed eyes missing nothing. Slumped in a chair, Dr. Willard sat with his eyes closed, his body relapsed in uncomfortable repose.

On down the corridor past the locked doors of the rooms originally assigned to Linda Holliday and Silver Logan, a state trooper leaned against the wall on two legs of his chair, his body slumped in apparent boredom and weariness, his eyes alert and suspicious.

At the far end of the corridor, Jack came to another locked door and knocked softly.

"Yes, who is it?" came the weary, discomfited, familiar voice of Jerry Booker.

Jack responded softly and the door was thrown open.

"How to have fun and frolic in Las Vegas," she grumbled, reseating herself on the platform chair at the switchboard and slipping the headphone over her blond hair.

Jack closed the door. "Nothing from Doc?"

"You'd have gotten it, if there had been," Jerry said sourly, sighing heavily. "Brother, have I had it. Last night playing footsy with card sharks and wrestling a female tiger. Tonight, giving my life's blood to a nest of cords and switches."

"It should have taken Doc fifteen minutes at the most from the Las Palmas to the hospital. It's been an hour and a half." A dissatisfied frown darkened Jack's face with unnamed anxiety.

The switchboard buzzed. Jerry plugged in. Her face lighted with interest as she listened. "Just a moment, please." She turned to Jack. "Night Supervisor Holden. She wants Emergency, fast."

"Plug her in and switch on the speaker," Jack snapped, standing by impatiently as Jerry's nimble fingers flew to a cord and flipped a switch.

Both of them heard the rush order for an ambulance and a wrecking car to 17443 Lost Hills Road.

"That's Holden's address, all right," Jerry said.

Jack turned to a telephone directory, ran through the pages, then his finger slid down a page. "Jerry, get me this number." He jotted it on her note pad. "Plug me in on the phone over here." He sat down at a small table and pulled the phone toward him and waited.

Suddenly Jerry's eyes widened. "Heeey, that's the Las Vegas airport. We making reservations for home?" She plugged in a cord with new alertness and dialed. Jack's phone jingled. He picked up the receiver.

"Come on, Jack, give!" Jerry persisted. "Does this mean Doc's got our man and the show's over?"

"When does the next plane leave for Carson City?" Jack inquired into the phone.

"Carson City!" exclaimed Jerry. "We live in Hollywood."

"Not until six in the morning? Uh-huh. Now can you tell me whether any plane has left for the north since 9:00 this evening? Right. Nothing to Carson City, huh?" There was satisfaction in his voice as he asked to be transferred to the luggage department. As he waited, from somewhere close by outside came the low moan and then the swelling wail of an ambulance. In the moments of listening to the shriek, Jerry missed all but the tag end of Jack's second conversation. It was not informative.

"That's right, do *not* send it out, as originally scheduled, ahead of my flight. I now wish to take it with me on my plane. That's right, thank you." Jack stood up, stretched and grinned.

"What are you so smug about?" demanded Jerry vindictively. "You told me to pack an overnight bag for Las Vegas. How many items of intimate girlish doodads do you think I can get into an overnight case? I'm about as prepared to go to Carson City . . . "

Jack grinned. "Jerry, how would you like to have dinner tomorrow night at the Tahitian on La Cienega, then drinking and dancing at the Millionaire's Club until the small hours?"

"You mean it? Back in Hollywood tomorrow?" Jerry's eyes sparkled with pleasure and then shone with something more intimate. "Thank you, Jack, I'd *love* it."

Jack nodded and opened the door. "I'll speak to Doc about it. The two of you should have a big evening."

"Why, you . . . " The door closed hastily. Jerry picked up the biggest phone book within reach—the Los Angeles business directory—and hurled it at the door.

39

In the corridor again, Jack passed the somnolent trooper with the lazy, watchful eyes. He was past the nurses' desk when he turned back sharply. In the room behind, State's Attorney Lambert was lying with his face in his arms upon the desk, which was not too unnatural at this late hour, except for the ugly red gash—like a gaping red mouth smirking out of his graying hair. In front of the desk, Dr. Willard's rough tweed overcoat was sprawled on the floor and his neat homburg was trampled into the carpet beside it.

Without stopping to enter the room, Jack walked swiftly back to the state trooper. "Did you see Dr. Willard leave the room down there with anyone?" he demanded sharply.

The trooper eyed him nonchalantly. "Sorry, I didn't see him leave the room with or without anyone. Why? Isn't he there?"

Jack looked at the man in disgust. "Then I don't suppose you heard any row in the room?"

"If I had, do you suppose I'd be sitting here?" The trooper, stung by Jack's aggressiveness, dropped the fore-legs of the chair to the floor and stood up. "What's this all about?"

"Nothing much," said Jack dryly, "except that Lambert has a hole in his head, and Dr. Willard's coat and hat're on the floor, but he's not."

The trooper took Jack's arm with authority. "You come along with me, Bud, and let's have a look." Jack went with him as far as the desk. "Holy jumping . . . " He dropped Jack's arm and dashed into the office. Jack didn't follow.

"Call one of the interns down in Emergency," he advised, turning quickly down the corridor.

"Heeey, fellow, where you going?" yelled the trooper.

"Where do you think?" Jack called back. "Dr. Willard's missing, isn't he?" He headed for the room where Linda Holliday and Logan were secreted under guard, but at the door of the second-floor Federal man's lookout he caught sight of Denton. He was lying in the open doorway, blood dripping from an ugly wound in his forehead. A young nurse came out of a patient's room and would have brushed past him, but Jack caught her arm and whirled her around. "Look what you've got here," he said. "Another case."

The nurse gasped.

"Get him some help, fast." Jack walked swiftly down the corridor, turned in through the operating amphitheater, through a second door into the isolated corridor to room 299, shared jointly in the emergency by Linda Holliday, Silver Logan, a federal guard, and at this hour, if schedules were followed, by Chief Supervisor Westover.

The door was ajar, not enough to permit looking in. Cautiously Jack pushed it wider, inhaled suddenly and deeply, and reached for his gun.

40

At 1:45 a.m., with the hospital normally at its lowest ebb of activity, and after a short, decisive interview with the second-in-command, Night Supervisor Coleman, Miss Westover had made one final survey of the second and third floors and, according to plan, had vanished into the operating amphitheater and retired to room 299. At first glance she had been startled by the apparent absence of the federal guard, but was quickly relieved as the door swung shut. Behind it had been a tense, alert figure, gun in hand. He relaxed, grinned a cheerful greeting, and thrust the gun back in its holster.

The round-faced, pink-cheeked supervisor watched with startled eyes, shivered slightly, then nodded and turned abruptly to her two patients.

There was a suspicious tension in the figure beneath the sheet and blanket pulled up under the chin of the calm, sleeping face of Linda Holliday. Gently Miss Westover reached beneath the covers, took a softly relaxed wrist and silently counted pulse beats. She thrust the wrist back and leaned over the face in repose and said softly, "Are you resting comfortably, Miss Holliday?"

There was no response, only quiet breathing. The supervisor frowned dubiously, hesitated, then turned to the guard. "Has Miss Holliday shown any signs of restlessness or waking?"

He shook his head, but looked at the bed with interest. Miss Westover nodded and crossed to Logan. Wide awake, unblinking, he lay on his back, his hands linked behind his head on the pillow, staring at a fixed spot on the ceiling. She took one hand and sought his pulse. Logan gave up his wrist, but without other acknowledgment of her presence.

"You should try to sleep, Mr. Logan," she murmured, releasing his wrist.

The moody eyes in the sullen face turned indifferently from the ceiling to the supervisor. In them was a sudden flash of sardonic mockery. After the briefest recognition, they returned to the spot on the ceiling.

Miss Westover rustled across to the bathroom and returned with a capsule and a glass of water. "This will help," she urged. Logan paid no heed. "Mr. Logan!" the supervisor said in sharp undertone.

Again the angry, suspicious eyes shifted, first to the yellow capsule in the tiny shot-glass in her left hand, then to the glass of water, and then to her face. Again the eyes swung back to the ceiling.

With an exclamation of impatience, Miss Westover set the two glasses on the bedside table. She walked to the far side of Linda Holliday's bed, nearest the wall, and sat down on a straight-back chair, looking wearily at her watch.

For three, four, five minutes, there was blank silence. Abruptly from behind the corridor door there was movement. The federal agent drew quickly back to be hidden should the door open, his hand on the butt of his revolver, which he did not draw. Miss Westover's momentary relaxation vanished and she sat erect, her eyes on the door. In the bed beside her, a head turned restlessly on the pillow. There was a faint sigh. Logan's eyes came away from the ceiling with a jerk and fixed on the door, fear gleaming. Slowly his body turned on the side and drew up in a knot, as though ready to spring.

The door pushed open cautiously, then abruptly swung wide, and the undersized figure of Dr. Willard stood in the doorway, blinking with owlish, sleepy eyes. In his hand was a small metal hospital tray containing a small bottle of alcohol, a daub of cotton and an injection syringe.

"Dr. Willard!" exclaimed Miss Westover, rising to her feet.

The doctor nodded, smiled wryly and moved a step into the room. "Hasn't Mr. Packard come yet?" he inquired. "He told me to meet him here." He looked inquiringly first at the sleeping girl and then at Logan, who lay shrunken and still, his eyes fastened on Dr. Willard as though hypnotized.

The doctor nodded again. "Good," he murmured, "I'm glad to see our patient is awake. Perhaps his lips will make sense now that he has rested." He moved towards Logan's bed, releasing the door so that it swung closed. Behind him the agent's gun slipped silently from its holster; he waited.

With an air of professional absorption, Dr. Willard set the tray beside the two glasses that had been placed on the night table by Miss Westover. He frowned down at the capsule in the smaller glass and turned to Miss Westover, who had moved around the end of Miss Holliday's bed. "You have been giving the patient sleeping capsules?" he said with a faint show of irritation.

"He was offered one, but refused to take it." There was a note of perplexed uncertainty in the supervisor's voice.

Dr. Willard nodded, relieved. "Good," he murmered. "First we will again attempt to read the patient's lips. If he still does not make sense, it is suggested we try the serum." He glanced at Logan's stricken face and smiled. "Truth serum to you, young man." He looked again at Miss Westover. "I have used it with some success at the Institute on mutes who previously had been unable to speak."

The expression of anguish and appeal in Logan's face restored Miss Westover's sense of confidence and authority. "I'm sure, doctor, you don't mind waiting until either Mr. Packard or Mr. Denton arrive."

Dr. Willard eyed Miss Westover with distaste. "It isn't my custom," he said brusquely, "to take my instructions from the nursing staff." Before Miss Westover could protest, he continued irritably, "Neither is it my custom to be kept from my bed, which I missed entirely last night and which seemingly I am being unnecessarily deprived of tonight."

"Just the same, doctor," the little medical man whirled at the sound of the guard's voice, "I think we'll follow Miss Westover's suggestion."

The sleepy owlish eyes of Dr. Willard were cold and menacing at the sight of the federal agent and his drawn gun. "This nonsense has gone far enough!" Dr. Willard's tone of authority carried weight. "Young man, put that gun in your holster and get Packard on the phone immediately. As for Denton, I have not seen him all evening." His voice, blurred and harsh, raised. "Quickly, man, move!"

The agent grinned and shook his head. "Sorry, doc, but on higher authority than yours . . . "

With an exclamation of impatience, Dr. Willard moved abruptly toward the phone, brushing past Miss Westover with such impetus as to throw her off balance. She grasped his arm to save herself and for an instant's pause, his back was to the guard. There was a gasp and a strangled cry from the chief supervisor and suddenly she collapsed against the doctor and slid through his arms to the floor.

"Quick, man, quick!" Dr. Willard exclaimed, bending over the insensible woman, his hand on her pulse. "She's had a heart attack. Call Emergency at once. Use the phone."

Momentarily off guard by the collapse, the agent moved toward the telephone. As he passed Dr. Willard, a sharp needle appeared suddenly and Willard lunged, sending it deep in the man's buttocks.

A sharp cry, a swift whirling, a swaying gun shot, and the agent fell heavily. Dr. Willard staggered momentarily, recovered, then cast aside the now empty syringe at the same instant that Silver Logan leaped from his bed, cowering in a cringing, desperate crouch to face the advancing doctor.

At the doctor's back, a white figure in a hospital gown slipped from the other bed on bare feet, picked up the revolver from the limp fingers of the guard and thrust it uncertainly into Dr. Willard's back. She pulled hard on the trigger, but nothing happened. It still was on safety. With a snarl, in one movement the little doctor swept the second syringe from the night stand and turned on the girl, knocking the gun from her hand and grasping her arm.

It was precisely at this moment that Jack pushed open the door to room 299. The crouching Logan was on the doctor's back, his arm twined about his throat and deflecting the needle approaching Linda Holliday's arm, but also protecting the desperately struggling man from Jack's gun.

Swiftly Jack reversed his revolver, moved quickly upon the milling trio and crashed the gun with precision on Dr.

Willard's skull. He collapsed with Logan atop him. The latter scrambled to his feet, his own brief hospital gown giving his bare, hairy shanks a knobby, grotesque, storklike length. He stood with the transfixed Linda looking down on the three sprawled bodies on the floor.

Jack picked up the telephone. "This Garden of Eden effect is tantalizing," he said dryly, "but hadn't you two semi-nudes better get back into bed?"

Startled, Logan fixed his eyes on Linda, then at his own shanks, shuddered and dove for the bed. Linda laughed shakily and retired without apparent discomfiture.

Jack jiggled the phone impatiently.

"All right, all right!" came Jerry's petulant voice. "The switchboard's lit up like Hollywood on a world premier night and there's only one of me."

"Jerry, this is Jack. Send up . . . "

"Hey, Jack," Jerry interrupted, "Emergency's picked up Lambert and Denton with bloody heads, and now every patient in the back end of the second floor is reporting they heard a gun shot . . . "

"Never mind that," Jack snapped. "Listen to me. Get Emergency up here to 299 fast, and I mean fast!"

"Oh, brother, is this a hospital or a slaughter house? Do you realize— " But Jack hung up and knelt first beside Miss Westover and then the federal agent. There was evidence of heartbeat, but it was fading under his fingers.

41

The hospital Board of Directors' room, air-conditioned, with an eastern exposure, and sheltered from the red welter of the sinking sun, still did not entirely escape the desert heat that bounced off paving, rock, and sand held close to earth by a steel-blue sky. On the long conference table in front of each chair was a sheet of hospital letterhead containing a typewritten list of names under four headings: the Dead, the Injured, the Suspects, and the Known Guilty. They read:

THE DEAD

Skip Sullivan
Lois Pallaski, alias Lilly Montrose
Lieutenant Tracy Holmes
Hilliard Holliday
Nurse Martha Rodin
Chief Jeff Jordan

THE INJURED

Linda Holliday
State's Attorney Gordon Lambert
Chief Supervisor Ruth Westover
Police Detective Perry Faber
Dr. Avery Willard, Director of the Nevada
    Institute for the Deaf, Dumb and Blind
Max "Silver" Logan

THE SUSPECTS

Linda Holliday
Max "Silver" Logan
Night Supervisor Grace Holden
Police Chief Jeff Jordan
Captain Jessie Michaels, Assistant to Chief
   (missing)
Members of the Las Vegas Police Department,
   now under investigation by the District
   Attorney and the State's Attorney
Members of the staff of the Nevada Institute
   for the Deaf, Dumb and Blind, now
   under detention and under investigation
   by the Reno District Attorney and the
   office of the State's Attorney

THE KNOWN GUILTY

Dr. Avery Willard
Police Detective Perry Faber

At one end of the long table the Las Vegas district attorney presided. At his right elbow sat State's Attorney Lambert. A neat, efficient bandage topped the latter's high, bony brow, much in the effect of a skull cap. At the district attorney's left was a neat young man with a stack of dictation notebooks and a row of ball-point pens.

At the other end of the table Jack sat, his small black pocket notebook before him. At his right was Joe Denton, also wearing the mark of last night's fray, a white gauze skull cap bandage. At Jack's left sat Jerry Booker, crisp and fresh, and armed with a single pencil and two folds of white paper, her blonde hair attesting to a recent visit to a beauty parlor. Next to her was Doc Long, his long legs sprawled beneath the table, one long arm hooked over the back of his chair, the other on the table. The dissatisfaction on his long, horsey Texas face made itself apparent in a scowl of displeasure. Between Doc and an empty chair,

Max "Silver" Logan hunched in mute resentment, his eyes wandering restlessly about the table. When he had first been seated, he had picked up the list before him, read it with a scowl and then thrust the paper from him.

Directly across from him was Doc's waiter of the Las Palmas, Charles O'Dell, and on his right was Night Supervisor Grace Holden, his sister-in-law. Between Lambert and O'Dell, on the latter's left, was Linda Holliday in neat, expensive black, a memorial for her dead brother. She sat pale, beautiful, reserved, save for the small sardonic turn of her expertly attended lips.

Jack looked down the table and received the barest nod from the district attorney. Before he spoke he looked down at his pocket notebook. "The business at hand will include testimony by Mrs. Holden, Miss Linda Holliday, and others, including a lip-reading statement by Max Logan, also known as "Silver" Logan, and statements by State's Attorney Lambert and federal agent Joe Denton." Jack glanced at Denton and added dryly, "Actually, Denton should be sitting in my place, but even after twelve hours he attests to mild headache as the result of a too close contact with Dr. Willard. I think we might offer our condolences also to Lambert."

"Get on with it," Lambert growled with distaste.

Jack nodded. "Also, some of you may not have heard that both Chief Supervisor Westover and Denton's federal man, who were given the needle by Dr. Willard, are resting nicely and will recover, due only to the fact that the attack took place in a hospital where immediate first aid was available. Fifteen minutes more and both would have been dead."

"Brother!" muttered Jerry, shivering.

"As a matter of fact, the same may be true for Miss Holliday, a victim of an earlier attack. That and the fortunate circumstance that the needle which killed her brother contained a lesser dosage for her, the attacker apparently having misjudged the amount intended for Hilly Holliday."

Linda's face paled slightly. Otherwise she gave no sign that she had heard.

"Now, then— " Jack's voice indicated he was ready to get down to business, but was interrupted by the district attorney.

"Before you begin, Mr. Packard, would you explain the empty chair? Are you expecting someone else? If so, why isn't he here?"

Jack nodded. "He will be here before we're finished." Then without pause, "Mrs. Holden, I suggest you begin the testimony."

Grace Holden hesitated. "Will it be question and answer or should I just tell my story?"

"Tell your story. If there are questions, they will come afterwards."

Mrs. Holden's hands, linked on the table, gripped until the knuckles whitened, but she spoke calmly, precisely. "Night before last, the evening of August eighteenth, two patients were brought into the hospital by the police. They were Lilly Montrose and Mr. Hilliard Holliday. A police guard was placed on the room of the Montrose girl, none on Mr. Holliday. That was about midnight. Then about one o'clock, police detective Perry Faber came to the hospital and disguised himself as the arthritic and gout patient, Sven Peterson, who for weeks had been allowed to prowl the halls at night in his wheelchair, when he could not sleep lying down.

"Detective Faber must have known of Peterson's habits, because he immediately ordered me to take Mr. Peterson to the isolation ward and he took over his room and his wheelchair. He said it was necessary to have this added guard on the Montrose girl's room, as one attempt already had been made to kill her and it was felt another would be made. He showed me an order signed by Police Chief Jordan.

"No one was supposed to know of the disguise but myself. However, I suspected nurse Martha Rodin was aware of it. She is . . . she was a nosy, inquisitive girl, and very little went on in the hospital that she didn't know about. I believe her murder was proof of it. Anyway, I took her aside and warned her she was neither to appear to notice anything unusual nor to mention it at any future time. At the time I simply thought I was protecting a normal police procedure."

Mrs. Holden paused and cleared her throat. "A great deal of my night duty is with records and charts in my office on the first floor. I should have mentioned that the Montrose girl and Mr. Hilliard Holliday were on the third floor, which at night is under the supervision of nurse Martha Rodin and nurse Grace Parker. Unfortunately, the guard at Miss Montrose's door was officer Mike Stern, who I now know to have been secretly engaged to nurse Parker. I understand that at one moment, unknown to me at the time, nurse Parker and officer Stern retired to one of the vacant rooms for about ten minutes. I think it was at this time that Detective Faber slipped into the Montrose girl's room and killed her."

Again she hesitated. "As Mr. Holliday's room was not under guard, it was quite possible for Detective Faber to enter his room at any time that both nurses were in patients' rooms and out of the corridor. I cannot say why he wasn't seen by officer Stern, if he was on duty at all times, as the door he was guarding was only about five doors down the corridor on the opposite side. . . .

"It was about 5:00 in the morning," her voice shook for a moment and then recovered itself, "when we discovered the body of the Montrose girl. I must have shown my suspicion of Detective Faber, for very shortly after the discovery he spoke to me privately and said under no circumstances was I to mention his being in the hospital in disguise. He said it was a police matter and made it quite plain that for me to speak out was certain death for me." She hesitated, then with a quick glance at the district attorney, continued. "Knowing the conditions in our police department and the previous murders of officer Clyde Smith and Sergeant Luke Bowman—"

There was a startled exclamation from the district attorney. For a moment he seemed about to speak and then waved his hand for Mrs. Holden to continue.

"Anyway, I felt I was in a difficult and dangerous position and I decided, for the moment anyway, to keep silent. Besides, I did not know whom I could trust with the story."

Jack nodded encouragingly. "And now we come to Lieutenant Holmes's murder, shot down at the entrance to the hospital from a second-floor restroom while handcuffed to a policeman and surrounded by several others, including Chief Jordan."

Grace Holden's clasped hands moved from the table top to her lap. She said tightly, "As you know, Mr. Packard, I was with nurses Martha Rodin and Grace Parker in the first-floor chief supervisor's office being interviewed by you and Mr. Long when the shot was fired."

"It also is true, isn't it, Mrs. Holden," Jack said softly, "that I was the first to run upstairs?"

The night supervisor's eyes lowered a moment as she nodded; then she raised them and looked steadily at Jack, as he continued.

"It also is true, is it not, that you came up right behind me? That you heard the disguised Faber in the wheelchair say he heard a shot from the women's restroom, that he saw a nurse dash out and run down the corridor after hearing a woman scream? Also, you saw one of the floor nurses looking as though she were about to protest something and you silenced her with a sharp look of warning?"

There was a slight hesitation, then Mrs. Holden nodded.

"And further, in the confusion, suddenly you and Faber and the wheelchair were gone?"

Again Mrs. Holden nodded.

"What was it the nurse was about to protest, when you stopped her?"

Her eyes swept the table and then returned to Jack. "I didn't know what she was about to say at the moment. I talked to her later and found that she knew it couldn't have been one of the second-floor nurses. She knew where they were at the time. Also, she had heard the scream and she at the time had thought it was a man's voice."

"And why were you so anxious to have this information checked?"

Mrs. Holden's shoulders, which had begun to sag under the examination, straightened, her voice dropped a tone, and her eyes suddenly were bright with urgent appeal.

"This you will have to take on my word, Mr. Packard, but beneath the shawl around Detective Faber's shoulders and across his lap, his hands moved, and in one of them I saw the revolver with which he had just killed Lieutenant Holmes. I knew he was desperate and I was afraid for the nurse."

"Was that why you wheeled him away?"

"I think he meant for me to see the gun, because he caught my eye and nodded for me to take him down the hall. I was afraid to cross him. I took him back to Mr. Peterson's room, where he threw off the Peterson disguise. He told me to get hold of a nurse's uniform, fast, and plant it in the dirty bedding at the foot of the chute in the basement."

"Which you did?"

"Yes. It was an old one, which I had brought with me from the East two years before and knew couldn't be traced." She hesitated. "In his own clothes and as himself, he walked out of the room, and being a police detective, simply nodded to the police guard and walked out of the hospital."

"And you felt justified in keeping all this from the police? Or if you were afraid of the police, you felt right about not telling Doc, or me, or Joe Denton, representing the federal government?"

42

Charles O'Dell, who had been following the inquisition with growing nervousness and indignation, spoke up in a husky voice. "I can answer that for you. No, of course my sister-in-law didn't feel right about it. She's been on the point of collapse ever since it happened. Can't you men get it through your heads that she and she alone, knew that Detective Faber was loose in the hospital and apparently had killed three people? That she knew the same awaited her if she crossed him in the slightest? Since the three hospital deaths she has been home in constant terror of Faber. We all have been. Why do you suppose I stuck my neck out at the Las Palmas trying to stop Miss Rodin from talking so recklessly to Mr. Long? I could read her lips, every word she was saying, and I knew she was in as much danger as Grace . . . Mrs. Holden. I also had seen Detective Faber at the bar."

Jack looked at O'Dell with interest. "Mrs. Holden had told you and your wife the whole story?"

"She had." O'Dell's face was grim.

Jack turned again to Supervisor Holden. "Do you also read lips? I mean, if your sister . . ."

"I'm learning, but I'm not good at it. I had been in the East until two years ago and had seen my sister only once in the years since she lost her voice and hearing."

She hesitated a moment. "I—I think that is everything I can tell you."

The district attorney said smoothly, "If you will come with me to my office at the close of this conference, Mrs. Holden, there are some details I'm sure you can fill in for us." His face grew grimmer. "I'm especially interested in your reference to officer Clyde Smith and Sergeant Luke Bowman. Your reference to murder seems somehow to involve the police department, rather than criminals outside the department, as the records show."

For a moment a kind of ague seemed to grip the woman. Then she recovered and tried to speak, but without success. She simply nodded her understanding that her tribulations were not yet over.

"Thank you." The district attorney's voice was dry and menacing.

"If you think to persecute my sister-in-law for something she could not help knowing as a member of the hospital staff and yet had nothing personally to do with . . . "

O'Dell's anger was broken off sharply.

"I'd like to see you, too, Mr. O'Dell," the district attorney snapped.

O'Dell looked sullen and defiant, but held his peace. Across the table, Silver Logan grinned wryly and his lips moved. O'Dell's eyes, on the moving lips, hardened and his face darkened.

"Will you translate for us?" Jack asked.

O'Dell moved uneasily in his chair. "He simply said 'Cheer up, pal. It's always rough on witnesses when the police department is under fire'. "

The district attroney's eyebrows went up.

Lambert cleared his throat. "I want it understood that I do not believe the district attorney's office is in any way involved in this police mess. Also, the state of Nevada will be taking an active interest in everything that goes on in the prosecution of this case. There will at no time be any injustice done to anyone and it is my intent to see that no one involved shall escape the full penalty of the law." He looked sharply at the district attorney, who smiled vaguely and nodded.

Jack brought the session back to matters at hand. "Mr. Lambert, now that you have the floor, will you fill us in with your interest in the case?"

Lambert's face settled into a grim mask. "It is simply told. We in the state's attorney's office have been cognizant for some time that matters in Las Vegas were reaching an intolerable state. We also were aware that the viciousness which from time to time was showing up in the Las Vegas police department was headed by someone close to the official state family in Carson City.

"From time to time I have had men on the matter, making a quiet investigation. Nothing had come of it; however, as time went by we had begun to feel, without anything definite to put our fingers on, that the trouble was centered in one of our departments of Health and Welfare in Reno.

"Checks on these departments gave us nothing. We watched communications between Las Vegas and Reno wherever possible without tipping our hand, and still nothing. Then came the phone call from Jordan to our Institute for the Deaf, Dumb and Blind asking for a lip reader. Now, there are a number of subordinates who are experts at the Institute, but when Dr. Willard chose to come himself, rather than sending the request through routine channels, I had a hunch. I decided to also come to Las Vegas.

"I gave as an excuse my concern over the shooting of Lieutenant Holmes and the involvement of the police in the two-hundred-fifty-thousand-dollar Chicago bank robbery loot. This was legitimate, especially with the Feds snooping around." He nodded at Joe Denton and received a cheerful grin in return.

"My endeavor had been, upon arrival, to keep Dr. Willard under close surveillance, keeping him with me as much as possible and trying at other times to watch his movements, except when he was in his hotel room. That, actually, was my reason for not going to the airport to meet my men with Jordan. I had seen Dr. Willard to his room and then had waited in the lobby, in case he should go out. That was my mistake. He may or may not have been aware of my close surveillance. In any case, he chose to find a safer exit from the hotel. After three hours of waiting, which seemed reasonable inasmuch as he had said he was going to take a siesta, I called the room and got no answer. I then went to his room with a bellboy. He was not there. I had lost him.

"Whether we'll ever prove it or not, it is my belief that he is guilty of knocking Joe Denton's man over the head in the airport parking lot and then murdering Jordan."

"Heeey, I thought that was Detective Faber," Doc exclaimed.

"No," Jack shook his head, "I have definite proof that Dr. Willard was at the airport."

"You have definite proof?" The exclamation came in unison from Lambert and the district attorney, both staring at him suspiciously.

Jack nodded. "We'll go into that later. Go ahead, Mr. Lambert."

Lambert grunted. "Well, there's not much more. I didn't see Dr. Willard again until he came to the hospital. My second mistake was nodding off while sitting with him in the second-floor office of the hospital. It was well after midnight and I'd had a hard day, but I had never for a moment intended drowsing in his presence." He shrugged glumly. "However, I did and got exactly what I deserved. A crack on the head."

"You could have saved me a crack on the head," Joe Denton murmured, "if you hadn't played your cards so close to the vest and had given us an inkling of your suspicions."

"Yeah, what about that?" Doc asked with a grin. "Letting Willard get close enough to you to swing the base of a table lamp!"

Denton shrugged. "I was in my second-floor lookout. I cautiously stuck my head out and there he was, waiting. He simply swung before I could dodge."

Doc grinned. "He was actually waiting to slug you?"

Jack looked up from his little black book to where Charles O'Dell sat in a black cloud of resentment beside his sister-in-law. "Before we have you go into your lip-reading act on Logan, Mr. O'Dell," he suggested, "suppose you give us your version of this business."

O'Dell turned his eyes on Jack in surprise. Then the sullen, resentful· defiance closed in again. "I?" he exclaimed. "What should I know about it, except my sister-in . . . Mrs. Holden's life's been threatened and my house has been a living hell for the past two days."

Doc had turned in his chair and was eyeing the man with lazy curiosity. At the moment it was hard to see him as the obsequious serving man, bowing and scraping at the Las Palmas as he had been the night before.

43

"Tell 'em about what happened at the Las Palmas last night, Mr. O'Dell," Doc drawled, sliding more comfortably down in his chair. "Tell 'em about our trip out to your place."

The waiter's eyes went blank and slid away from Doc. He looked appealingly about the table to the state's attorney, Denton, Linda Holliday, and ended with the district attorney. He lifted his shoulders wearily. "What's there to say that already isn't known?"

"Just your version, Mr. O'Dell," Doc murmured softly.

Again the man shrugged. "Somewhere about midnight, this gentleman, Mr. Long, and a young woman I recognized as one of the nurses from the hospital came into the Las Palmas and took one of my tables."

"Matter of fact, you came forward and *led* us to your table, right?"

"I simply was following the custom of the Las Palmas, taking care of new patrons when the head waiter was occupied in another part of the room."

"What's all this got to do with this investigation?" the district attorney snorted. "Good God, we can spend days over all this trivia! I have five assistants to sweep up all these loose ends. Right now I want basic facts."

"I think we may bring out a couple of basic facts, Mr. district attorney, if you'll just bear with us a moment," Jack said dryly. He nodded to O'Dell. "Please continue. You recognized the nurse with Doc as Martha Rodin, one of your sister-in-law's night nurses."

O'Dell shrugged. "Apparently she and Mr. Long had been to a number of other places before they arrived. Miss Rodin was a little intoxicated and somewhat, I should say, inclined to be both confidential and—er—cozy."

Doc grinned. Under her breath and for his ears only, Jerry Booker muttered viciously, "So that's your technique! Get 'em fuzzy and unable to defend themselves. My hero!"

O'Dell was continuing. "Being able to read lips, I was appalled to see Miss Rodin giving out dangerous informa- tion—the same dangerous information which my sister-in- law had and which was threatening her life. In her own behalf, I tried every way within my power to warn her and stop her."

Doc agreed, "Yeah, steppin' on her foot and whisper- in' to her to clam up and get out."

O'Dell nodded. "Exactly, but it was useless. The young woman insisted on talking."

"So," suggested the state's attorney, "the moment Mr. Long left the table you put a stop to it with a hunting knife."

O'Dell stiffened and sat mute for a moment. Then slowly he turned hot, angry eyes on Lambert. "This is just what I expected," he said bitterly. "When members of the police department are cutting each other's throats, it's like a family fight. An outsider is insane to step in and give a helping hand to either side. They'll both turn on him and make him the goat."

Mrs. Holden reached over and touched his arm gently. "Hush, Charles, you're just making matters worse." He turned to stare at her. She smiled wanly. "Just tell them the facts."

After a moment, O'Dell's contorted face smoothed out into a blank mask and he continued in a monotonous tone. "Mr. Long went to the telephone booth in the entrance corridor, asking me to keep an eye on Miss Rodin, who had gone to sleep at the table. Unfortunately, I was required to go to the bar and fill an order for another table. When I returned, someone had pulled Miss Rodin's coat up around her shoulders. I took up my regular station where I could keep an eye on all my tables until Mr. Long returned.

"He came to the table, lifted Miss Rodin's coat as though about to get her to her feet, then dropped it again before I had reached their table. He said he just remembered he had another phone call to make."

"At that time you did not know the knife was sticking in Miss Rodin's back under her coat?" Jack asked.

"I did not. I did not know it until after the shooting in the entrance corridor, when Mr. Long miraculously escaped death. He told me as he was paying his bill, and said he would meet me outside as soon as I could get away."

"Why did he want to meet you outside?" asked the district attorney.

"He had discovered I had been reading Miss Rodin's lips and he said he had an urgent job for me at the hospital."

"So," the district attorney's voice was heavy with sarcasm, "you two gallant men simply walked out of the Las

Palmas, leaving a girl dead at the table with a knife between her shoulderblades."

"That's about it," Doc said cheerfully. "Miss Rodin didn't need us no more and we had other fish to fry, namely, to break loose and get a tracer on brother Faber, who took a couple of shots at me in the phone booth and, it looked like, had put the knife in the nurse. Doc turned to O'Dell. "I never *did* get a chance to ast you how come you didn't wait for me in the parking lot like we'd planned, but hightailed it out like a scairt cat so's I durn near missed climbin' aboard."

"Naturally, I was frightened. I had no knowledge you were in the back." O'Dell looked at Doc, puzzled. "How did you get in?"

"By the skin of my teeth, and I got a skinned shinbone to show for it. Anyhow, so you thought you'd ditched me, and was considerable surprised when I popped up on the road and jarred Faber's nerves and spoilt his aim when he drove up alongside and turned loose on you. Now, what I'd like to ast you is, what was you intendin' to do if you had ditched me and friend Faber hadn't been on your tail?"

Again O'Dell's eyes went blank, but his voice was the same defensive monotone. "I was trying to reach home fast and warn my sister-in-law that Miss Rodin knew the whole story at the hospital and had been killed for talking. I was going to urge her to let me hide her somewhere else until she could get out of Las Vegas."

"You didn't know I had a man watching your place?" Joe Denton queried.

"No, sir." O'Dell licked his lips. "And I want to thank you for having him there to drive off Faber when he got there ahead of us."

"By the way," Doc threw in, "how is Faber? Anybody know?"

"Unfortunately for him, he is expected to recover sufficiently to face trial and the firing squad. At the moment he still is unconscious," Lambert said with satisfaction.

Doc nodded. "And poor little squint-eyed Dr. Willard who Jack rapped on the noggin? He still out, too?"

"Dr. Willard has quite recovered from his misadventure, but so far has chosen to keep his own counsel." The barest sparkle, which might be taken for humor, twinkled for a moment in Lambert's frosty eyes.

Doc's eyes wandered from Lambert to Linda Holliday, who throughout had sat quietly waiting, the tiniest quirk of a disdainful smile on her lips. From Linda, Doc's eyes went to Jack. He nodded.

"Yes, Miss Holliday, I'm quite sure both the state's attorney and the district attorney would like to hear your part in this affair."

She looked at Jack with the naive expectancy of a bright but uncertain child. "You mean, how I came to be in Las Vegas?"

"That might be interesting as a start," Jack said dryly.

"Well," she said readily, "as you boys of the Triple A agency know, I called you for help last—let's see, day before yesterday, I guess it was . . . Anyway, the same day you came to Las Vegas for Mr. McCracken."

Jack nodded and added for the record, "Head of the Investigation Department of the Home and Farm Mutual Insurance and Indemnity Company."

"Yes," nodded Miss Holliday, smiling, "it turned out apparently that my call and Mr. McCracken's had to do with the same matter. That is, in a way. He was interested in recovering two hundred fifty thousand dollars of stolen Chicago bank money which had found its way to Las Vegas. I was interested in a second two hundred fifty thousand which my brother, Hilliard, had obtained from our mutual bank account which had been set aside for income tax purposes and required both of our signatures to withdraw funds."

"You are suggesting that your brother forged your name and embezzled the funds?" the district attorney asked.

Linda looked pained. "My brother is dead. I think the least said about that, the better; however, it was not the first time, as Mr. Packard and Mr. Long know." She looked first at one and then the other for confirmation. Jack was looking at his little black book, but Doc nodded vaguely. "Anyway, I followed as soon as I could, arriving here on the 6:30 a.m. plane yesterday morning."

"Checking in at the Desert Palace at 7:10," Jack verified.

Linda smiled wryly. "Oh, checking up on me, huh?"

"But," continued Jack, "how did you know your brother would be coming to Las Vegas?"

Linda shrugged. "Knowing Hilly, where else would he go with a hatbox full of money? Anyway, I checked the airlines."

"Yes, I've heard about these hatboxes of money," interrupted Lambert. "Doesn't that seem to you a curious way for a man to act who was embezzling a quarter-million dollars? Putting it in a hatbox at the bank and making a stunt out of it, which was sure to reach the newspapers?''

"You didn't know my brother,'' shrugged Linda. "Anything for publicity—from a broken romance with a wealthy and notorious young widow to just such a mad caper as this. He loved seeing his picture in the papers.''

"But, as I understand it, the hatbox idea was not his. It had been arranged by the Holmes-Faber-Dr. Willard gang to have him bring the good money in a hatbox and then, unknown to him, it was to be replaced by a similar hatbox containing the two hundred fifty thousand of hot bank money.''

"I think I can explain what happened,'' Jack said. "It had been intended that Holliday withdraw his money quietly and then at the airport for him to transfer it from some unspectacular container, such as a suitcase, to the hatbox for the switch in Las Vegas. Holliday couldn't resist the big gesture. It was a chance for a big playboy show and he took it.''

"Who was the contact man in Hollywood who gave him the hatbox and arranged for the lure to get him to bring so much money to Las Vegas?''

Jack looked at Linda Holliday questioningly. "Some vague party friend of Holliday's. He fell out of a window to his death in Hollywood within a few hours after Holliday arrived here. Would you know his name, Miss Holliday?''

Linda blinked and looked surprised. "Why, no, why should I? Hilly's friends weren't mine.''

Jack nodded. "Reggie is checking it in Los Angeles. Now, after you arrived and signed in at the Desert Palace, you came to our hotel, right?''

"Yes, it was just five minutes to eight in the morning by the clock in the lobby as I came in."

"Then you went to the hospital with us when Chief Jordan notified us Lilly Montrose had been killed. Your brother also was in the hospital recovering from one of his frequent seizures brought on by fright or excitement. You asked permission to see your brother and went to his room. About an hour later we checked his room and found your brother dead and, yourself, stripped of your clothes, on the bed in a coma."

"I think that's disgusting," the girl flared, her face suddenly aflame.

"What had happened from the time you left us until we found you unconscious?"

"I've told you already."

"Tell it again for Mr. Lambert and the district attorney."

Linda shivered, was silent for a moment, and then spoke in a low, harsh voice. "I knocked on the door and then walked into Hilly's room. He was lying on the bed, fully clothed. At first I didn't see the horrible old man in the wheelchair. Then he spoke and I saw him sitting around an angle in the room near Hilly's bed.

"I said, 'Who are you? What are you doing in my brother's room?' He said, 'Oh, are you Miss Linda Holliday?' I thought it was strange. He looked so old and decrepit and yet his voice was quite young. Then he said, 'Your brother doesn't seem to be sleeping normally. Do you suppose he's all right?'

"I bent over the bed and my back was toward him. Suddenly he was out of the chair and on me. One hand was around my arms, holding them down, and the other over my nose and mouth. It was as though steel bands were around me. I never felt anyone so strong. I couldn't move and I couldn't breathe. Whether I lost consciousness from lack of breath or from fear, I don't know."

"Then you were not aware when he gave you the injection?"

A horrible tremor ran through her body. "No," she said faintly.

"Why do you suppose," the district attorney asked, "you were stripped of your clothes? According to the doctor you were not molested."

The deep flush again suffused Linda's face and neck. "He was just that kind of man, I suppose," she said, resenting every eye that was upon her.

"Now, one more thing," Jack picked it up quickly. "Can you give us any reason why Max Logan here, or Silver Logan, who was wanted by the police, should have taken refuge in your room at the Desert Palace and was waiting for you with a gun?"

There was a movement of indignant protest from Logan. Linda eyed the sharpfaced man with the streak of yellow in his hair. "I cannot," she said with a touch of hauteur. "I have never seen him before in my life."

"Before we get away from Holliday's hospital room," put in Lambert, "I suppose it is obvious to everyone that Miss Holliday's attacker and her brother's killer was Detective Faber."

"Obvious," shrugged the district attorney, "but I doubt whether we can prove it unless Miss Holliday can recognize him despite his disguise. Do you think that's possible, Miss Holliday?"

"I don't know," she said dubiously. "I might know his voice. All I'm sure of is, he was the strongest man . . . "

"That's it!" exclaimed Lambert. "His tremendous strength in his arms."

The district attorney shrugged. "And how would you go about proving that? Of course, we have Mrs. Holden's word that Faber was in the wheelchair at the time this took place, but . . . " He shook his head. "No, I think we'll have a better chance going after him for Lieutenant Holmes's murder." He looked at Jack expectantly.

44

"Now, then," murmured Jack, "we come to Silver Logan's story, which will be interpreted for us by Mr. O'Dell." He looked at Logan, who was eyeing O'Dell with disfavor.

In the moment's silence which followed, all eyes centered on the silver-tipped, pokerfaced, pint-sized figure between Doc and the empty chair, who barely could write his own name and who, temporarily at least, had lost his voice. His cat's eyes left the face of O'Dell and moved quickly about the table, the mask of the professional poker player—calm, bored and watchful—replacing the scowl. When his eyes reached Jack, his lips moved.

O'Dell's eyebrows raised. "He wants to know how many people in this room are armed and who they are."

"What in hell . . . " snapped Lambert, but retired with a mutter as Jack slipped a gun from his belt and laid it on the table. "This, by the way, is the gun found on Dr. Willard." He looked at the district attorney. "When I'm finished with it today, you will want it to check it against the bullet they found in Jordan, inasmuch as the police department seems to be without a head at the moment. Incidentally," he added, "has anyone seen Captain Jessie Michaels, supposedly the acting chief when Jordan is not available?"

There was a blank negative silence.

Jack nodded. "Anyone else armed?"

Doc put two guns on the table with a laconic, "The one that shoots two ways at once is mine. The other's the shootin' pistol Detective Faber was a carryin' when we picked up the pieces after the wreck. I was a wonderin' who I should turn it in to." He nodded to the district attorney. "You, I reckon, later." Doc slipped the one back in the shoulder holster, the other in his waistband, and grinned.

"Anyone else?" Jack asked.

"Of course not," snapped the district attorney.

Jack's eyes rested for a moment on the slight, boyish secretary next to the D.A. who was jotting shorthand curlycues assiduously into a half-filled notebook. Suddenly he looked questioningly at Jerry Booker with her half-sheet of notes and received a big, amused wink. His eyes passed on to O'Dell. "We know you don't have a gun because you were frisked." Jack gave the waiter a clean bill of health and passed on to Lambert.

"Certainly not," said the latter testily, "and I agree with the district attorney. This is getting to be a damned bore. If you think we have nothing else to do . . . "

"You agreed to let me handle this my way," Jack said shortly, "the both of you." Jack turned to Joe Denton, who nodded, grinned, and laid his own gun on the table for a moment and then replaced it in its holster. Jack then looked questioningly at Logan. Again the man's lips moved in a blank, unreadable face.

O'Dell snorted. "Now he wants to know 'how about the dames?' "

Jerry laughed. All eyes turned on her. She shrugged. "I just was thinking, in this hot-day garb Miss Holliday and

I are wearing, a gun would add a very unfeminine and unflattering lump."

There were momentary glances of amusement, but not from Linda Holliday. "I hate guns. I've never touched one in my life."

"And you, Mrs. Holden?"

A prim, severe expression of distaste and indignation sealed her lips, but she shook her head.

Still no expression on his face, Logan's lips began to move and O'Dell began to interpret.

"I was number two man in Skip Sullivan's floating poker game. I was payoff man to the police department. Almost always to Lieutenant Holmes of the racket squad or else to Detective Faber, who was known in Sullivan's crowd as the hatchet man. According to the word, it was Faber who took care of officer Clyde Smith and Sergeant Luke Bowman, who got onto Lieutenant Holmes's racket and were about to expose the police department graft.

"But the Holmes activities went beyond the police department, big deals beyond petty graft from unlicensed gambling."

"You mean," Jack interrupted, "Holmes was top man in the police end? It went no higher than Holmes?"

"We suspected it went much nearer the chief's office, but if that was so, we never were able to finger it."

"You say it went beyond petty graft," Jack encouraged. "Can you be specific?"

Logan's eyes surveyed the table watchfully. His lips moved with greater care. O'Dell's eyes were fastened on his face with sharp intensity. Suddenly he said in a grating voice. "You'll have to repeat that. I didn't get it."

"I think I did," Jack said. "It was perfectly plain." He turned to Logan. "Didn't you say, 'there were big deals in girls and dope and that the Chicago bank robbery was not the only hot money that was siphoned off through the Holmes gang?' "

When Logan nodded, every eye at the table was on Jack. O'Dell had jerked around, his head back as though he'd been slapped. Mrs. Holden's hands were clenched white on the table. The district attorney stared the length of the table stonily. Even the D.A.'s secretary had looked up, startled, his pen suspended in midair.

"Holy cow, Jack," Jerry murmured in the deathly silence. "Are you reading his lips or his mind?"

If Jack heard, he paid no attention, in fact he seemed entirely unaware of the tension he had created.

Doc, completely relaxed, sighed happily, a cheerful grin on his horsey face. He folded his arms across his chest and sat watching.

"Keep your eyes on Logan's lips," Jack counseled O'Dell. "I don't want you to miss the answer to this next question." He turned to Logan. "Of your own knowledge, was any other branch of the local Las Vegas official family involved with the Holmes gang?"

Logan's hesitation had that hypnotic suspension of the born gambler weighing his cards before deciding whether to push in his stack or throw in his cards. Very slowly he turned his head and looked at the district attorney.

A green tinge colored the D.A.'s jowls and red streaks of anger shot up the bony structure of his face and settled as white-hot heat in his eyes. The secretary unobtrusively laid down his pen and seemed to be fumbling in his pocket for a cigarette.

When the district attorney found his voice, it was hot and vitriolic. "Why, you little fourflushing, two-bit card shark! I'll bury you so deep in the state prison you'll never see daylight again! Why are you looking at me? What are you implying?"

Logan shrugged and his lips moved.

The district attorney looked at O'Dell, who shrugged, "He said, 'Isn't it obvious the district attorney would know more about what has been going on in this town than I do?' "

The D.A.'s eyes protruded.

Jack broke the tension. "Then you wish to imply that someone, perhaps not the district attorney himself, but someone in his office is connected with the police renegades?"

Logan nodded, his watchful eyes still on the official at the end of the table.

"You know this of your own knowledge and can give specific details which can be proved?"

Logan, his head still turned to the head of the table, nodded. In the same instant a gun appeared, a gun exploded, and Logan vanished from his chair, crouching beneath the table. But it was not the gun from the D.A.'s office that had exploded, but one from the far end of the table in the hands of Joe Denton, and the body that sprawled grotesquely on the table was not that of the district attorney, but that of his secretary, the unused gun still in his nerveless fingers.

Doc rose cheerfully, jamming his own gun back into its holster. "It had to be you, son," he said to Denton, "on account Mister Logan was between him and Jack and me, and my shootin' pistol which shoots two ways at once ain't trained yet to shoot around corners." He came to Logan's chair and leaned down. "Okay, Mister Logan, you can come out now. Shootin's over."

Logan scrambled out, a look of fury on his face. His lips moved in a snarl of words.

"Huh?" Doc asked of O'Dell. "What's he a sayin'?"

O'Dell grinned stiffly, but there was no humor in his eyes. "He's using some pretty bad language, but the gist of what he says is that you and Jack Packard promised him he'd be safe in this room and to hell with you."

Doc grinned, patted Logan on the shoulder and pushed him back down in his chair. "Cheer up, son," he encouraged, "the worst is yet to come."

During this exchange, Jack had made a quick phone call to Emergency downstairs. The district attorney and Lambert might have been figures of shock and disbelief frozen in ice. Of the three women, none had screamed, but Jerry sat bug-eyed, gasping for air, and Linda Holliday sat with head down and eyes closed, her fingers on the table tearing a fragile handkerchief to shreds. Mrs. Holden's head was in her arms on the table within inches of the young secretary Forbes's lifeblood, which was spreading slowly over the surface.

There was a sharp rap at the door. A white-jacketed intern burst in, followed by two ambulance bearers in white jackets. Without a word the young doctor bent over the sprawled figure. After a moment he raised his head and looked inquiringly around.

"Well?" asked Jack.

He shook his head. "Nothing I can do."

"Take him outside in the chair and call the morgue," Jack ordered. "And swab up this table. We're not through in here yet."

The intern hesitated doubtfully. "I'm not supposed—"

The district attorney came to life. "Take him out of here, damn it! I'll see to the routine myself, when I have the time."

"Yes, sir," agreed the intern readily and nodded to the two bearers. He followed them out and in a moment returned with a big roll of absorbent cotton and a sheet. Quickly and efficiently the conference table was restored to its former pristine neatness.

When the door closed, the district attorney looked at the empty space beside him. "If there's going to be more testimony, I want it taken down for the record."

Jack nodded. "Jerry?" he said.

"Well," said Jerry with forced cheerfulness, "I'm not in the same league as my predecessor, but neither am I going to pull a gun on anybody." She arose, and sat down beside the district attorney.

Jerry pulled the open notebook towards her, then pushed it away. "Heeey, it's got blood on it!"

"Start a fresh one," the district attorney said grimly, nodding at the pile in the center of the table.

45

"Now, then," the district attorney said harshly, "I want this for the record. Apparently I'm going to have to do some housecleaning of my own. Whether Forbes was in this alone or with others, I intend to find out. And I wish to add that at no time had I even suspected the boy. He has been with me two years and was thoroughly efficient. I'm sure he was straight when he came to me and if I ever find out who got to him, I'll personally wring his neck."

"He was sure desperate and an amateur to pull a gun in here," Doc agreed. "He must have been in over his head."

A rumble came from Lambert's throat. He cleared his larynx and said, "Not that I don't believe your skirts are clean, Mr. District Attorney, but also for the record I want Logan to state whether his information implicates you or only your office."

Logan shook his head and his lips moved.

"Only your office," interpreted O'Dell, "but because it was your personal office, it was supposed it was the district attorney himself, although it just as well could have been his secretary."

Lambert nodded. "Good." He looked with less friendly eyes at the district attorney. "We'll settle the rest of it between ourselves."

Jack seemed satisfied. "Now, then, Logan, are you aware of any other city department being implicated?"

Logan shook his head. Again his lips moved, but with hesitancy.

Suddenly O'Dell's face stiffened. He glanced down at his sister-in-law, who still lay with her head in her arms, then said harshly, "I don't read you. You'll have to speak more distinctly."

Logan's eyes, which had been on Jerry's pencil flying across the notebook page, suddenly flew to O'Dell's face with resentment and suspicion. His lips moved and O'Dell's face darkened.

Again Jack broke in. "Didn't you say, Logan, that it was suspected by Sullivan that Holmes and his boys had strong connection in the Morrison Hospital, which, of course, is a city institution?"

Again Logan nodded. O'Dell's startled glance fixed on Jack, and Mrs. Holden's haggard face lifted from the table to stare at him.

"A doggone lip reader right in our own family circle," marveled Doc. "Honest to goodness, Jack, sometimes I suspect you of bein' one of them seven-day wonders."

Jack ignored him. "And isn't it a fact that some of the narcotics which were going to the trade were being distributed from the hospital?"

Logan looked dubious and moved his lips.

Jack looked at O'Dell, who shrugged his shoulders. "He said, as you apparently already know, that he had no knowledge of it coming from the hospital. It was always suspected of coming from Reno. He says, of course, this is just rumor and he has no definite knowledge."

Jack nodded. "From Reno. That would be Dr. Willard and your institute for the deaf and blind, I imagine, Mr. Lambert."

Lambert nodded grimly.

"Then," asked Jack of Logan, "what was the connection of the hospital with the Holmes gang?"

Logan's lips began to move, his eyes moving from O'Dell to the night supervisor beside him.

Suddenly Mrs. Holden stood up. "It's a lie! Every word he's speaking is a damned lie out of a vicious mouth!"

Logan stopped, an expression of surprise in his eyes. O'Dell grabbed her and tried to pull her back in her chair, but she was gripped by hysteria. "I've been with the Morrison Hospital since before it was rebuilt," she cried out, "and there's no better hospital anywhere. There's nothing wrong at the hospital—nothing—nothing—nothing!" She burst into tears and dropped into her chair, again burying her face in her arms, her body shaking with emotion.

After a pause Jack said softly, "Then you also can read lips, Mrs. Holden."

She raised her ravaged face. "No, of course not."

"Then how did you know what Logan was saying?"

"I didn't, but I knew he was saying something against the hospital. That's what he was talking about."

"It isn't what he might have been saying against the hospital that was worrying you, was it, Mrs. Holden?" Jack suggested quietly. "It is what he might have been saying about you?"

The woman looked at him in fright for a moment, then buried her face.

"That was an unnecessarily cruel thing to say," O'Dell said hotly. "Logan was saying nothing at all about Mrs. Holden."

"I don't think he has to," Jack said dryly. "I think Mrs. Holden is witness enough against herself. Especially in view of the report Mr. Denton has from Washington concerning yourself."

O'Dell half arose to his feet. He started to speak, then dropped back into his chair and shrugged his shoulders. "What would that be?" he asked wearily.

Jack looked at Denton.

Denton took several telegrams from his pocket and shuffled them.

Across the table, Doc stretched his arms above his head, yawned vigorously, murmured " 'Scuse me," and slipped a hand under his coat, scratching his ribs vigorously.

Denton ran his eye down the selected paper and began to read. "Fingerprint report: nurse Martha Rodin, negative; nurse Grace Parker, negative; police officer Mike Stern, negative; State's Attorney Lambert, negative— "

Lambert snorted. "What the hell! Sending my fingerprints in!"

Denton grinned and continued. "Jack Packard and Doc Long, negative; Police Chief Jordan, negative; police officer Clyde Smith and police Sergeant Luke Bowman, negative;

Chief Supervisor Ruth Westover, negative; Dr. Asa Willard, negative; police detective Perry Faber, former member of Chicago police racket squad, dismissed three years ago on charges of indiscretions unbecoming to a police officer in connection with three separate homicides."

"In plain words, a killer in uniform," Jack murmured.

Denton nodded. "Skip Sullivan, former member of Florida and New Orleans small-time rackets with emphasis on floating gambling games; Lois Pallaski, alias Lilly Montrose, female shill and hanger-on of same gang; Max Logan, alias Silver Logan, confidence man and card sharp with two records of convictions."

Logan eyed Joe Denton with neither surprise nor chagrin, nodded and shrugged.

Denton looked amused and continued. "Charles O'Dell . . . " He paused, frowned, and after a slight hesitation went on, " . . . alias George Meriam, on the list of the ten most wanted criminals as head of the Meriam bank robbery syndicate."

O'Dell sat unheeding, his eyes fixed on the window at the far end of the room, brooding over the freedom that lay so close and yet so far away. Supervisor Holden moved convulsively, a dreadful moan issuing from the face hidden in her arms.

Denton shot a quick glance at the pair, an intelligence passing between him and Jack, which Doc interpreted, and lazily his chair slid from the table.

Denton read on. "Latest robbery accredited to the Meriam syndicate was a two-hundred-fifty-thousand-dollar heist from Chicago Stockyard's First National Bank."

"Oh-oh," exclaimed Doc. "Same two fifty I was a playin' poker with last night—or was it the night before?"

Denton nodded. "Obviously O'Dell, alias Meriam, brought the hot money to Las Vegas, turned it over to Lieutenant Holmes, who arranged the shift in hatboxes through Lilly Montrose, giving Meriam's syndicate Hilliard Holliday's clean money."

"Only Mr. O'Dell never got the clean money," Doc observed.

"Or perhaps he did," Denton said softly, looking at O'Dell. There still was no sign from the latter that he was listening. His eyes were on the hot, open desert outside the window. "We have men going through his house out on—"

O'Dell's eyes flew to Denton's face, an expression of hot, passionate anger suffusing his features. "If you so much as lay a hand on my wife . . . "

Denton nodded sympathetically. "That's all right, O'Dell. Everyone understands she can neither hear nor speak—"

Mrs. Holden's head came up sharply. "That's a lie. That's a coverup . . . "

O'Dell's hand shot out and slapped the woman sharply, so that her head snapped against the back of her chair. A drop of blood oozed from her lip.

"That's all right, Mrs. Holden. You can save the rest for the district attorney."

Mrs. Holden rose unsteadily to her feet.

O'Dell reached to jerk her back, but Doc said gently, "Hold it, Mr. O'Dell, just slide back easy and keep your hands folded on top of the table." Doc's gun was resting negligently in his hand.

"I can give it to the district attorney right now." Mrs. Holden supported herself upright with one hand on the table. "I've lived in hell with my sister and O'Dell here for the last ten years. My sister is the real head of the Meriam syndicate. She was a nurse in a school for mute children and learned lip reading. Then she met Meriam, or O'Dell here. Only she was smarter than O'Dell and she was made for money. She pretended to be a deaf-mute and was able to case a bank without suspicion. She would set up the whole plan of operation and coach O'Dell and his men in what they were to do. She even taught O'Dell lip reading so . . . " She took a deep trembling breath and swallowed.

"You'd better sit down, Mrs. Holden," Jack suggested.

"No. I was a nurse in Chicago and didn't know what my sister was doing until—until she roped me in—until suddenly I found myself a member of the syndicate—at least an accessory. I was terrified and slipped away to come here to Las Vegas; they didn't find me until three years ago. Then they moved here and it began all over again, using me whenever they needed a cover. Just the way Detective Faber used me the other night to get into the hospital to kill Lilly Montrose, Mr. Holliday and Lieutenant Holmes. And I didn't dare open my mouth because I was implicated. But I swear I didn't know Faber was going to commit murder when I helped him disguise himself in the hospital. I swear it."

"Then Faber actually was working for O'Dell?" the district attorney put in.

"Everybody was working for O'Dell. I don't know what he had on Dr. Willard, but he had something and that's where the narcotics were coming from. Lieutenant Holmes was working for him. Everybody. And when Mr. Packard and Mr. Long came here and fouled up the exchange of hatboxes and began to cooperate with Chief Jordan and Joe Denton, then O'Dell and Faber decided that everyone who knew anything about the inner workings of the syndicate had to be eliminated."

Doc sat up straighter. "Heeey, then it could have been O'Dell hisself who stuck that hunting knife in nurse Rodin in the Las Palmas."

The woman turned deliberately to her brother-in-law, her eyes mad with vindictiveness. "If I were to see the hunting knife, I think I could identify it as the property of this man."

O'Dell crouched in his chair as though about to leap.

"Hold it, feller," Doc said softly. "I owe you a lot for stabbing my girlfriend in the back, so just make one move . . . " There was a pause and then Doc complained, "But, Mrs. Holden, it don't make sense. If O'Dell here and Faber was in this together to bump off everybody else, how come Faber took a potshot at O'Dell in the car when we was a goin' out to his house?"

Mrs. Holden gave a short ugly laugh. "Oh, I hadn't heard about that. They used that trick again."

"Trick?"

"Well, Faber didn't hit him, did he? But it made O'Dell here look pretty clean. He must be on the right side if the killer was trying to get him, too."

"Or maybe Faber did try to kill him," Joe Denton said thoughtfully. "If everyone else was eliminated, then with O'Dell out of the way that would make Faber top boy and he'd inherit both the bank loot and Holliday's money. Want to give an opinion, O'Dell?"

O'Dell was looking out the window again.

Lambert cleared his throat. "Mrs. Holden, are you able to give Chief Jordan a clean bill of health in all this?"

"Poor old Jordan," Mrs. Holden said with a bitter smile. "He was an innocent lamb among the wolves. He didn't know from nothing." She shook her head. "No, the top man in the police department who was taking orders from O'Dell was Captain Jessie Michaels, the acting chief, when Jordan was away."

The district attorney sat up straight. "Did you say Michaels? You know this?"

"I was wondering," murmured Joe Denton, "why Michaels hadn't put in an appearance since Jordan was killed. You don't suppose he saw the handwriting on the wall and vamoosed across the Mexican border?"

"No," said Jack, "I think I know where Captain Michaels is."

All eyes swung to him.

"I think you'll find him in the morgue."

"The devil!" exclaimed Lambert.

"I've had no such report," the D.A. protested. Even the eyes of O'Dell turned from the window in surprise.

"Dad blame it, Jack," Doc complained, "you seem to have your fingers on everybody and everything except the missin' half a million cartwheels, plus two thousand five hundred in which I got a personal interest."

Jack grinned. The D.A. rose and walked to Jack's end of the table, picked up the phone receiver and dialed a number. He asked a question, then a second, hung up and went back to his chair. "The list of dead in the morgue consists of Lilly Montrose, Lieutenant Holmes, Hilliard Holliday, an unidentified woman picked up on the desert this morning, Paul Forbes, my ex-secretary, and Chief Jordan."

"There must be some mix-up in the names," Jack said, rising and going to an office door. He opened it, and stood back.

Chief Jeff Jordan stalked in, surveyed the table grimly and walked to the empty chair between Silver Logan and Jerry Booker.

46

It was a tie between the D.A. and the state's attorney as to who was on his feet first, whose eyes started farthest from his head, and whose mouth dropped open the widest. Supervisor Holden swayed on her feet and her mouth opened and closed as though in some silent incantation against the walking dead as she sank weakly back into her chair.

Jerry Booker, her eyes wide and shining with excitement, instinctively drew her chair chair nearer the D.A. and farther from the chair now so unexpectedly occupied.

On the other side, Silver Logan gulped and said in a perfectly audible voice, "Like everything else in this town, a substandard morgue! Letting their corpses walk the streets in broad daylight!"

From Linda Holliday's lips burst a wild, hysterical laugh, which she smothered with the torn handkerchief in her left hand, while her right pointed at Logan, her voice quavering behind the fragment of lace. "He's got his voice back!"

Logan, startled, gave Jack a chagrined, apologetic glance.

Jack nodded. "It's okay, Logan. We've accomplished what we set out to do."

"Jack," complained Doc in an outraged voice, "you mean to say you can't read lips after all? That Logan could talk all the time and you was just pretendin'?"

Jack nodded. "He got his voice back this morning. He told Denton and me his story. We kept up the lip-reading gag in hopes O'Dell here would trip himself up."

Doc looked at O'Dell, who no longer was looking out the conference room window and seemed to have shriveled. "Looky at him," Doc said. "Since Jordan come back to life, he reminds me more of a sack of old bones than Charlie O'Dell, bank robber."

The D.A. had sunk back in his chair, still staring at Jordan, who, seated, had taken a sheaf of papers from his pocket, thumbing through them and waiting for order to restore itself.

Lambert was still on his feet. "Never mind Charles O'Dell!" His voice rasped with indignation. "I demand to know the meaning of this farce. If Jordan was not shot and killed at the airport last night, then who was?"

Jack met Jordan's eyes and nodded.

Jordan cleared his throat. "That's fair enough, Mr. Lambert. It was Captain Jessie Michaels, my assistant chief, dressed in my uniform."

"Michaels!" exclaimed Lambert. "Why Michaels?"

"Because I had reason to know he was overly friendly with Lieutenant Holmes. When it came out that Holmes was double-crossing the department, it seemed obvious Captain Michaels was involved." He nodded at Jack. "That's why I asked Packard and Long to give me a hand. It was Packard's suggestion that I send Michaels to the airport ahead of me. Then I drove out and we went to the Men's room and changed uniforms. Personally, I thought—and Packard went along with me—that I wasn't meant to come back alive." He looked grimly at Lambert. "Actually, I thought it was your men from Carson City who were to do the job."

"What?" exclaimed Lambert, sinking down into his chair.

"I apologize. But suspecting your men and knowing they didn't know me by sight, I preferred to have a man who I knew was double-crossing me put on the spot."

"Captain Michaels was willing to take your place?" The D.A.'s voice was heavy with disbelief.

The chief shrugged. "I merely told him I had another job to attend to and wanted him to represent me in meeting Lambert's men. Why shouldn't he? Being on the inside, he knew quite well that Lambert's men were not involved. But what he didn't know—what none of us knew—was that there was a killer waiting for me in the parking lot. In the dark he mistook Michaels for me."

"And so a bloody end for another crooked cop, huh?" murmured Doc.

"This doesn't make sense," protested the D.A., frowning. "The body identified both at Emergency and at the morgue was yours."

For the first time a glint of humor showed in the chief's eyes. "That was another of Packard's ideas. When Michaels was shot at the airport, I called him, and at his suggestion I then called Emergency and the morgue and told them to identify Michaels as me. It was done to a man, proving that there were no traitors in either department. So I carried it further. I sent every police officer I could lay my hands on to the morgue, one at a time, also with instructions to identify Michael's body as mine. Out of the more than hundred men given this instruction, only two tried to get on a telephone and pass the word that I wasn't dead."

"Pass the word to whom?" asked the state's attorney sharply.

The chief's eyes surveyed the table. "One call was made to the home of our friend O'Dell here." O'Dell, sunk in a stupor, seemed to hear nothing. The chief smiled. "I'm afraid Meriam, alias O'Dell, was pretty severely shocked when I walked into the room. He was expecting last-minute help from Captain Michaels."

Then his eyes switched to the district attorney. "The second call was made to your office." The D.A. flushed and started to protest, but the chief nodded. "I know. I heard what went on in here earlier. It was your secretary who was meant to get the message."

"But what was the object of killing you? If the O'Dell-Meriam gang was on a rampage to wipe out all their underlings who might talk . . . "

Again the chief broke in on the district attorney. "I supposed my death would link me with the others who had been killed and it would be assumed that I must have been tainted, too; however, Packard and I went through my office earlier this morning and," he held up a sheaf of papers, "in my files we found letters, memoranda, names, facts, and figures, which, upon my death, would have condemned me as the brain, not only behind the Meriam bank robbery syndicate, but the ringleader in pushing narcotics, white slavery, and the cleaning of money. Here even is a notation indicating I was responsible for the two quarter-million-dollar hatboxes which were stolen from the police department strongbox."

"You suspect these were put in your files by Michaels?"

The chief shrugged. "Had I been killed and these papers found and delivered to the right parties by Captain Michaels, I feel quite sure he would be your chief of police today."

"Which would have put the whole police department right into the hands of Charlie, here," Doc said admiringly. "Son," he said to the man across the table, sunk in blank, morbid indifference, "you got quite a brain hid behind your guise as a lowly waiter in the Las Palmas."

For the first time since Jordan had entered, Supervisor Holden raised a bitter voice. "You're giving O'Dell here too much credit. He'd still be a small-time racketeer and hashhouse waiter if it hadn't been for my sister." She looked around the table with haggard eyes. "Look," she cried out, "aren't you going to do something about her? If you let her go free after what I've told you today, my life . . ." She began to shake. "Don't sit there gloating over Charlie," she pleaded, near hysteria. "Charlie's nothing without Lorna."

Jack looked at the chief and received a nod, then at Joe Denton, who grinned and nodded. "I don't think, Mrs. Holden," he said softly, "you're going to have to—"

The ringing of the phone reverberated through the room. Jack picked up the receiver, listened for a moment, then shoved the phone over to Joe Denton. He turned to Chief Jordan and said with satisfaction, "It worked!"

47

"What worked?" growled Lambert.

Denton hung up the receiver with a cheerful grin. "They're bringing in two hatboxes of long green disguised in oversized suitcases."

"The missing half-million?" Lambert demanded.

"Plus my twenty-five thousand dividend pin money?" Doc interjected hopefully.

"Two thousand five hundred, Doc," Jerry reminded. "And it's Triple A's pin money, not yours."

"Honest to goodness, Jack," Doc said bitterly, "gettin' a female secretary in our office was just plain fatal. We ain't been able to call soul, body, nor a paycheck our own since she come into our lives. And as for rubbin' two nickels together— "

"Doc!" Jack interrupted.

"Huh?"

"Turn it off. This is a business conference."

"Is there anyone here," asked the D.A. impatiently, "who wants to tell the district attorney's office what's going on?"

"I think that would be a good idea," nodded Denton cheerfully, "and I hereby delegate Packard to carry the ball, inasmuch as he spotted the cache and set the trap."

Denton looked inquiringly at Jordan, who nodded. "In view of the fact that the Triple A Detective agency will get no public mention for its part in this business, this is a good place to give Packard, Long, and . . ." with a glint of humor in his nod to Jerry Booker, "their fascinating secretary, recognition."

"Thanks," Jack said dryly. "Our job with Chief Jordan is gratis, as we're already collecting, over and above the recovered loot, twenty-five hundred won by Doc in the poker game, a thousand from Miss Holliday as a client, and another five thousand from McCracken of the Farm and Home Insurance Company."

"Eight thousand five hundred," breathed Jerry, her face flushed, her eyes shining.

Denton laughed. "You've made Miss Booker very happy. However, haven't you forgot to include the five thousand reward for the capture and conviction of the leader of the Meriam bank robbery syndicate?"

"No kiddin'!" Doc sat up straighter.

"Brother!" exclaimed Jerry. "The Triple A's bank account's going to look like a real bank account for once."

Jack shook his head. "We're not greedy."

"Whatcha *mean,* we're not greedy?" protested Doc.

Jack ignored him. "There've been too many working on the case. If the five thousand comes through, divide it between the chief's loyal men.

"All right, all right, now you've cut up the pie," growled the district attorney, "what about the half-million cache and the trap?"

Jack nodded. "When the two hatboxes disappeared from the police strong room so close upon the arrival of State's Attorney Lambert and—"

Lambert let out a roar. "Are you still trying to implicate me in this affair?"

Jack said blandly, "You didn't let me finish, Mr. Lambert. When Mr. Lambert and Dr. Willard arrived here simultaneously, it occurred to me the money might be earmarked for a flight north. A check with the baggage rooms at the airport revealed two suitcases had been checked through to Reno in the name of the Nevada State Deaf, Dumb and Blind Institute. They were scheduled for the 11:00 flight this morning."

"Another count against Dr. Willard," the D.A. nodded with satisfaction.

"I met Denton, here, at the airport baggage room with the necessary credentials and we examined the cases. The hatboxes were inside. We left the cases intact and Denton put his men on watch. Two others had been assigned to search O'Dell's house, which they did. Actually, it was only a pretext for keeping an eye on Mrs. O'Dell—or Mrs. Meriam."

"Then you suspected Lorna all the time!" exclaimed Mrs. Holden, who had been listening avidly.

"Not actually," Jack admitted, "but we couldn't pass up the wife of a known bank robber. Anyway, after Denton's men had left the house, Mrs. O'Dell waited for the mailman. She received a letter and immediately drove to the airport and bought a ticket for Reno. This was enough. Denton's men grabbed her and found the two baggage check stubs in her purse, still in the letter."

"But who sent her the stubs?" Lambert demanded.

"Funny you should ask that," Jack said softly, but his eyes were hard and watchful.

"Why, in heaven's name?" Lambert exclaimed indignantly.

"Because you did."

"What?"

"You sent the stubs."

"Ridiculous!" Sweat had popped out on his forehead.

Jack shook his head. "No, you made a stupid mistake. You addressed an envelope at the airport, after you'd checked the suitcases, in your own handwriting."

Lambert's mouth fell open. For a moment he seemed dazed by the unexpected blow. Then his mouth snapped shut. "You couldn't possibly know that. You haven't seen the envelope. For all you know, it may be typewritten."

Jack looked at Joe Denton, who shook his head. "No, Mr. Lambert, it's handwritten, all right, and in your hand. One of my men is a handwriting expert and . . ."

Lambert's right hand moved suddenly to his mouth. Linda Holliday seemed unaware, but Denton, sitting at her left, reached across her in an attempt to grab the frenzied man's hand. Then he was bodily on Lambert, forcing his head back and desperately trying to pry open his teeth. As suddenly as he had acted, Lambert relaxed. The smell of bitter almonds pervaded the hot room, and his body slumped grotesquely in his chair.

No one else had moved. For a moment there was not a sound and then from the throat of Charles O'Dell came a deep, ugly chuckle. He glanced over at the dead man and said with dreadful malice. "He could pass it out, but he couldn't take it."

Supervisor Holden shivered, and Linda Holliday, in a daze of horror, slid her chair back against the wall, staring at the thing which a moment before had been a man.

"I don't get it." The district attorney swallowed hard, finding his voice. "I thought Dr. Willard had knocked him out in the hospital waiting room and gone berserk, trying to kill Logan."

Jack nodded to Doc, who pulled the phone to him and said laconically, "Emergency . . . Another suspect's bit the dust."

Jack answered the D.A. "Berserk's just the word. If you'll check with Chief Supervisor Westover, you'll find Dr. Willard is suffering, not from the blow I struck him on the head last night, but from an overdose of narcotics. That sleepy, inattentive look of his should have told us at once what he was. Anyway, when the pressure got to him he gave himself a big dose, and then he cracked his boss over the head and went out to get Logan."

Doc stirred uncomfortably. "Jack, *now* have we reached the top? First we thought it was Lieutenant Holmes, then we thought it was Detective Faber, then Dr. Willard, and *now* we got Lambert. Honest to Christmas, son, we've been a sittin' here so long this chair's a gettin' butt-sprung. Besides, it's past twelve and I'm hungry." Before Jack could answer, he was on his feet and walking around to Linda Holliday, who still sat with her chair backed against the wall, staring. "Come on, honey," Doc said persuasively, "you don't have to sit next to no corpse. You can have my chair."

"No," whispered the girl in a hoarse, agonized voice. "I don't want to see any more. Take me out of here."

There was a tap on the door. Jack called, "Come in." The door swung open and two of Denton's operatives came in, a woman between them. The woman, an older, harder replica of Mrs. Holden, came with reluctant defiance.

The two operatives stared at the deceased Lambert, at Denton, then at each other and grinned.

The woman's eyes went first to O'Dell and then to the dead man. "Well," she said indifferently, "I'm glad he's out of our lives, anyway."

Again the door opened and the intern with his two assistants entered. The intern's eyes opened wide at the sight of Lambert. He crossed quickly, sniffed the air, leaned over and sniffed the dead man's mouth, shrugged, and motioned to his assistants.

As the chair containing the body was wheeled out the door, the intern hesitated again beside the district attorney. The latter looked up and growled, "I'll be along presently to give you a report." The intern nodded and closed the door behind him.

"There's just one more thing I want to know," the D.A. said, turning back to Jack.

"Just one?" Joe Denton grinned broadly. "Man, you've got six months of digging before you bring this case to trial."

"One more at the moment," growled the other. "How did Lambert get the money he took to the airport?"

Jack shrugged. "That's something you'll have to dig for, as Denton suggests. However, I suspect that Captain Michaels, the chief's assistant, got it out of the safe. And there's something else you haven't asked, but I imagine it will come to light when you get to digging. I think it wasn't Dr. Willard or Detective Faber who killed Michaels when they were gunning for Jordan. I think you'll find it was one of Lambert's boys he brought down from Carson City. They didn't know Jordan by sight. Anyway, it's worth looking into."

"Now can we go to lunch?" demanded Doc. "Honest to gran'ma, Miss Holliday's so weak in the knees she can't hardly stand."

"I'll never eat again!" declared Linda shakily.

"Miss Holliday, honey, don't never say that," protested Doc. "Folks just has to put something in their stummicks between drinks or the whole world'd be as drunk as jaybirds at corn-squeezin' time."

Epilogue

It was a hundred and two in the Triple A-One Detective Agency's Hollywood office; a glaring ninety-eight on the shady side of Hollywood Boulevard; a dizzy, blinding ninety-nine in the smog and fumes of the wearisome, slow-moving traffic of Wilshire Boulevard; and a tingling, pneumonia-inviting, air-conditioned sixty-eight in the Waverly-Carlton cocktail lounge, where Jack and Doc sat in comfortable summer tropics with the Home and Farm Mutual Insurance and Indemnity Company's McCracken in his black woolen coat, beneath which was a heavy vest of some past era unsuccessfully covering a dark gray woollen sweater.

McCracken sipped at a cup of black, steaming coffee, eyed Doc's tall, frosted milk punch with two raw eggs beaten in as a gesture to breakfast, and shuddered.

Doc grinned. "Whilst Jack is workin' his brain over that shyster release you want me and him to sign before you reluctantly turn over your company's check, Mr. McCracken, why don't me and you have a heart-to-heart talk on how come you always seem to have a froze-up radiator."

McCracken scowled and turned an impatient eye on Jack. "It's a company form, Packard, same as you've signed a dozen times before. It simply asks acknowledgment that you release the insurance company and the Chicago bank from any and all damages, or damage suits which may in the future arise out of the Triple A's activities in recovering the quarter-million dollars."

Jack sipped his iced tea laced with rum and nodded. "I like this typed-in paragraph to the effect that 'there shall be no liability on the part of the insurance company nor the bank in the deaths of Lois Pallaski, alias Lilly Montrose; Hilliard Holliday; Lieutenant Tracy Holmes; Miss Martha Rodin, R.N.; Captain Jessie Michaels of the Las Vegas Police; Paul Forbes, secretary to District Attorney Joseph Smythe; or State's Attorney Gordon Lambert. Nor shall the insurance company nor the bank be held liable nor made active participants in the arrest and prosecution of Dr. Asa Willard; Police Detective Perry Faber; Lorna O'Dell, alias Lorna Meriam; Charles O'Dell, alias Charles Meriam; Max Logan, alias Silver Logan; and Mrs. Grace Holden, R.N.' "

"Heeey," protested Doc, "Silver Logan and Mrs. Holden are only being held as material witnesses. They ain't a comin' up for trial."

"We would prefer to have their names included in our release." McCracken's voice was final.

"Just like that, huh?" Doc's light blue eyes glinted with amusement.

"And this paragraph," Jack continued. " 'It is understood by all parties that the payment of Five Thousand Dollars for the recovery of the two hundred fifty thousand dollars shall in no manner imply either moral or legal obligation of either the insurance company or the bank in the action or manner of the Triple A-One Agency in connection with its recovery of the said two hundred fifty thousand dollars.' "

"Just plain tippy-toe cautious," grinned Doc. "You'd think, Mr. McCracken, that you suspected me and Jack of operatin' down below the belt someplace and dealin' in sin and shame."

McCracken's mouth closed in a tight, thin line. "We neither ask you where, when, or how you operate, nor do we make any specifications. We neither know, nor want to know. Therefore, we are in no sense responsible. We have considered that clause before. It has always been in the releases and will stay in now."

Jack took out his ball-point, saying casually, "Especially in this case."

"Especially in this case," McCracken confirmed. "Do you realize how many people died violently in Las Vegas after your arrival?" The words had a sense of querulous complaint, but the tone merely hinted at a prim disapproval.

"Well, don't look at us," Doc said. "We didn't kill none of them. My shootin' pistol was only out of its holster twice. Once when I shot the front tire of Detective Faber's getaway car. The other time was in the conference room when the D.A.'s secretary pulled a gun, only Jerry and Logan was between him and me, and Joe Denton had to take him."

Jack scribbled his name on the release and passed it, and his pen, to Doc.

"Okay to sign, huh?" Doc asked, eyeing the paper suspiciously.

Jack nodded. "We've kept McCracken long enough in this comfortably cool atmosphere."

"Too long," McCracken grunted.

"Yeah, you'd better go right home and soak your hummels in a pan of hot mustard water." He wrote his name with a flourish, making the two short words "Doc Long" twice as long and important as Jack Packard.

McCracken took an envelope from his inside coat pocket and handed it across the table to Jack. Jack opened it and took out the check. "Heeey," protested Doc, "they was s'posed to be *two* checks, twenty-five hundred to Jack and twenty-five hundred to me. Makin' a check out just in Jack's name makes me feel inferior and . . . " He had taken the check from Jack's hand and broke off abruptly. " . . . Why, doggone it, it's made out to the Triple A and that means it's gotta have Jerry Booker's signature, too . . . "

"I had specific instructions from your office to make it out in the firm's name."

Jack grinned. "Apparently Jerry intends to see we keep a large enough bank balance to assure her of a salary for the next ten years."

"Honest to my grandma on my mama's side, Jack. Sometimes I wonder if she belongs to us or we belong to her!"

When Jack and Doc entered the Triple A office, Jerry looked up with an expectant smile of welcome. Doc, first through the entrance gate, ignored her completely, yanking off his coat and hanging it with deliberate care on a hanger, his back to her. Jack, following through the gate, walked around to Jerry's desk and laid the check before her with an amused grimace.

Jerry's eyes glowed at the amount as she turned it over and saw with approval Jack and Doc's endorsement. She added her own small neat signature below.

"Some nest egg!" she gloated, rising to cross to the filing cabinet and then paused for a moment beside Doc, who had thrown himself in an office chair, disgruntlement on his face, a cool unfriendliness in his light blue eyes. "Something eating at your vitals, Texas boy? Or is the heat getting you?"

"Me and Jack a workin' our fingers to the bone and what for? So's a bank, already bloated with money, can gobble up our take."

"Oh-oh!" murmured Jerry, amused.

"Well, what's so all-fired funny about it? It's our money, ain't it?"

Jerry agreed. "After Uncle Sam gets his share, and after I've taken out my back salary and earmarked enough to be sure I don't get behind again, and after you've paid me a small sum for clothes, shoes, medical bills and incidentals due me for what happened in Las Vegas."

Jerry passed on to the filing cabinet, Doc's eyes following her. That lightly covered wiggling behind made Doc feel good all over.

"Jack," he rhapsodized blissfully, "I take it all back. I ain't mad at nobody! What's money when you got a secretary like Jerry!"

Jerry whirled in time to see Jack pick up a waste basket and shove it down over Doc's head.

"Well, now if that ain't a dog-in-the-manger trick!" Doc complained indignantly, pulling the basket off his head. "Just because you ain't capable of enjoyin' the beauties of nature . . . ''

Jerry, returning, a bank book in one hand, paused to brush pencil shavings and paper-punch confetti out of Doc's hair. "Yes, Jack," she said, "give lover boy a break. After all, what's fair in giving the man with the green eyeshade in the window across the street all the pleasure?"

Jack crossed to the window and pulled down the dilapidated shade.

"Just because we have a shameless hussy for a secretary doesn't mean we have to advertise it to the world." Jack nodded at the bank book in her hand.

"I'm taking the money down to the bank during lunch hour, which is right now, and will deposit eight thousand five hundred dollars, of which twenty-five hundred is poker winnings—"

"*My* poker winnings, doggone it," protested Doc.

"One thousand from Linda Holliday," she continued, unheeding, "and five thousand from the insurance company. Oh yes, one more thing, my esteemed employers." From between the pages of a book she removed a pink oblong slip, which was a Triple A check, to which was attached a notation list. "I'd like you boys to sign this check for fourteen hundred and ten dollars, which was the total of my misfortune on the Las Vegas expedition. Would you like to review the items before you sign?"

Jack grinned. Doc yelped, "Fourteen hundred . . . '' He took the slip from Jerry's hand and read: "Evening shoes $25, cocktail dress $225, Lingerie $35 . . . honey, you need lingerie like an eel needs legs!"

"Every girl likes a drawer full of beautiful lingerie whether she wears it or not."

Doc grunted and read on. "'$125 for fingernail claw marks and a bruised instep from Lilly Montrose; $500 for public humiliation by being torn to shreds and denuded in a hotel lobby, and $500 for Jack's crude remarks to the effect of my being 'starved for love.'"

"And furthermore, if the check wasn't already made out, I'd tack on another $250 for being called a 'shameless hussy,'" Jerry added with a defiant look at Jack.

"I agree to everything," Doc said, rising and taking the check from Jerry's hand and picking up a pen on her desk. "Especially Jack's snide remarks." He affixed his signature and handed the check to Jack. "And maybe this'll teach you not to get fresh with the hired help in the future."

Jack looked at the check, but made no effort to take it.

"Now looky, Jack," Doc urged, "after all, what's money *for*?"

"I'll sign it, on one consideration," Jack said, looking at Jerry with amusement.

"Well?" she asked.

"That this small gesture of blackmail doesn't become a habit."

Jerry thought a moment, then grinned. "It's a deal."

Jack nodded and took the check.

"And now, honey," said Doc contentedly, "now I helped you, how about sittin' down and writin' out a check for me?"

Jerry eyed him coolly. "How much?"

Doc shrugged. "Oh, say two-fifty."

"For what?"

Doc looked surprised and hurt. "How do I know what for until I see it?"

"The answer is no." Jerry's voice was flat and final as she took her check from Jack, blotted it and put it between the pages of the bank book.

"And after what I just done for you!" Doc was deeply hurt. "Jack, we got a doggone female reptile in our bosom, which bites the hand that feeds it."

Jack nodded sagely. "You'll learn sometime, Doc. Women are not to be trusted with money."

Jerry smiled smugly, nodded and went out to lunch.

"Oh, well," grumbled Doc, "there's always the floating poker game somewhere in town. But you'd think *sometimes* you could get a little pocket change at home without havin' to go out and milk the professionals."